THE ROSIE RESULT

I was standing on one leg shucking oysters when the problems began . . . Don and Rosie are back in Melbourne after a decade in New York, about to face their most important project. Their son, Hudson, is having trouble at school: his teachers say he isn't fitting in with the other kids. Meanwhile, Rosie is battling Judas at work, and Don is in hot water after the Genetics Lecture Outrage. The life-contentment graph, recently at its highest point, is curving downwards. For Don, geneticist and World's Best Problem-Solver, learning to be a good parent as well as a good partner will require the help of friends old and new. It will mean letting Hudson make his way in the world, and grappling with awkward truths about his own identity. And opening a cocktail bar.

Books by Graeme Simsion
Published by Ulverscroft:

with Anne Buist
TWO STEPS FORWARD

GRAEME SIMSION

◆

THE
ROSIE RESULT

Complete and Unabridged

AURORA
Leicester

First published in Great Britain in 2019 by
Penguin Random House
First published in Australia & New Zealand in 2019 by
Text Publishing

First Aurora Edition
published 2019
by arrangement with
Penguin Random House and Text Publishing

HEREFORDSHIRE
LIBRARIES

A catalogue record for this book is available
from the British Library.

ISBN 978–1–78782–136–1

Published by
F. A. Thorpe (Publishing)
Anstey, Leicestershire

Set by Words & Graphics Ltd.
Anstey, Leicestershire
Printed and bound in Great Britain by
T. J. International Ltd., Padstow, Cornwall

This book is printed on acid-free paper

To the many people in the autism community who have inspired and supported these books.

We are all special cases.

ALBERT CAMUS

1

I was standing on one leg shucking oysters when the problems began. If I had not been a scientist, conscious of the human propensity to see patterns where they do not exist, I might have concluded that I was being punished by some deity for the sin of pride.

Earlier that afternoon, I had been completing a performance-review form, and was presented with the question *What do you consider to be your key strength(s)?*

It was a vague construction which specified neither context nor level of generalisation. *Expertise in genetics* was the obvious answer, but this was implied by the job title Professor of Genetics. My knowledge of myxoid liposarcoma would soon be of minimal relevance, as my research project in that area was nearing completion. *Objectivity and intelligence* might suggest that I thought some academics lacked these attributes, which was true, but probably tactless. I needed to avoid tactlessness.

I was still searching for an answer when Rosie arrived home.

'What are you doing in your pyjamas?' she said.

'Preparing dinner. Which I'm time-sharing with solving a problem. And single-leg dips.'

'I meant, why are you wearing pyjamas?'

'There was a minor cooking accident involving

1

an exploding chestnut. I was attempting to speed up the process by increasing the temperature. Hence the oil on various surfaces.' I indicated the splashes on the ceiling. 'My clothes were also affected. I avoided further loss of time by switching directly to pyjamas rather than putting on an intermediate costume.'

'You haven't forgotten we've got Dave and Sonia for dinner?'

'Of course not. It's the second Wednesday of the month. The day I change my toothbrush head.'

Rosie performed her impression of my voice, a sign that she was in a good mood: 'Guests. Pyjamas. Not a valid combination.'

'Dave and Sonia have seen me in pyjamas. On the Cape Canaveral trip — '

'Don't remind me.'

'If there's time to change my costume, I should devote it to the performance-review form.' I explained the problem.

'Just write whatever you wrote last year.'

'I didn't do it last year. Or the year before. Or — '

'Twelve years at Columbia and you haven't had to do a performance review?'

'I don't complete the form. There's always some higher-priority task. Unfortunately, David Borenstein insisted. If it's not on his desk tomorrow, he's threatened to take some unspecified punitive action.'

'You're stuck on the question about strengths?'

'Correct.'

'Just say *problem-solving*. It's a good answer

and it won't come back to bite you. If you don't find a cure for cancer, they're not going to say, 'But you said you were a good problem-solver.''

'You've encountered the same question?'

'Only about twenty times in the last month.'

Rosie's current medical-research project was also finishing, and she was seeking a more senior position. It was proving difficult, as most roles involved clinical work. Her argument was: 'I'm a crap physician but a good researcher. Why waste time on stuff I'm not good at?' I had applied the same logic to the performance-review form.

'Presumably, you also gave the optimum answer,' I said. '*Problem-solving.*'

'I usually say *team player*, but in your case . . . '

'It might have returned to bite me.'

Rosie laughed. 'I'll finish filling it out and you'll have time to make yourself respectable. Teamwork, see.' She must have noticed my expression. 'You can review it when I'm done.'

As I processed the remaining oysters, I reflected on Rosie's suggestion. It was satisfying that my partner recognised an attribute that I had not previously articulated. I *was* a good problem-solver.

I had the advantage of an atypical — the word used by others was *weird* — approach to analysing and responding to situations. Over my twenty-five-year career, it had enabled me to overcome day-to-day obstacles and initiate major break-throughs. It had also delivered benefits in my personal life.

At twenty, I had been a computer-science

student, socially incompetent even by the standards of twenty-year-old computer-science students, with zero prospect of finding a partner.

Now, largely due to the deliberate application of problem-solving techniques, I was employed in a stimulating and well-paid job, married to the world's most beautiful and compatible woman (Rosie), and father to a talented and happy ten-year-old child (Hudson), who was showing signs of becoming an innovative problem-solver himself.

I had identified Rosie's biological father from sixty-five candidates, rescued my friend Dave's refrigeration business from financial failure, and, after detailed analysis of customer preferences in the bar where Rosie and I worked part-time, designed a cocktail which won the New York People's Choice Award.

I was in excellent health, in part because of regular martial-arts classes and a fitness program which I had integrated into other activities. Psychologically, I had the support of my local men's group: Dave and a retired musician named George.

Creative thinking had, over twelve years of marriage, produced a routine which accommodated Rosie's requirement for spontaneity without unduly sacrificing efficiency. I would have liked more sex, but the frequency was above the mean for our ages and relationship duration, and infinitely better than it had been prior to meeting Rosie.

The only significant blemish was the loss of my long-standing friendship with my mentor,

Gene. But even taking that factor into account, if I had maintained a graph of my contentment with life, the curve would now be at its highest point.

I returned to an oyster that had not offered an entry point for my knife. In the bottom drawer was a collection of tools, including pliers. If I used them to break the edge of the shell, I would create a gap into which the knife could be inserted. I allowed myself a moment of satisfaction. Don Tillman: World's Best Problem-Solver.

Rosie appeared with my notebook computer. 'What do you want to say for areas you'd like to improve? I put *fashion*.'

'You already mentioned the pyjamas.'

'I'm kidding. But there's always room for improvement. Those are bushwalking socks you're wearing, right?'

'Multi-purpose. Extremely warm.'

I turned towards her, in accordance with the convention that people look at each other while conversing. Concurrently, I was lowering myself on one leg to access the pliers, extending my free leg to keep my supporting shin vertical as required for the leg-dip exercise, while holding the oyster and knife in my other hand.

As I reached into the drawer behind me, I felt a pervasive stickiness. Reviewing the situation later, it was obvious what had happened. Rosie had recently instructed Hudson to put away his breakfast ingredients after use. He must have been concentrating on some other topic as he cleared the table and had stored the maple syrup on its side in a random drawer without replacing the lid.

I retracted my hand, rapidly — a primitive response to the unexpected. As a result, I lost my balance.

The best solution would have been to return my raised foot to the floor, but, instinctively not wanting to abandon the exercise, I grabbed another drawer, which was not an effective fixed support. I may have slipped in oil from the chestnut explosion. The net result was that I fell, though not heavily.

Rosie was laughing. 'Multi-tasking,' she said. 'Your multi-tasking could definitely do with improvement.' Then, 'Oh, shit, you've hurt yourself.'

Rosie's diagnosis was correct. I had trapped the oyster knife behind my knee. She knelt to examine the injury.

'*Don't move him!*' Hudson was standing in the doorway, also wearing pyjamas, as he did after school on Wednesdays.

'It's okay,' said Rosie. 'He hasn't hurt his spine.'

'How can you tell?' said Hudson.

'I'm a doctor, remember?'

This was an unconvincing argument, given Rosie's own assessment of her clinical competence. The knife had entered to some depth, and a pool of blood was forming on the floor.

'We need to call 911,' said Hudson.

'Excellent idea,' I said.

'Where's your phone?' said Rosie.

'In its holster. I'm lying on it.'

'*Don't move!*' said Hudson, placing himself between Rosie and me.

'Can we use your phone?' I asked Rosie.

'Hudson, go look in my handbag.'

'You promise not to move him? *Promise?*'

'Promise. Just get my phone.'

'Presumably they'll take me to the hospital,' I said. 'By then, the difficult oyster will probably have relaxed sufficiently to open conventionally.'

'Don, forget about dinner.'

'You'll need to submit the performance-evaluation form. The deadline — '

Hudson returned with Rosie's phone. She tapped the screen, and said, 'Shit.' I assumed her battery was flat — a common occurrence, due to lack of a charging regimen.

Fortunately, the doorbell rang. Dave and Sonia were, respectively, self-employed trades-person and financial controller. It was almost certain that one of them would have a functioning phone. Hudson activated the electronic lock.

Sonia was predictably hysterical, critical and practical. 'Oh my God, I knew you'd have an accident one day. It's crazy you coming home from work and having to cook. Can you move?'

'Don't go there,' said Rosie. 'Just call 911.'

'I'm on it,' said Dave. 'You're good with that, Don?'

'Correct.'

Rosie was staring at her phone.

'Is everything okay?' said Sonia. It was a strange question, but Rosie must have interpreted *okay* as *okay except for Don lying on the*

7

floor bleeding while Dave calls an ambulance.

'I got the job.' She said it again, more loudly, and began to cry. 'I got the job. The one I thought I had no chance of getting.'

'Which job?' I asked, looking up from the floor.

'Working for Judas.' Judas was Professor Simon Lefebvre, a former colleague in Australia who had been 'seeing' our friend Claudia for several years until being discovered in an act of infidelity.

'Judas is coming to New York?'

'No, the job's back in Melbourne. I knew you weren't listening.'

I probably had been listening, but I would have ignored the personnel and location to focus on the important parameters. I could find university employment wherever we lived, particularly as I was unconcerned about status, and it was Rosie's turn to advance her career after undertaking the majority of the Hudson-rearing task.

'Is that going to be a problem?' asked Rosie.

'Of course not. Excellent news. And I won't have to complete the performance-review form. We should have a drink to celebrate. Immediately.'

Rosie was shaking her head. 'We're going home. I need to call Phil.' Phil was Rosie's father.

Rosie's success more than compensated for the pain behind my knee. The life-contentment curve moved upwards again. It was the last time. Hudson was standing in the doorway holding his head with both hands.

8

Perhaps it was the unusual visual perspective created by lying on the floor, combined with the fact that Hudson was wearing pyjamas, but I was struck by how tall he had grown and, simultaneously, how young he still looked. With his dark hair, longer than typical for his age, and black-rimmed glasses, he could have been me at age ten. His obvious distress added to the identification.

The kitchen had gone silent and we were all looking at him.

'Are you all right, Hudson?' said Sonia.

'No. I don't want to go to Australia. I don't want to change schools. I don't want to change anything.'

2

By the following June, our situation had changed dramatically. We had relocated to a three-bedroom house in the 'hip' inner-Melbourne suburb of Northcote, a short bicycle ride from the university. Our new home featured a garden, garage and sufficient space for Hudson's collection of science-fiction novels, which now spilled from his room into the hallway.

My hamstring tendon was healing. Rosie was working for Judas, Hudson was attending school and I had secured employment as a professor of genetics. This much was within the range of possibilities we had planned for.

But five new problems had developed. In increasing order of severity, they were:

1. *Curing Cancer.* I had joined a research project evaluating individualised approaches to cancer treatment, taking into account patients' genetic make-up. It was potentially valuable work, but I was underqualified. The chief investigator had been impressed by my computer-science degree, but the field had changed hugely in the twenty-nine years since I reconfigured myself as a geneticist. I had deferred all optional activities, including aikido and karate, to catch up, but the online courses were consuming time and intellectual resources that I needed for the more serious problems.

I discovered after accepting the position that

Laszlo Hevesi, my friend in the Physics department, had also applied. He would have been perfect but had, predictably, 'interviewed badly'. He could not have listed *team player* or *fashionista* as strengths. But cancer sufferers would be unlikely to complain that the cure for their illness had been discovered by a man working at a computer screen in bicycle helmet and goggles.

There was also a personal aspect. My father was suffering from advanced prostate cancer, and my mother had been pleased that we were returning to Australia. I explained to her that by the time my research influenced clinical practice, my father would be dead, if not of cancer, then of old age.

It was possible that the job-incompetence issue would resolve itself, due to the second problem.

2. *The Genetics Lecture Outrage.* As a result of an error of judgement on my part, I was at risk of being fired. I was due to face a disciplinary committee, and the task of preparing my defence had already consumed one hundred and twenty-eight hours, not including disruption to sleep.

Rosie had proposed a radical solution. 'Screw them. You can make twice as much in the private sector. And no lecturing.' She persuaded me to approach a small company working in genome editing.

'You love this stuff,' said Rosie. 'You're always talking about it; here's a chance to do it.'

'I don't have the necessary knowledge.'

'So, you learn. Isn't that what you're spending every evening doing now?'

The interview had gone unexpectedly well. My potential employer, Dang Minh, a woman of approximately forty with an enthusiasm approaching mania, had shown me the lab, noting that they would soon be moving to new premises.

'We're changing the world. Solving impossible problems every day. How could you not want to work here?'

The answer was that I was wary of risking my professional and interpersonal skills outside the academic world. Still, it meant that I had options. Unlike my friend Dave.

3. The Dave Disaster. Dave had also suffered a knee injury and was currently unable to function as a refrigeration engineer. As a result of the American system of workers' compensation, or his failure to take out insurance, or the fact that the accident occurred in a bar, he was in financial trouble. Sonia, who had recently given birth to their second IVF child, had to return to work ahead of schedule. Dave was now responsible for baby care, a role he was not happy with. Rosie had been critical. 'Tell him, 'Welcome to what women have been doing forever.''

Dave's weight, which was unhealthily high (estimated BMI on our departure from New York: thirty-five), was likely to be impeding recovery. I had encouraged him during our weekly Skype discussions to eat less and devote more time to rehabilitation exercises. His failure to do either seemed to indicate a problem with his mental state. As a member of his psychological

12

support team, I needed to find a remedy.

4. *The Rosie Crucifixion*. The name of this problem was Rosie's idea, derived from a series of novels by Henry Miller. The second word was in fact spelled *Rosy*, so I would not have made the connection.

Rosie had been recruited to lead a project on bipolar disorder, commencing with a pilot study. This was the 'dream job' that had prompted our relocation. Then, in our first few months back in Australia, Hudson experienced some difficulties with the after-school care program, and Rosie, *with the agreement of her manager, Judas*, reduced her hours to enable her to collect Hudson from school on three afternoons per week. Her father, Phil, covered the remaining two days.

Then, when the funding proposal for the main project was being prepared, Judas used Rosie's part-time status as a reason to replace her as chief investigator.

'No consultation. He just gave my job to Stefan.'

'You've been demoted?'

'My permanent position stays the same. But I don't get to lead the study.'

'So, no management? No committees? No people issues? All those things you've been complaining about. Incredible. And you achieved it without having to demonstrate incompetence. We should celebrate.'

'Don, I *want* to run it.'

'Then we should research alternative after-school programs to enable you to return to full-time work.'

'No. Hudson needs time with one of us. And we know who that has to be.' We had discussed this before. Being older than Rosie and having worked full-time without breaks, I had a substantially higher income. Rosie's reduction in hours to care for Hudson again had reinforced a vicious circle.

I was treating the Rosie Crucifixion as second in importance only to the happiness of our child.

5. *The Hudson Adjustment Problem*. Hudson's reaction to our relocation was predictable. Like me, he had an aversion to changes in routine. It was a rational response to the need to relearn and re-optimise something that was working well, but certain transitions are unavoidable. Hudson found these transitions — notably to child care, pre-school and school — traumatic, and the effects frequently continued beyond the changeover date.

Several weeks after he began school in New York, his teacher discontinued her practice of walking with the children to meet their parents at the end of the day. Hudson had not memorised the route from classroom to gate, nor made friends with anyone who might have. A wrong turn led to him becoming lost, fortunately within the school grounds, but by the time Rosie gained access and located him, he was extremely distressed.

It was the first of several incidents of this kind, most of which could have been avoided by giving Hudson notice that he would need to memorise landmarks and turns, but the school seemed to interpret it as deliberate behaviour on his part

— 'wandering off' — rather than a predictable consequence of his brain not being equipped with an unconscious track-recording function.

Rosie had not been able to work in a full-time job until Hudson was 'settled' at another elementary school. For some periods her only employment had been making drinks with me in the cocktail bar.

Hudson had demonstrated a substantial variation in aptitude for schoolwork. Maths: excellent; Sport: terrible. English: outstanding; Handwriting: illegible. Science: ready for more challenge; Art: challenged. At home, he enjoyed reading, to the exclusion of other activities.

In the adult world, an uneven distribution of abilities is more valuable than mediocrity at everything. It is irrelevant to me whether or not my doctor is adept at hitting a ball with a stick — or finding her way to work without looking at street signs — but I would like her to be as proficient as possible in the practice of medicine. Conversely, at school, being other than unobtrusively average in every area (with the exception of sport) is a distinct *disadvantage*.

But in New York, at his new school, Hudson's teachers and classmates appeared to accept his personal configuration. He had two friends, one male and one female, and interacted successfully with Dave and Sonia's child, Zina. All seemed to be well, in contrast to my own experience of school in the country town of Shepparton — the worst time of my life.

In Australia, we had enrolled Hudson at a private school which scored marginally higher

15

than the local public school in my spreadsheet analysis. With its associated secondary school, it had an accelerated mathematics program and claimed to embrace diversity.

The diversity included females — essential in Rosie's opinion. 'I don't want him regarding women as some other species.'

I pointed out that I had attended a co-educational public school and had ended up regarding the majority of the human race as another species.

'Maybe, but at least you had a chance to study both genders.'

Hudson enrolled for the fourth term of Year Five. Initially, he appeared to enjoy the academic component. Rosie was concerned that he lacked friends, but I thought it likely that she was using her own ease at establishing social relationships as a benchmark. Hudson's only complaint was the poor organisation of the after-school program — inconsistent from day to day, with no published timetable. It was this that led to Rosie's decision to withdraw him from it, and the consequent series of events at work.

But now, eight months later, with fifty per cent of his final year of primary school completed, we were convinced that something was wrong. His academic results had fallen, and though his report card used ambiguous language, Rosie was certain that it was intended to signal an 'issue'. We had booked an appointment with his teacher on the twelfth day of the third term.

Rosie also suspected that Hudson had feigned illness to avoid school attendance. Several times at home he had exploded in frustration at some obstacle. A problem was brewing, like the general malaise before the full symptoms of an illness appear, and I was waiting for it to declare itself. When it did, it would receive priority over all other matters.

3

The phone call signalling an escalation in the Hudson Adjustment Problem came at 10.18 on a Friday morning. At 5 a.m., Rosie had delivered Hudson to the school for a three-day excursion to the snow. He had been sharing information about it for several days and appeared to be excited and well informed.

I was at home preparing for the Genetics Lecture Outrage disciplinary hearing, scheduled for that afternoon.

The incident had occurred during the final lecture before the semester break. We had completed the prescribed curriculum with twenty-four minutes remaining and I saw an opportunity to implement a recommendation from a seminar I had been compelled to attend on making lectures more 'engaging'.

'Any questions?' I asked. There was a collective gasp, scattered applause and then conversation. It is traditional to encourage questions, but they typically reflect the concerns of one student and are of minimal relevance to the rest of the class. By banning questions, I am able to pack the maximum amount of information into each lecture.

A student who I guessed was in her early twenties raised her hand.

'Professor Tillman, do you believe that race has a genetic basis?' She looked to the woman

18

beside her, possibly to confirm that she had phrased the question correctly.

'It's an interesting topic, but outside the scope of the course and hence the exam.' I expected that would end the discussion, but, to my surprise, the other members of the class indicated that they would like an answer. It was an interesting topic.

I began by dealing with my interrogator's reference to belief, a concept that should be used sparingly in science. In the few minutes that it took me to repeat a practised correction, my subconscious produced a brilliant idea which I was sure would have impressed the convenors of the 'Engaging the Millennial Mind' seminar.

Melbourne is one of the world's most ethnically diverse cities, and the mix of students in the room was consistent with this. Many were studying genetics with the intention of enrolling in Medicine, a popular career choice for migrants and their children as well as international students.

I advised the class that participation was optional, then summoned to the stage an archetypal physical example of each of the 'three great races' as defined in the late nineteenth century: a tall, older woman from Ghana named Beatrice, whom I knew as an aspiring physician; the sole Scandinavian, a heavily built Danish male whose name I did not know; and one of the numerous Chinese students, Hui. Her small stature was in striking contrast to Beatrice's height and the Danish male's solidity.

Negroid, Mongoloid and Caucasoid. I knew

that these terms were no longer acceptable. Even as I acknowledged this, the class appeared shocked; I had delivered a powerful lesson on the subjectivity and evolution of classification schemes. The woman who had originally asked the question appeared to be making a video recording of the exercise on her smartphone.

The three nominated students looked at each other and laughed. I could see why scientists in the past had argued — incorrectly — that they represented distinct subspecies of *Homo sapiens*.

The second phase of the demonstration was intended to challenge this simplistic formulation. I directed each of my reference students to a corner of the stage and addressed the class.

'Consider the stage a two-dimensional graph with Beatrice at the origin, consistent with humans originating in Africa. Hui is positioned on the X axis and the male student with the pale skin and blue eyes is on the Y axis.'

Danish Student interrupted: 'I'm Arvid. Arvid the Aryan. My great-grandfather would be proud that I was chosen, but that is perhaps not so good.' There was scattered conversation. The millennials were definitely engaged.

I continued: 'I request all students to position themselves on the graph according to physical appearance.' Again, I remembered to add: 'Participation is optional.'

Almost everyone participated. Two of the exceptions were the woman who had asked the original question, now occupied with recording, and her friend. The others mounted the stage and began organising themselves, just as we had done in the 'line up in order of experience' exercise that had inspired me. After a few minutes, Beatrice left her place and approached me.

'Professor Tillman, are you sure this is a good idea?'

'You've observed some problem?'

'Not for me.' She laughed and pointed to a small group around Arvid the Aryan. 'It's killing me watching those guys arguing about who's the whitest.' The discussion among the Indian and Pakistani students was also animated.

When the positions of the students had stabilised, I began the debriefing, pointing out what was now obvious — that we were dealing not with categories but a spectrum — in fact, multiple spectra. I planned to follow by discussing explanations for the rapid evolution of local physical characteristics that were not directly linked to survival. Then my phone rang.

During lectures, my phone is programmed to respond to calls only from Rosie's work number, which by agreed convention, indicates an emergency.

'What the fuck is *happening*?' said Rosie.

This was confusing. 'You should be telling *me* what's happening,' I said. 'Presumably an emergency.'

'*You're* the emergency. It's all over Twitter. What are you *doing*?'

'You're using Twitter? At work?'

'A friend called me. From Columbia.'

'Someone called you from South America — '

'Columbia *University*. Where you *worked* for ten years.'

'Twelve.'

21

Now, to add to the confusion, there was a second interruption. Three security personnel entered the lecture theatre. One of them approached me, confirmed my identity and led me out. After that, I was not longer a witness to events, but from the disciplinary-committee summons, together with a visit from Beatrice, I was able to establish what had followed.

In summary, the Twitter posts portrayed me as an advocate for the exact theories of race that I was seeking to debunk, as well as for discrimination, eugenics and public humiliation.

All members of the class were offered counselling and one lodged a formal complaint. The social-media exposure prompted three opinion pieces in the press, misrepresenting the facts and arguing that my behaviour was representative of a general malaise. This was new to me: I was accustomed to criticism for being unusual rather than typical. Only one journalist contacted me, and the article he wrote seemed accurate and balanced. Unfortunately, he was, in Rosie's words, a 'right-wing nut job' and his views on unrelated matters meant he would have zero credibility with the university.

My defence occupied sixty-two pages, and Rosie insisted that I summarise it.

'This is the summary.'

She shook her head. 'You're saying that you were using a creative teaching approach to present a scientific argument to a scientifically literate audience, who were not required to participate, and, had you not been interrupted, your conclusions would have been not only in line with current scientific thinking but with progressive philosophical and political views. Is that basically it?'

'You're a genius. Incredible conciseness. It's true and completely exonerates me.'

'I wouldn't count on it. These things aren't decided by whether the science is right.'

I was allowed to bring a 'support person' to my hearing and had an offer from an unexpected source — the former Dean of Science, Professor Charlotte Lawrence, who was now the head of administration at another university.

Professor Lawrence and I had argued — *clashed* — on numerous occasions, almost always over conflicts between personal and scientific integrity (me) and the university's public image (her). However, she was an expert in academic administration and would have a high degree of credibility. I was amazed that she would want to have anything to do with me.

Her assessment of the situation was consistent with Rosie's. The university would not only be concerned with establishing the truth.

'Whatever the finding, they're worried that any future funding proposal with your name on it will attract the wrong kind of attention.' Professor Lawrence did not need to elaborate. In the academic world, the ability to attract funding ranks above all other qualities.

She recommended I solicit personal references. 'And not just from straight white males.'

'Why are gender and sexual orientation relevant? The accusation is of racism.'

'Don, don't make me argue with you on this

23

or I might change my mind about helping. You're a straight, white, middle-aged male who's spent his life in top western universities. You're the definition of privilege.'

A few days later, we met again, and my news was not good. David Borenstein, my former dean, had emailed to say that nobody from Columbia would be providing references. *When it comes to racism, there's no room for fine distinctions: we can't be seen to offer anything but unequivocal condemnation. Had this happened at Columbia, I would have had no option but to terminate your employment, despite my longstanding admiration for you professionally and personally.*

David's email only increased my perplexity about Professor Lawrence's willingness to defend me. Her explanation was remarkably similar to the newspaper article that had supported me, including the phrases 'professional offence-takers', 'outrage industry' and 'identity politics'. It appeared that she was also a right-wing nut job. I pointed this out.

'Don,' she said, 'we've known each other a long time. You're not always the most tactful or sensitive person, but I've never doubted your integrity and decency. I'm still a scientist and academic, and I don't ever want academics to be afraid to think and speak freely on questions of science.'

Rosie was impressed that Professor Lawrence was involved.

'I'm guessing that before Charlotte said all those nice things about academic freedom, she gave you a serve. A dressing-down.'

'I'm familiar with both colloquialisms. But no, there was no 'bollocking'.'

'Fuck, Don. She's gay, isn't she?'

'Presumably. Her partner is female. Why?'

'Because I'm a woman, and all my life I've had to deal with stuff: discrimination, attitudes, something in the paper or on TV or a billboard, little things that are too small to complain about without looking petty, but they add up. They make life not as good as it should be, every day, and you can't do anything about it. It's worse now I'm a mother as well — the way people talk to me when I'm with Hudson, and at work . . . not just Judas — everyone makes it part of my identity in a way they don't do with Stefan, who's got a four-year-old. I figure it'd be worse again if I was a lesbian.'

'I didn't suggest any race was inferior or superior. Which is the underlying definition — '

'Don, you're not listening. Imagine you're one of those students in your class from . . . it doesn't matter . . . India. Or with Indian parents. Every day, you're forced to be conscious of the colour of your skin and what it means. People ask, 'Where are you from?' when it's got nothing to do with anything. You do something good, or something bad, and the fact that you're Indian gets brought into it. Maybe you're studying to be a doctor, and after all your work, someone whose life you're saving is going to prefer you were white. And you'll know it.' Rosie stopped and laughed. 'Okay, maybe *you* wouldn't.'

'You're suggesting that I caused suffering to

students by reminding them of something that is . . . annoying to them?'

'I'm saying you added to their load. They go to class to learn about Huntington's disease and suddenly the lecturer's getting them to declare their race. If you don't play, you'll stand out. I know when you went on that course, they lined you up in order of experience, but that's not the same as doing it according to something that's problematic. Imagine if . . . I can't think of an example.'

I could. My primary-school teacher assessing our handwriting by lining us up randomly and then making comparisons. After each comparison, I would move down, until I reached my inevitable position at the 'worst' end. I wasn't ashamed of my writing. I never complained about the assessment approach, which was doubtless convenient and accurate.

But it was annoying. Like being 'accidentally' bumped when I was carrying books or having my pencil case emptied or my exercise book scribbled on or my lunch interfered with or my style of speaking mimicked or my gait imitated or my attempts to hit a ball laughed at or being referred to by my nickname or being the target of a teacher's wit. An accumulation of reminders that I wasn't average and didn't fit in.

'No example required,' I said.

★   ★   ★

'Don? It's Neil Warren, Hudson's teacher.'
'Is there a problem?' My immediate thought

26

was that Hudson had failed to bring a critical item for the snow excursion. The school had provided a packing list, but there had been some debate between Hudson and Rosie about its interpretation. Hudson had emptied his drawers into four large bags, which Rosie had reduced to one. Perhaps she had mistakenly discarded something.

'I'm afraid so. Hudson's had a bit of a meltdown.'

It took me a few seconds to interpret Mr Warren's statement, as the use of the term *meltdown* in the context of snow created a distracting image.

'He wasn't happy with the ski boots . . . Look, he's okay now, but he won't be skiing, and we don't have the resources to look after him if he's not with the group. I'm afraid someone's going to have to come and collect him.'

I was already on my way to the car.

4

The GPS indicated a drive of three hours and eighteen minutes to the mountain resort. I texted Rosie to explain the situation: *Hudson crisis. Gone to snow.*

In the absence of detailed information, there was little I could do to plan my response. Hudson's teacher could be using the term *meltdown* to describe anything from anger at an unreasonable rule to the near-complete loss of control that I had suffered sometimes as a child and less frequently as I grew older — only once in the thirteen years, four months and three days since I had met Rosie. Hudson had himself experienced some episodes of this type at home — several in the last few months — but they had been resolved with the time-out protocol.

I guessed that my job would be to reassure Mr Warren that a repeat was unlikely in the short term, assuming the triggering circumstances had been resolved. I recalled that he was about my own age. As a result of a habit I was finding difficult to break, I had also estimated body mass index: twenty-five. I could not picture his face. He had seemed friendly at the parent — teacher night, but I knew from experience that parents' superficial judgements of teachers are frequently inaccurate.

After negotiating the winding road to the resort, I parked in an 'emergencies only' car space, unfortunately failing to notice a bollard obscured by snow. The damage to the front of Phil's Porsche was only cosmetic. We had the car on 'permanent loan', as Rosie's father had realised that it was more sensible to buy a new Toyota than drive and maintain an old vehicle whose design appeared not to be based on any practical requirements. I texted Professor Lawrence to advise her that I would not be able to attend the afternoon's hearing, due to a family emergency.

There were multiple voicemails and texts from Rosie, but a single three-part message would have been sufficient: *What the fuck is going on? Is Hudson all right? Call me NOW.*

Rosie wanted the information that I was being prevented from finding out due to being on the phone to her. I explained this.

'Are you sure you don't need me to come up?' she said.

In conversation, it is impolite to say, 'Refer previous answer,' so I repeated, 'I need to assess the situation first.'

'You should have called me. You're not missing anything important? Oh shit, shit, *shit*.'

'The disciplinary-committee meeting has been deferred. I'll call when I have more information on the Hudson problem.'

An employee of the ski school directed me to Hudson, who was sitting on a bench reading *The Martian*. I was unable to detect any distress. Beside him was a thin white-haired girl of approximately the same age whom I assessed as albino. She was wearing sunglasses and eating a Snickers bar.

'What happened?' I asked Hudson.

'I have to go home. She does too.' He indicated his companion, who removed the earbuds she had been wearing.

'She also found the boots unsatisfactory?'

The girl answered the question herself. 'I'm vision-impaired.' Albinism is associated with sensitivity to light and compromised eyesight.

Hudson added, 'When Mr Warren found out, he checked her permission form and it wasn't on it, so she couldn't legally ski.'

'I'm new,' said the girl. 'I came to meet everyone. Now I've got to go home.'

'*Have to* go home,' said Hudson. My father did not approve of Hudson's use of *gotta*. Hudson had corrected the problem and had been sharing the advice with others.

'They haven't been able to call my parents because my dad's in Thailand and my mum's not in the shop. The masseuse minds it when my mum has to go out for something. My name's Blanche, by the way.'

It was an easy name to remember.

'Your mother's mobile phone is not responding?'

'She doesn't have one. Because of cancer. Neither does my dad.'

I was trying to work out what forms of cancer might prevent use of a phone — throat, larynx, possibly brain — and how likely it was that two members of a family had such forms, when Blanche explained. 'She doesn't *have* cancer, but she doesn't want to get it. From the microwaves.'

'Can we give her a ride — lift?' asked Hudson.

'We'll need to get permission, because on the form there's a question about . . . '

My brain was in danger of becoming overloaded before I had any information relevant to the primary problem. I drew my finger along my lips: the *zip it* signal. In communication with Hudson it meant *suspend talking to receive important input*.

'I need to know the exact nature of the problem.'

'It doesn't matter. I have to go home, that's all.'

'Mr Warren indicated that there was a problem with boots. If you explain it to me, possibly we can solve it.'

Hudson sat silently, a familiar indication that he wanted to sit silently. An interrogation would be unproductive. However, he was generally willing to argue.

'I presume there was some error on your part.'

'No way, Dad. I didn't do anything. It was their job to have boots that fitted.'

'Surely they would be equipped for all foot sizes within the normal range.'

Hudson explained that several sizes had been tried, but all were either painfully tight or too loose to enable control of the skis.

The ski-hire assistant had proposed alternative brands, along with supplementary socks and inserts, without significant improvement. The manager had been summoned and explained the necessity of a tight fit. Hudson had not been convinced.

Blanche interrupted. 'Everybody was putting it

31

on Hudson,' she said, 'because they all had their boots and wanted to get skiing.' It was easy to deduce the missing elements of the story, which Hudson might not want to reveal, due to embarrassment. I knew already that it had ended in a meltdown.

Hudson had a high sensitivity to pain and disliked many forms of physical contact, particularly if they were out of his control. I had the same problem as a child and was regularly mocked as a 'sissy'. I would likely have had a similar reaction to having another person tightening straps and closing buckles on unfamiliar rigid boots, especially under time pressure.

I tried to imagine myself in Hudson's current position. I would want to return home, immediately, as he apparently did. My own father would have taken me back to the ski shop, persisted with the boots and eventually become angry that I was 'being a sook'. I needed to do better.

The ski school would surely have dealt with this situation before. I found the employee who had been overseeing Hudson and Blanche and explained the problem.

'Talk to Lucy,' she said. 'I promise she will have a . . . solution.'

We waited at the designated location and Lucy appeared, travelling by snowboard. I guessed her age and BMI as twenty-two. She looked more like a science student than a ski instructor.

She addressed Hudson. 'I hear we don't like ski boots.'

'*I* don't like them. Every pair I tried hurt somewhere.'

'Right. You and me both. You okay with falling in the snow?' Lucy demonstrated by falling in the snow, firmly. 'Go on.'

Hudson stood still, but Blanche threw herself into the soft snow, then stood up again, laughing. I guessed Hudson felt pressured to conform. He collapsed, slowly, then performed the action twice more, each time with greater force. Blanche followed, harder again, and Hudson responded by crashing into the snow with what appeared to be maximum effort. Competition had stimulated behaviour that would otherwise be considered ridiculous.

'That's as much as it's going to hurt,' said Lucy. 'So, ready to go snowboarding?'

'I've got a vision problem,' said Blanche.

'Am I black or white?' said Lucy.

Blanche laughed. 'White.'

'Good to go, then.' She looked at me and said, 'And your dad won't have a problem either.'

I explained that I was not Blanche's father and that the lesson was only for Hudson. Lucy explained, in turn, that the tuition price was the same. The snowboard and boots would be covered by the credit for the unused skis. 'And you can come too, if you want.'

'I have no requirement to be able to use a snowboard,' I said.

'I'm thinking about the kids. Everyone's a bit uncoordinated at first, and if they see you falling about . . .'

'I'm recovering from an operation on my

hamstring tendon. It would be unwise to stress it.'

She nodded. 'Okay, then. And you won't look silly in front of the kids.' She laughed, but I sensed that I had been criticised.

'We could be sued if Blanche crashes and dies,' said Hudson. 'We don't have a permission form.'

Hudson was probably right. Blanche's mother was apparently irrational and might initiate litigation because I had exposed her daughter to radio waves or gluten or the chemicals in sunscreen, which it was obviously essential that she wear. But at that point the original ski-school employee appeared and advised that Blanche's mother was on the landline.

Blanche explained the situation, then thrust the receiver at me.

'Hello,' said Blanche's mother. 'I'm sorry, I don't even know your name.'

'No apology required. We haven't met. I wouldn't expect you to know my name.'

She left a long pause before saying, 'I'm Allannah. I can't believe I missed the disability question on the form. Sorry, I should be thanking you. You're being so kind.'

'I'm doing zero. Which should be reassuring to you. I've outsourced the problem to a professional. Her name is Lucy. Ski instructing is a highly competitive profession, so unless she obtained the job in some corrupt manner, she should be competent. However, I require you to absolve me of all liability if Blanche is injured or killed, whether or not I am partially or completely responsible.'

'Um, you're just being technical, right? You're not planning anything?'

'Correct.'

She laughed. 'I don't really know the teachers either, so I guess it's no difference. Sorry, I'm sounding rude.'

'Definitely not.' She was sounding rational, which was a surprise.

'I hate to ask this, but would you be able to bring Blanche back with you too? We're just in Thornbury.'

'I have a better solution. If I outsource the day activities to Lucy, she can return Hudson and Blanche to the teacher in the evenings. They will be able to participate in the non-skiing activities and Blanche will achieve her familiarisation goal.'

I could have added, 'And Hudson will not be embarrassed by having to return home,' but he and Blanche were listening.

'Are you serious? You'll organise all that for Blanche?'

'There's minimal incremental effort.'

'What can I say? Thank you so much. I'm so sorry . . . '

'Apology not required. Blanche will provide companionship for Hudson.'

'Well, thank you again. You're a good person. But can you make sure she doesn't eat any sugar?'

★ ★ ★

Complications arose. Rosie was impressed with my solution, but insisted I stay for the handover to Mr Warren. 'He may not be as excited as you are.'

Rosie was right, although he was initially friendly.

'Call me Neil. Actually, you can call me Rabbit. I used to play a bit of cricket and the name's stuck. Just don't say it in front of the kids. Listen, I really appreciate you driving all this way, and taking Blanche home as well. I was up to my arse in alligators.'

'Alligators?'

'You know, *When you're up to your arse in alligators, it's hard to remember that your original intention was to drain the swamp.*' Rabbit laughed. 'Busy.'

It seemed a particularly obtuse way of expressing a state that could be described unambiguously in a single word. I wondered how effectively he communicated with eleven-year-olds.

His friendliness disappeared when I advised him that Hudson and Blanche would be staying. It took fifty-seven minutes to work through his objections. I had already decided that I would remain to oversee the various handovers and periods between lessons.

I had a solution or counter-argument for all of his concerns: the lack of supervisory resources; the legal risk of including activities beyond those originally advised to parents; the need to avoid making an exception, which I pointed out was counter to the school's mission statement, which emphasised the importance of treating each child as an individual . . .

Rabbit interrupted me: 'By God, I see where Hudson gets it from.'

'Gets what from?'

'Doesn't matter. Listen, I've been running this activity for thirteen years. In the holidays, off my own bat. In exchange for that, I get to make the calls. I could send Hudson home. Blanche too. But she's just starting at the school, and she's got a disability . . . '

He stopped and tapped his hand on the table a few times. 'I appreciate what you're doing for the kids and your being prepared to stay here yourself. Otherwise I'd absolutely be asking you to take him home. But you need to know — and I'd like you to convey this to your wife — that it's not just about the boots.'

5

'What the fuck is that supposed to mean? 'Not just about the boots'?'

I was back home, debriefing Rosie, and did not have an answer for her question. The three days at the snow had been incredibly busy. Securing accommodation was straightforward early in the season, but I spent several hours at the laundromat, dressed in two towels, washing my single set of clothes, twice, and continuing my skills update. I also had to provide high-level supervision for Hudson and Blanche. Rabbit was unavailable for extended conversation, due to the alligator — swamp problem.

At the first end-of-day handover from Lucy, I sought clarification of her statement implying that I was happy she was white.

'You recognised me from a newspaper article?' I said.

'I'm an engineering student. I probably shouldn't have said anything but if you complain to the ski school . . . ' She shrugged. 'Not speaking out is the same as acceptance.'

I began to explain, but she cut me off.

'I don't want to discuss it. The kids are good: we'll just do a couple of lessons tomorrow and they can do the beginner slopes by themselves if you keep an eye on them.'

And there had been a disturbing call from Professor Lawrence.

'Don, the postponement has given me time to think, and . . . I don't want you to take this the wrong way. But you're an unusual person. Perhaps not so unusual in the Science and Mathematics faculties. But, I was wondering, have you ever seen a psychologist?'

'Why?'

'I think even a layperson might guess that you were on the spectrum — the autism spectrum. I imagine I'm not the first person to suggest that.'

'Correct.'

Professor Lawrence paused. 'This trouble you've got yourself into is all about oppression of minorities. Yet you yourself . . . '

It took me several seconds to comprehend what she was suggesting.

'You're proposing that I claim to have Asperger's syndrome. Making me a member of a minority entitled to special consideration.'

'A person with a disability — and one relevant to the mistake you made. You'd need a formal diagnosis, if you don't already have one.'

My initial feeling was of relief. If I did obtain a diagnosis, I would have a simple explanation to give to people like Lucy. But within minutes of terminating the call, I began to feel uncomfortable.

It seemed to me that claiming Asperger's syndrome as an excuse for the Genetics Lecture Outrage was cowardly. It would reflect badly on others with Asperger's who might not have done what I did. And, despite Professor Lawrence's informal assessment, I did not consider myself 'on the spectrum'.

In New York, a psychiatrist had argued, after

one of our lunch companions had made that suggestion, that I would not qualify for a diagnosis: my personality did not cause me to suffer socially or professionally. The 'professional suffering' criterion had now been met, but only as a result of a change in my employer's attitude to me. I was not prepared to accept that I could acquire a syndrome without any change to myself.

On the other hand, based on my experience of the psychiatric profession, it was likely that we could find someone who was prepared to add Asperger's to the list that I had accumulated in my early twenties.

In the morning, I called Professor Lawrence.

'Don, it's 6.30 a.m.'

'This may take some time, and I have an immovable family commitment.'

'Are you getting help with this family crisis?'

'Of course. Professional help.' Lucy was doing an excellent job with the snowboard lessons, which both Hudson and Blanche were enjoying.

'Go on, then.'

'You're suggesting we argue that because I have a particular brain configuration, a result of genetics and possibly environmental factors . . . '

'We won't be required to deliver a paper on the causes of autism.'

'What if it were some other neurological variant?'

'Such as? I'm sorry, I can't see what point you're making.'

'The point is that everyone's brain configuration is a combination of genetic and environmental factors. We only give names to variations that are

40

easily described and relatively common. My behaviour at the lecture was a result of my brain configuration. It should be irrelevant whether or not that configuration has its own name.'

'Don . . . I hear what you're saying, but you're making a philosophical argument about free will. Maybe you can take it to a conference, but it's not going to fly at a university disciplinary hearing. You'd just convince them that you were crazy.'

'Isn't that the idea? Not guilty by reason of insanity?'

'Disability.'

'I don't consider myself disabled.'

I agreed to let Professor Lawrence know if I changed my mind. And unless that happened, there was no reason to report the conversation to Rosie.

★   ★   ★

The meeting with Rabbit Warren to discuss Hudson's report was brought forward, at the school's request, to the first week of the third term. 'Something else had come up' and the principal would also attend.

Rosie met with Hudson, without me ('We don't want him to feel like it's an inquisition'), to conduct an inquisition in advance of the meeting. He was unable, or unwilling, to provide any useful information. Rosie assured him that we would be concerned only about his best interests, as would the school. I was confident about the first part.

As Rosie and I proceeded along the corridor

of an educational institution for a meeting which was presumably about some form of misconduct, it struck me that Hudson's life and mine were following similar trajectories.

We were seven minutes into the interview when Neil Warren (who, despite the absence of students, now did *not* want to be addressed as Rabbit) added another — stunning — element of commonality.

'I've seen quite a few boys like Hudson. Most of them have subsequently — or in some cases already — been diagnosed as autistic.'

'As *having* autism,' said principal, whom I judged as being approximately Rosie's age — forty-two. She addressed Rosie and me: 'When we're talking about disabilities, we try to use person-first language.'

I was not sure whether to address her as Ms Williams or Bronwyn. My attempt to suppress the estimation of her BMI had had the usual opposite effect. Approximately thirty-five. She had seemed friendly as she commenced the ritual of emphasising positives before delivering bad news.

'Hudson does well in the science subjects.'

'He was top of his class in science and maths in New York,' said Rosie. 'One of the reasons we chose this school was the advanced maths program.'

'Well,' said the principal, 'that's one of the things we wanted to talk about. He has good mathematical intuition, and an excellent memory, but — ' She pointed to Neil.

'Not keen on doing the working. Sees the

answer. Can't explain how he got there. These kids do well at first, but when the problems get harder and they have to follow a process, quite a few of them drop back. And he's not interested in doing it any way but his way.'

'In his report, you mentioned public speaking,' said Rosie.

'He certainly gets enough practice. And he's confident. But it's always space travel. Flights and dates. Not necessarily stuff that captivates a Year Six audience. And he's not keen on reading.'

'*Not keen on reading?* What planet are you guys on?'

'I'm his teacher. We're doing *Harry Potter* in class . . . '

Rosie laughed. 'He hates *Harry Potter*.'

I explained. 'It contains magic. Hudson objects to all books that rely on magic. But he reads hard science-fiction. And non-fiction.' Hudson had read *one* non-fiction book, multiple times. We had purchased it on a trip to Cape Canaveral and he was familiar with every fact that it recorded. Rosie and I had also become familiar with those facts.

'Thank you for that,' said the principal. 'We can't always judge a child by what we see in class. It's wonderful he's reading, but we may all want to work on broadening his scope.'

That was when Neil mentioned autism.

'But first things first,' said the principal, giving him a look which I interpreted as annoyance. She had delivered good news, then Neil had interrupted with bad news, and now she would need to deliver two pieces of good news to complete the first bad-news sandwich and begin the second, before she could deliver her own bad news. She seemed to be struggling to think of sufficient good news, as I frequently did when applying the formula, and moved directly to the bad news.

'The reason for bringing this meeting forward is that we've had a complaint from the parents of one of Hudson's classmates. I can't officially identify them, but the circumstances make it obvious who they are. I understand you spent some time at the snow with their daughter.'

Rosie looked at me and I detected horror. She had warned me — too late — of the risks of a middle-aged male taking responsibility for a pre-teenage girl whose family he did not know. Was I about to have *paedophile* added to *racist*?

As frequently happened, the reality was less serious than my fears. Hudson had asked Blanche what form of albinism she had and informed her that at least one variant was associated with a reduced lifespan. Blanche had, in turn, asked her parents, who had complained to the school.

'I understand you're a scientist, Don, and I can see why you might want to explain this to Hudson, but he may need some guidance with tact,' said the principal.

'I can second that,' said Neil. 'It's one of the things with autism. Not his fault; it's the . . . disorder.'

'I didn't discuss it with him,' I said. 'It's likely he researched it himself. I presume Blanche has the less-desirable form of albinism. Or her parents would have given her the good news and there would have been no complaint.'

'I wouldn't presume anything,' said the principal. 'Blanche has just joined the school and, given she seems to have latched on to Hudson, and . . . You're a medical doctor, Rosie?'

Rosie nodded. This was not the time to bring up the 'crap physician' characterisation.

'Well,' said the principal, 'you can see for yourselves from the parents' list that he's some sort of naturopath. So . . . I wouldn't assume any level of consultation with your profession.'

'Do we now discuss the Asperger's hypothesis?' I asked.

'Autism. Excuse me correcting you, but psychiatrists don't use the term Asperger's any longer and it's important that we stay up-to-date,' said the principal. 'What we used to call Asperger's we now understand as a milder form of autism. Which is what Neil is suggesting Hudson may have.'

Rosie responded before I could argue about the terminology. 'Thanks for the heads-up. We're glad we chose a school that values diversity. If it ever becomes a problem — if there are particular things we need to support him with — I'm sure you'll let us know.'

She began to stand, but Neil already had some particular things. Multiple particular things.

'He's behind socially. He doesn't really have friends. Except possibly Blanche, and that's early days.'

Neil paused, apparently to search his mind for more faults. 'He's a bit of a smartypants — someone's taught him more grammar than he needs at this stage of his education. And combined with what we refer to as 'no filter' when we're talking about . . . people with autism . . . I'd appreciate it if you told him that correcting the teacher is not appropriate. He can't help having an American accent, but he has a strong voice and it all adds to the effect. Does he do that at home?'

'No,' I said, 'but Rosie and I don't generally make grammatical errors.'

'Right,' said Rabbit and paused again. 'He really struggles at sport, especially team sport. He runs like . . . doesn't run tidily, can't catch. And the meltdown he had at the snow wasn't the first. Two or three times I've had to send him to the time-out room — '

'You have a dedicated room for time-outs?' I asked. It seemed like an excellent idea.

'It's actually the sick bay, but it functions as a time-out room too.'

'A message there,' said Rosie.

'As I was saying, he had a couple of . . . I didn't see them as meltdowns then, but — '

'Now that you're seeing him through the lens of autism . . . '

'Look,' said Neil, 'I know what goes on. He was being wound up, which is going to happen when you're . . . different. But I have to let the kids know that you can't go crazy because someone's niggling you. At this level they've got to start building some resilience.'

Resilience appeared to be the equivalent of toughening up, which, when I was a child, was a general excuse for bullying.

'I think we've got enough to think about,' said Rosie. 'Unless there's something more serious. Good academically, a bit young socially, fights back when he's attacked.'

'It's more than that,' said Rabbit. 'We say 'social skills' but they're really life skills. Developing friendships, playing in a group, dealing with conflict and anger. Knowing when to stop talking. The uniform.'

Hudson preferred to wear the summer uniform, with shorts, throughout the year. The school rules specified that Years Five and Six boys were to wear long trousers in the cold season, other than in exceptional circumstances. Hudson had argued that as he was the only student who wanted to wear shorts, he was exceptional, and therefore should be accommodated. After extensive discussion, the school had agreed.

'I thought we'd sorted that one,' said Rosie.

'I'm not going to make him wear long pants,' said Rabbit, 'but it's another sign of him being behind socially. Next year . . . '

The principal interrupted. 'The bottom line is that we think it would be a good idea if you looked at getting a diagnosis.'

'You want him tested for autism?' I said.

The principal nodded. 'We can't make you, but it'll be easier for everyone if we know what we're dealing with. Especially, as Neil was saying, being ready for high school. If there's a diagnosis on the record, we can get some help. Maybe a teacher's aide.'

'For Hudson specifically?' said Rosie.

'Not necessarily. But additional funding, and the more we have, the more we can do for everyone.'

Funding. I was right. Hudson and I were living parallel lives.

6

After the school interview, we drove to Jarman's Gym, owned by Rosie's father. Hudson was the youngest VIP member, despite using the facilities only for homework and reading. Rosie gave Phil a summary of Rabbit's observations and the principal's recommendation.

Phil was opposed to any professional intervention. In his day, children ate peanuts and played in the streets. Hudson was a good kid. Both his parents were eggheads, so what should we expect? Let him be himself. He might have a tough time at school, but in a few years the jocks would be working for him.

'How's your old man doing?' asked Phil.

'Physically, badly. Psychologically, well. He purchased a book on Beethoven and is listening to everything in chronological order. It's his final project.'

'You've seen him, then?'

'Not this week.' The family home in Shepparton was a two-hour-and-eighteen-minute drive in each direction and there were multiple other issues needing attention. It had been several weeks since our last visit.

My mother wanted to see us more often and my father was particularly insistent about spending time with Hudson. He complained that he had seen little of his only grandchild when we lived in New York, and now would not be around to watch him grow up.

'Who's going to teach him to ride a bike?' my father had said. It was a reasonable question, as Hudson had resisted learning to ride in New York. Buying him a bike for Christmas had demonstrated the folly of the Santa Claus deception: 'I *told* Santa I wanted Lego. Did I do something bad?' The bike had been returned and Hudson had reached the age of eleven without an important life skill.

★　★　★

We time-shared dinner with discussion of the book Hudson had read prior to *The Martian*. As a result of the conversation with Rabbit, I decided to introduce a new element to the meal routine. Hudson initially objected to the change, but quickly became involved in the interesting-number game, the goal of which is to find unique properties for each successive integer.

We suspended the competition at fifteen (the product of the first three odd numbers) and proceeded to the second issue.

'I recommend not interrupting your teacher with grammar corrections.'

'Not fair. Mr Warren dobbed me in.'

'Mr Warren spoke to us because he wanted our help in teaching you something,' said Rosie. 'Even in adult meetings, people can't just talk when they feel like it.'

'We're allowed to ask questions, as long as we put our hands up. Maybe I could make it a question, like *Why did you say less instead of fewer?*'

'Excellent idea,' I said. 'Particularly as I can save you significant effort by giving you the correct answer for all occasions, which is *Because I made an error that the whole class now knows about, which is embarrassing to me and will make me annoyed with the person who exposed me*. Since you now know the universal answer, there will be no need to ask in future.'

Hudson did not have an immediate counter-argument and went to his room either to formulate one or to read.

'Nice work,' said Rosie. 'Sometimes, just sometimes, you've got his number.'

I was still thinking about the autism issue. So, apparently, was Rosie.

'I think we need to accept the possibility that Rabbit has seen something. But before we send him off for a diagnosis, we should try to get a sense of what the impact would be — what it would be like for him. I'll see if I can find some support organisations.'

It was possible that I could contribute. Prior to meeting Rosie, I had delivered a talk on genetic precursors to Asperger's syndrome to a group of 'sufferers' aged between eight and twelve. I had minimal expertise on the subject but had been persuaded to cover for my then-friend Gene, who was using the time to commit adultery. The convenor, a woman a few years younger than me, had telephoned afterwards, seeking a discussion over dinner. At the time I had been focused on my project to find a life partner and had declined. But I had her phone number. I called the following morning.

'Julie Sykora.'

'I thought your name was Reed.'

'I'm sorry, who's calling?'

'It's Don Tillman. You called me to discuss the Specialisterne program — the Danish program — for employing people on the autism spectrum as software testers. I was busy at the time, but I'm now available.'

There was a long pause, then, 'My God, I remember. How could I forget? The kids standing on the tables shouting *Aspies rule!* like something out of *Dead Poets Society*. That must have been . . . ten years ago.'

'Thirteen.'

'You didn't want to go for a drink afterwards because you had to clean your bathroom.'

It was an odd detail to remember. 'Correct. Are you available for a discussion about autism? We could time-share it with a drink if you wanted.'

'You want to catch up? Is that why you're calling?'

The conversation continued in this unfocused manner, but we eventually established that Julie was still working in the field; that she had since been married and divorced; that I was now married and *not* divorced; that I was not considering leaving Rosie; that I was not seeking help personally but for Hudson; that there was no point in getting together for a drink (Julie's conclusion); and that the solution to the autism-familiarisation problem was to attend a support group which she would be chairing the following week. Rosie and I would meet members of the autism community and hear from two speakers.

'One of them's a bit of an activist — autistic rights and everything. We're seeing more of that, and I guess you'll relate to it, but it's tough on the parents who've got really difficult kids. Still, you were a bit ahead of your time.'

★   ★   ★

In parallel with lunch at the University Club, I undertook some preliminary research on autism diagnosis.

'Thought you might be here,' said Rosie, standing behind me.

'Totally predictable. This is where I have lunch on Thursdays.'

'I had another call from the principal.'

'More problems?'

'Ostensibly she wanted to check that we were happy with the discussion — she said that Neil Warren can be a bit abrasive but it's hard to get male teachers, so we have to cut him a little slack. See how it works? When men are the majority, they make the rules; when they're a minority they get special treatment.'

'Do I get to argue, or will that interrupt the briefing?'

'It'll interrupt the briefing. I'm right anyway, so no point arguing. What she really wanted to do was check whether we were getting an assessment. I told her we were looking into it.'

She pointed to my laptop screen, displaying the diagnostic criteria for autism. 'I see you've gone straight to the psychiatrists' bible.'

'*Bible* seems an inappropriate term for a document that should be evidence-based and regularly revised.'

Rosie laughed. 'Anyway, it's a medical model. Not even the only medical model.'

'Correct. And the principal was *incorrect*. The term *Asperger's* is still in use.'

'Not for much longer. It's going the way of manic depression and dropsy.' She laughed. 'I knew that'd be the first thing you looked up. Anyway, I've been talking to someone I went to school with who's got a son with autism.'

'Professionally diagnosed?'

'By a specialist. Anastasios — her son — really struggled, but he had a lot of support and he's doing way better. He's at uni and he's got a partner.' Rosie made the stop signal. 'Information. Let's just take it in for now. And there's a seminar next Wednesday. We'll have to miss the play.'

'Already in my calendar. I've given the tickets to Laszlo and Frances the Occasional Smoker. Can it still count as date night?'

7

Rosie's discussion with her former schoolmate had yielded useful background information and an exercise to get Hudson to 'open up'.

'The idea is that we discuss our own school experiences, including a few negative ones,' said Rosie.

'Listing negative experiences won't be difficult.'

'It's not a competition, and we don't want to paint too dark a picture. And we need to let him find his own way into the conversation.'

Hudson was highly skilled at finding his way into conversations.

As it was a Thursday, dinner was crumbed whitefish (flathead), a green vegetable from the approved list (peas) and an acceptable farinaceous component (mashed potatoes with twenty-eight per cent celeriac, which I was gradually increasing to accustom Hudson to the taste). Rosie was a pescatarian and Hudson had a number of aversions. It had been a stimulating challenge to design meals suitable for all of us.

The solution was the reinstatement of the Standardised Meal System, with variations to make it less obvious. It had been in place five months before Rosie noticed.

'How was school?' Rosie asked Hudson.

'Fine.' This was not part of the opening-up exercise; it was a conversational ritual. 'I finished *The Martian*. Five stars. It's about an astronaut.

His name is Mark Watkins and the name of his ship is the *Ares 3*. Before that there was the *Ares 1* and . . . '

Over the main course, we continued the interesting-number game.

'Sixteen,' I said. 'The smallest power of four, other than one.'

Hudson thought for approximately ten seconds. 'You can't say 'other than' or I could say, 'Seven hundred and ninety-nine, the smallest number other than one, two, three, four, five, six, seven — '

'We get it,' said Rosie.

Hudson's criticism was reasonable and demonstrated an intuitive grasp of proof by induction. I modified my answer. 'The smallest power of four which is not also a cubic number.'

'What's a cubic number?'

I explained, then gave him the next number. 'Seventeen.'

He was silent, not eating, for about a minute, then put two thumbs up. 'Sixteen plus one, so the sum of the first two powers of four.'

'Very neat,' I said. 'Rosie's turn: eighteen.'

'That was how old I was when I left school,' she said.

'Doesn't count,' said Hudson. 'That's about you. It has to be about the number.'

'Correct,' I said. 'Not accepted.'

'Right,' said Rosie. 'The smallest number whose digital root is the same as its largest divisor other than itself. Will that do?'

Hudson stared at her.

'I'm not just the lady who does the laundry,'

said Rosie. 'Did you play that game at school, Don?'

I assumed the response Rosie wanted was 'yes' but I'd had no one to play it with at school. 'No. I played it once at home. With my sister. She was older than me and became a maths teacher, but I still beat her.'

'You played before,' said Hudson. 'You know the answers. You never told me you had a sister. Where is she?'

'Dead,' I said.

'What did she die of?'

'She just got sick,' said Rosie.

'AIDS,' said Hudson.

'What?' said Rosie.

'When people say someone just got sick and died, it's probably AIDS. Mr Warren's brother died of AIDS and nobody's supposed to mention it.'

'You just did,' I said.

'Which is fine,' said Rosie. 'Family is where we can share that sort of stuff.'

'So, what did Dad's sister die of?'

'Undiagnosed ectopic pregnancy,' I said.

The word *pregnancy* would have terminated my enquiries at Hudson's age. It appeared that times had not changed.

Instead, he asked, 'What was she like?'

'World's best person . . . you and Rosie excluded, obviously.' I had a moment of inspiration. 'At school, everyone called her Edna.'

'Why?'

'An old-lady name, due to her being conservative and wearing glasses.'

'There's an Edna in *The Incredibles*,' said Hudson. 'Old but okay.'

'I had coffee today with a friend from school,' said Rosie. 'They used to call her Miss Piggy.'

'Pretty mean,' said Hudson. 'Was she ugly?'

'Your dad would say *not conventionally attractive*, which is a good way of putting it, because what people think is attractive is not the same everywhere. In some cultures, being overweight is considered attractive.'

'You're saying that in some countries, Ms Williams would be attractive. No way.'

'Don, you can answer that,' said Rosie.

'Attractiveness is irrelevant to performing the duties of a principal. Also, as an eleven-year-old, you are not configured to assess attractiveness in middle-aged women. It's unlikely you would consider the principal for the role of girlfriend.'

'Aaargh,' said Hudson. 'Gross.'

'What did they call you at school?' Rosie asked me.

'Data,' I said. 'From *Star Trek*.' I added an impression: 'I remember every fact I am exposed to, sir.' I could see the kids laughing, probably *at* me. But it was better than having nothing to say at all.

Hudson, being a kid, was laughing too, and Rosie took advantage of his lowered defences.

'What about you?'

'We're not allowed nicknames. Counts as bullying.'

'I'm not going to report it,' said Rosie. 'Unless you want me to.'

'Promise.'

'Promise,' said Rosie.

'Nasty,' said Hudson. 'Everyone calls me Nasty. Except Blanche. Can I be excused, please?'

★ ★ ★

We arrived early for the autism seminar so that I could introduce Julie to Rosie, who considered unstructured conversation a legitimate research method. Julie saw us arrive and intercepted us.

Before I could begin my interrogation on the topic of the evening, she asked, 'Are you still in touch with Gene?'

'No. We're no longer friends.'

The falling-out with Gene had occurred in New York, where he had been on sabbatical after separating from his wife, Claudia. During that year, he had established a romantic relationship with an American social worker named Lydia.

They had invited Rosie and me to drinks, which Rosie refused, on the basis that she needed to wash her hair. Hair-washing was a standard excuse for avoiding Gene, whom she considered a misogynist pig.

'She's missing out on champagne,' said Gene when I arrived at his apartment. 'Lydia and I have a little announcement. Go ahead, Lydia.'

'Gene has asked me to come back to Australia with him. And I've accepted.'

'Have you investigated visas?' I asked.

'Yes,' said Gene, 'but in case Lydia wasn't clear, there shouldn't be any problem. She'll be coming as my partner — my life partner.'

I felt a shock of disappointment. The announcement was the final blow to the possibility of two of my closest friends reconciling. I had privately — and publicly in our men's group — encouraged him to consider that option. Lydia was a pleasant person, most of the time, but Gene seemed no happier with her than he had been with Claudia.

'Are you sure?' I said.

Gene smiled. 'This is why Don's my dearest friend. Not afraid to test me, and I assure you he has done so assiduously. And my answer has never wavered.' He lifted his glass in a toast.

'I think that question is for me, too,' said Lydia, incorrectly but usefully. 'I *have* had my moments. Gene's made mistakes in the past, but we've had full disclosure and he's making a fresh start.'

'Full disclosure?' I said. 'Incredible.'

'He's told me everything.'

'Including the map?'

Lydia looked at Gene. Despite my incompetence at interpreting expressions, I knew instantly what hers meant. *What map?* She confirmed it by saying, 'What' — unnaturally long pause — 'map?'

Gene hesitated, and Lydia looked at me. 'Tell me, Don.'

'Oh, for Christ's sake,' said Gene. 'You know Claudia and I had an open marriage. I had a little game, keeping a tally of the women I'd . . . been with. By nationality.'

'You put pins in a map,' said Lydia. 'Didn't you? And you hung it in a public place. Your

60

office. Am I right?' It was an impressive demonstration of her understanding of Gene, and in other circumstances it might have strengthened their relationship. But it was obvious Lydia was not happy.

Fortunately — I thought at the time — I was in a position to make amends. Gene had revealed to our men's group that his entire history of encounters with women had been a fabrication.

'He was just showing off,' I said. 'He's only actually had sex with five women other than Claudia.' I realised the information was out of date. 'Plus you, presumably.'

'I don't believe you,' said Lydia.

As I considered her response, which seemed inappropriate and even aggressive, I had a flash of insight. *I* didn't believe me either. I had believed Gene because it was automatic to trust a friend. But his story was, I now realised, ludicrously unlikely, given the vast evidence to the contrary, including the constant searching for foreign nationals to increase his tally.

At Gene's instigation, I had communicated the lower number to his son, Carl, and it had been instrumental in saving the father — son relationship. I realised now what had happened and was so shocked that I blurted it out.

'You lied to me. You manipulated me to convince Carl — because he'd believe me but not you.'

'Yes, Don,' said Lydia. 'He lied to you. His best friend. It seems his children don't trust him either. And nor do I.'

Gene presumably finished the champagne

61

alone, because I walked out with Lydia.

There were two outcomes of the event that were continuing to affect my life. I'd had no further contact with Gene. And my position on social skills had changed. I had previously regarded them as unimportant, and still considered them overvalued, but I had to accept that in this case my ineptness had caused terrible damage. Gene and Lydia had generously invited me to celebrate an important moment in their lives. I had responded by destroying their relationship and preventing my best friend from making a new start.

Once, I would have been unconcerned by Hudson's delay in acquiring social facility, but now I understood that the deficit might lead to behaviour that he would be ashamed of, such as causing distress to marginalised students.

It could even get him killed. I had twice had a gun drawn on me by law-enforcement officers — in a New York playground where I was suspected of being a paedophile, and in New Mexico when I exited my vehicle after being pulled over, as recommended in *The Naked Ape*.

Julie did not pursue her enquiry about Gene. A crowd was building, largely adults. We had left Hudson with Phil, but I had been hoping to meet some children of his age to make an informal comparison. 'It's a support group, so it's mainly parents and carers,' said Julie.

Before Julie excused herself to prepare for her chairperson role, she checked that I had updated her name correctly in my contacts list.

'After two marriages, I decided to go back to my maiden name,' she said.

'Wise move,' I said. 'Stable no matter how many more marriages you have.'

'Sykora,' said Rosie. 'Where's that from?'

'I was born in Czechoslovakia,' said Julie. 'Funny thing: I think that was what Gene found most interesting about me.'

8

'Remember,' said Rosie, as we selected our seats, 'we're not here to debate the diagnosis and treatment of autism, but to get a sense of the community. Are they talking about kids like Hudson? Are those kids benefiting from whatever interventions are happening?'

'You're suggesting I avoid contributing? What about asking questions?'

'Let's just keep a low profile,' said Rosie.

There were two speakers. One was approximately forty, female, BMI approximately twenty-four, conservatively dressed. I guessed the other was fifteen years younger, with a BMI of thirty and short blond hair dyed partially purple. She was wearing a black T-shirt with the slogan *Autistic Lives Matter*.

Julie introduced the older woman as Margot, the mother of a girl with autism. Margot began by expressing solidarity with the autism parents in the audience, and sympathy for their challenges and sacrifices. She thanked Julie for using 'person-first' language, rather than calling her daughter 'autistic'. 'She's a girl with autism, but a lot less of it than she started with.'

Margot's daughter, who was now sixteen, had failed to develop language skills at the expected age and was diagnosed before her third birthday. After researching treatment options, Margot and her partner engaged professionals to provide intensive therapy. This all seemed rational and uncontroversial, but someone had a question. That person was Rosie.

'You used the word *intensive*. How many hours a week?'

'About twenty-five.'

'That was in addition to her schoolwork?'

'Yes, once she started school.'

'And for how long?'

'She's still doing it. And she's continuing to improve. I'm going to talk about this, but she's at a mainstream school; she has friends. Yes, it is a lot of work, for her *and* us, but if you want — '

'How do you motivate a three-year-old? To do all that therapy?'

'The system we use — and I'm going to get to that — has built-in rewards.'

Black T-shirt leaned into her microphone. 'And punishments. Remembering that withholding a reward is punishment too. You're using ABA, right?'

Julie expanded the acronym: 'Applied Behaviour Analysis. For those who are new here, it's widely regarded as the gold standard for autism treatment. But we're getting — '

Black T-shirt interrupted. 'I can't let that go. Psychologists and parents love it. Of course they do, because that's who it's for — not for the kids being trained like puppies.'

Now we were in Rosie's area of expertise. Her research project was comparing therapists' and patients' perceptions of success in treating bipolar disorder.

'What sort of work is being done to get

feedback from the kids?' she asked. 'And, Margot, how does your daughter feel about her progress?'

'She's getting the dog treats, so how can we tell?' said Black T-shirt. 'She's being trained to spend her life seeking approval from others. Ask her how it's working out when someone uses her fucked-up reward system to abuse her.'

This was excellent. Rosie's questions had shifted the discussion from a single, possibly unrepresentative, case study to a discussion of contentious issues, with two opposing views being articulated. Unfortunately, Julie felt obliged to let Margot finish her prepared speech, which reiterated that her daughter had made impressive progress in acquiring speech and transitioning into a more socially acceptable person.

Black T-shirt was introduced as Liz, and she immediately identified herself as both lesbian and autistic.

'I'm not a person with autism any more than I'm a person with lesbianism. I'm lesbian. I'm autistic. When I get a cold, I *have* a cold; I'm a *person with a cold* and I want to get rid of it. Medical help appreciated. But being autistic and lesbian — that's who I am, and I'm not interested in anyone trying to cure me of who I am. If they force me into conversion therapy — because that's what ABA is — for being lesbian or for being autistic, they're abusing me. If they do it to a child, they're abusing that child.'

Liz continued with a list of things not to say

when speaking to autistic people (examples: *You seem pretty normal to me* or *What's your special talent?* or *We're all on the spectrum*) and explained the idea of social disability with a brilliant example. Imagine everyone used wheelchairs except you and society was designed to accommodate them. You'd knock your head on door frames and have to ask for a chair at restaurants. I thought of Hudson and the ski boots.

Julie called for questions. The first came from a male of approximately forty. 'I know you said not to say it, but you seem pretty normal to me.' He laughed. Liz did not. 'I mean, you're obviously at the high-functioning end of the spectrum. How does what you say relate to — '

Liz didn't let him finish. 'See,' she said, 'this happens. I ask you not to say something — I *tell* you it's hurtful and insulting — but you treat it as a joke and say it anyway. So, let me say something hurtful and insulting to you. Fuck off. Arsehole.'

Julie attempted to interject, but Liz raised her hand in a stop sign and spoke over her.

'You didn't shut him down when he was offensive, so don't shut me down. But, yeah, some other people might want to know if what I said applies to all autistic people, and it does. Yes, there's a spectrum, but it's multidimensional and people's place on it changes over time. Sometimes because of 'treatment'.' Liz used the air-quotes convention.

'Some days I'm doing well in some areas and not in others, and the next day it's different. But

I'm always autistic. It's my identity, my permanent way of being, and those of us who can speak out have to do it for those who can't.'

'Perhaps we have a question for Margot,' said Julie.

Rosie had already breached our agreement by asking six questions, so I considered it reasonable to ask one of my own. I began to raise my hand, and caught Julie's attention, but Rosie pulled it back. Julie smiled, but Liz pointed to me.

'Most of you won't have seen what just happened,' she said. 'A man in the audience put his hand up and Julie nudged Margot. I can tell you what that nudge meant: watch this guy, *he may ask something weird*. Because he's . . . maybe, oh fuck . . . *autistic*. Am I right, Julie?'

Julie attempted a response, but it was difficult to make sense of it, and Liz continued. 'Then the lady beside him who asked the questions before tried to shut him down. Didn't you?'

I was expecting Rosie to respond aggressively. Instead she said, quietly, 'You're absolutely right. I apologise.'

'Okay,' said Liz, 'I'm guessing you're neurotypical. I know Julie is. I know Margot is. And we autistics aren't always great with the non-verbal stuff. What we just saw was the neurotypicals using *their* secret language . . . like, 'Hey, do you want to take the d-o-g for a w-a-l-k?' They used it to send a warning about one of us. To shut us down. To oppress us.' She looked directly at me: 'Anyway, you had a question?'

'Correct, but what you said was so spectacular that I may have forgotten it.' The audience laughed, but I sensed in a positive way. I remembered the question.

'The question was for Margot, as Julie requested.'

'You can ask Liz a question if you prefer,' said Julie.

'Excellent. Can I have one each?'

'That's fine.'

'Margot, you said your child attends a mainstream school and has friends. Is she socially accepted?'

'Thank you,' said Margot. 'And I've no wish to shut you down. It's a good question, and a tough one to answer. Her friends are mainly people like her, people she's met through therapy. It's not ideal, and sometimes we feel they're holding her back, but it's a stepping stone.'

'You didn't answer the second part,' said Liz. 'About acceptance.'

'I hadn't finished. I'm not here with any agenda except to share my experiences in the hope that it will help others, so I'll tell you honestly that she's struggling. She's far, *far* better than she was, but she's not there yet and she's having a tough time at an age when she should be having fun and . . . My husband and I wonder every day if we're doing the right thing.'

She turned to Liz. 'We know what we're doing is traumatic for her; we know it could damage her; we know she might even end up committing suicide and we'd have to live with the fact that our decision might have been responsible. But she was three and we were her parents and we decided it would be worse if she could never speak or look after herself. Maybe you think that would be okay, and maybe it would be if the world was different. But I don't care if you've got the same diagnosis — you've never been the same as she was and you can't empathise. So, say whatever you like for yourself, but don't stand up here, full of confidence with your smart words that my daughter would never have had in your perfect world, and say you speak for her.'

There was loud applause from the audience.

I expected my second question would have been forgotten: we had reached the scheduled end time and facilitators generally think that finishing with applause is more important than completing the agenda. But I was unused to having an autistic person monitoring proceedings.

Liz pointed me out again. 'You also had a question for me. I wouldn't like it to get lost in the chorus of sympathy for parents burdened with children like us. I'd like to ask everyone who clapped when Margot said that I couldn't speak for another autistic person: who does speak for her? Someone with *no* experience of what it's like to be different?' She pointed to me again. 'Your question.'

'Are you saying there's a clear division between autistic and neurotypical?' I said. The second term was new to me, but I expected I would find it useful in the future. 'The instruments for identifying autism seem to be inexact; you stated that it's a multidimensional spectrum, so it seems simplistic to reduce it to a binary.'

'You're a scientist?'

'Correct.'

'Well, I'm the first to say that we need more science — good science that doesn't begin with a model of autism as a disease or a disorder or a deficit. But I'm not a scientist. I'm an activist. And for me, for the fight I'm in, you're either autistic or neurotypical. And it's not dictated by what you score on some scale invented by neurotypicals any more than you'd use an instrument to decide if you were gay or Indigenous or a Bulldogs supporter. In the end, it's your choice, your identity. Diagnosis is for diseases.'

⋆   ⋆   ⋆

'Fuck,' said Rosie after we had exited the hall. 'I think we saw more drama than Laszlo and Frances did. Hey, I'm sorry I tried to shut you down. Really sorry.'

'Totally reasonable. You were helping me keep my side of the silence agreement, even after you'd been unable to resist speaking. I should have shut you down, but I was too slow, and anyway, your questions were excellent.'

'You sure you didn't feel oppressed? You seemed to be supporting Liz when she beat me up. Justifiably.'

'No, no. I was supporting her in general. What she had to say was so interesting.'

'Like the civil-rights movement in the sixties. *Which side are you on?*'

'Neither. I consider tribalism one of the worst

71

aspects of human behaviour. A major contributor to confirmation bias, lack of innovation in public policy, war . . . '

'I didn't mean it as a question. But where are we at with Hudson?'

'Our goal was to decide whether we should seek an autism assessment. My provisional conclusion is that he could be misdiagnosed as autistic, in which case he would be subjected to unnecessary treatment and possibly discrimination. If he is autistic, the outcome may be the same.'

'First, do no harm.'

'Correct. Also, analysis of the problem should precede action.'

'We are as one. Shall we get a drink before we go home? It's supposed to be date night.'

'I'd scheduled the time for study.'

'And you could ring your parents.'

'Drink.'

As we walked to the cocktail bar I had located on the internet, I reflected that if I decided to plead the autism defence for the Genetics Lecture Outrage, Liz would be the perfect support person.

9

'I have some good news,' said Professor Lawrence, who had called me as I rode home from work. 'Someone who was at your lecture wrote a piece for the student newspaper, which they refused to publish. She's cried foul, and — '

'Presumably it was critical of me.'

'Hardly, or the newspaper would have eaten it up. No, it was titled something like *Why Are Snowflakes Always White?* and it was written by a Ghanaian woman.'

'Beatrice?'

'That's the name. The one you selected as the blackest of the black. Jesus wept. Seems she doesn't like a white person — it's common knowledge that the complainant is the student who asked you the question — taking umbrage on her behalf. For whatever reason, she's on your side, her article's done the rounds anyway, and it's now a divisive issue that won't be solved by firing you. They're looking for a way out and they'll accept the autism explanation without a diagnosis. As long as you identify as being on the spectrum.'

Rosie's call from the school was less positive.

'Another so-called meltdown. I had to collect him and he's clammed up. Do you want to . . . ?'

'You're vastly better at interrogation. Also, I'm falling behind with study.'

'This isn't about interrogation; it's about

knowing his father's there to help. Think about what you would have wanted at his age.'

The answer was 'not to be interrogated by my parents about something that happened at school which they would not understand'. If I had given that response, Rosie would have told me to 'think harder', so I moved directly to doing so. I time-shared my thinking with a run, followed by water for rehydration, and a pisco sour to stimulate creativity and stay in practice with cocktail-making.

What would I have wanted of my parents at Hudson's age? Their single helpful initiative had been to enrol me in a karate class, but their motivation had not been to provide me with a lifelong fitness regime, improved co-ordination and a place to go in my early twenties when I had no other social life. Their goal was to enable me to 'fight back', an unrealistic scenario given the dynamics of the schoolyard, classroom and changing room.

I needed a generic answer, since the ideal responses to specific events — meltdown, complaint from school, discovery of packed lunch uneaten — were different. It came as I poured a second pisco sour and thought that, in seven years, I could be offering it to Hudson, legally if not ethically.

I would have wanted to be treated as an adult. Not to be allowed to drink pisco sours, but to be properly informed, listened to and involved in decisions affecting me.

★ ★ ★

'You've been drinking alcohol. I can smell it. It's irrational to drink alcohol.' The intonation of the last sentence was suspiciously reminiscent of Data from *Star Trek*.

Hudson liked to point out examples of what he perceived as irrationality on my part. However, I was, in a traditional psychological ploy, demonstrating the opposite behaviour to that which we wanted to encourage. Hudson would rebel against his parents by becoming a teetotaller.

'Correct,' I said. 'But even for irrational behaviour, there is generally a rational explanation, based on an understanding of the human psyche. Do you have a rational explanation for why you refuse to have your hair cut?'

'That was when I was a little kid.' Hudson pointed to his hair or possibly his brain. 'Little kids are less rational.'

'What about today's incident? The principal stated that you had been given a time-out for some unspecified infraction, and that when your sentence was reduced due to good behaviour, you responded with anger.' This was where the *meltdown* word had been used.

'I wasn't being irrational.'

'Anger is intrinsically irrational. And it's irrational to respond with hostility to an act of generosity.'

'It wasn't generosity. The time-out was supposed to be all day. Mr Warren came to check on me, and I'd finished my work because it was quiet and nobody was annoying me. I was reading, which we're allowed to do if we've done

75

all our work. But he said I had to go back to the classroom. I told him he was breaking his promise.'

'Leading to anger and an argument?'

Hudson nodded. 'He didn't actually say, 'I promise,' so it wasn't an official promise, but it was a deal. In the end he let me stay.'

'Obviously you prefer the time-out room to the classroom.'

'Not all the time. There's a kid in the other Year Six class who wants to go there all the time. But he's seriously weird.'

'In what way?'

'All ways. He's got autism.'

★   ★   ★

Rosie laughed when I conveyed Hudson's explanation to her. 'Poor old Neil the Bunny. Don't tell me Hudson doesn't have social skills. He pulled the meltdown so he could stay in the time-out room.'

'If your hypothesis is true, then it wasn't a meltdown. Meltdowns are not amenable to being pulled. It's likely the correct term is *tantrum*.'

'Or just stating his position in a way Rabbit didn't have a good answer for.'

'It must be incredibly difficult being a teacher. So many parallel interactions.'

'Neil wouldn't have had a problem if he didn't see the timeout room as punishment. So, what are we going to do about it?'

'I recommend forgiveness, hence no action. The behaviour was inappropriate, but the situation was complex. I doubt I would have performed any better than Rabbit.'

★   ★   ★

When I arrived at Jarman's Gym the following evening, there was a woman (estimated age thirty-two, estimated BMI twenty-one, unconventionally attractive) waiting outside with a boy of about four. In addition to my involuntary estimate of BMI, I was in danger of developing a habit of placing interesting looking people on my racial-characteristics graph. This woman would have been somewhere between Hui and Beatrice.

To my surprise, she intercepted me and said, 'Mr Tillman? Hudson's father?'

'How did you know?'

She laughed. 'You and Hudson are peas in a pod. I'm Blanche's mother. Allannah.' She extended her hand and I shook it, matching the light pressure that I knew to anticipate from most females and trying to suppress the thought that we were facilitating virus transmission.

She smiled. 'You just did something that almost nobody does. Actually, it's something you *didn't* do.'

I was thinking she was referring to my getting the handshake intensity correct and not crushing her hand, but she continued, 'There's a look everyone who's met Blanche gives me, like *you can't be her mother*. Because of her colour.'

'That's ridiculous. Blanche is albino . . . a person with albinism. Which do you prefer? Which does *she* prefer?'

'Person with albinism. Thanks for asking. But I just wanted to thank you face-to-face for everything you did on the snow trip. Blanche had the best time.'

I knew the formula for dealing with thank-yous. 'No problem.' I waved my right hand upwards and over my shoulder as if flicking rhinoviruses from the back of my fingers.

'No, no,' she said. 'You heard that the other kids were jealous and wanted to go snowboarding instead of skiing? Blanche said Hudson talked nonstop about it on the bus back. Sounds like their teacher had his hands full.'

'Up to his arse in alligators.'

Allannah laughed. 'Exactly how he put it. Gary — my husband — said to come in for a healing session or a massage anytime that works for you. As a thank-you. He was pretty unhappy that the school was going to send her home because of her vision problem, which they already knew about. We've spoken to the principal.'

'Excellent. The system seemed inadequately designed for handling predictable exceptions.'

Allannah laughed again, an odd response to a serious problem that had affected her daughter. 'Did you know that Hudson said something to Blanche about genetics?'

'Of course. We were required to visit the principal's office because of your complaint.'

'Oh. I'm so sorry. It wasn't meant to be a . . . complaint. Gary just thought we should mention it. Blanche says that's what you do. Genetics.'

'Correct. Currently I'm trying to find a cure

for cancer. It's proving extremely difficult.'

'Well, you don't fit my idea of the evil genius working for big pharma.'

'I don't work for big pharma. I'm a university professor.'

'I'm sorry. Like I said, you don't fit. If you ever meet my husband, please don't mention I asked this, but . . . the different kinds of albinism that Hudson told Blanche about. Is there any way of telling?'

'A simple genetic test — '

'Is there any other way? I mean, something I could look for myself?'

'Is there some problem with genetic testing?'

Allannah took a few seconds to reply. 'If I got a sample, could they just do the test and let me know? They wouldn't need to see Blanche?'

'I can give you contact details for a laboratory, but I recommend consulting a medical specialist. The medical profession is less evidence-based than it should be, but I would trust them ahead of all alternatives.'

'Thank you, but I guess 'trust' is the word. We have to decide who to trust with our children. And we believe there are better ways. Gary's a homeopath.'

A homeopath! Not only zero evidence, but no realistic possibility that there ever would be.

Allannah laughed. 'That's the expression that you didn't do when I told you I was Blanche's mother. Blanche was home-birthed and we didn't know she had albinism until after we'd named her. My husband is very fair, so we just thought . . . '

'Is she receiving treatment for her eyesight?'

'When she was born, she was almost blind. Gary treated her and she got a lot better. I'm her mother and I saw it. So did my mum. Since then it's settled, and I just think, what he's doing is working, my child is all right, and that's all that matters to me.'

'That shouldn't preclude — '

'You may as well have the whole story. We don't believe in vaccination. We're terrible people. *Anti-vaxxers*.'

'People who oppose vaccination.' It would be interesting to know the thought process that had led to her position so I could explain the error. But the child, who I assumed was Blanche's brother, was tugging at his mother's arm.

'I'd better go,' she said. 'I have to collect Blanche.'

'Blanche is here?'

'You didn't know? The kids arranged it. Hudson spoke to his grandfather. It's frightening, isn't it, how they've got to the age when they start making their own lives.'

10

I was facing a complex problem with too much information to process and not enough to support an evidence-based decision. I had learned that this was to be expected in all situations involving human interaction.

Fortunately, I could rely on my friends: a group of people from diverse backgrounds who cared about my welfare, yet were sufficiently detached that they would not be overwhelmed by emotions. They had helped me find the perfect partner, prepare for fatherhood and save my marriage.

I prepared a schedule to contact all six of them.

★   ★   ★

I began with Claudia, Gene's ex-wife, as we already had a meeting arranged. I had continued to seek her advice, even after the falling-out with Gene, taking advantage of her background as a clinical psychologist. She did not consider it appropriate to meet in her rooms, and we discussed psychological issues over coffee.

In keeping with the informality, I began the conversation with small talk.

'Are you still single?'

'No change from three months ago. And I know what you're going to say next and the answer is that it's not up for discussion. It's been twelve years. We've both moved on.'

'Not successfully. In terms of finding a new partner. You do still want a partner, correct?'

'It's not at the top of my list. Anyway, I thought you were after advice.'

'I thought I should reciprocate by offering you some advice. I was right about Judas. Simon Lefebvre.'

'Everyone was right about Simon. If anyone in my family needs genetic counselling, we'll come to you and I'll expect it delivered over coffee for nothing. But *I'm* the psychologist. Simon's in the past, Gene and I are living our separate lives, Eugenie and Carl are adults. We're fine. Now, what's happening with you and Rosie?'

I explained the Hudson situation.

'I see a lot of this,' said Claudia. 'On the one hand, I think that teachers are in a wonderful position to notice if something is going on, and we absolutely have to listen and respect their experience and observations. But they're not qualified to diagnose autism, let alone the full range of disorders that it might be mistaken for.'

'Excellent point.'

'If you decide to get a diagnosis, give the psychologist an open brief, not 'Does he have autism, yes or no?' '

'Obviously. As a consequence of your previous point.'

'Another thing,' she said. 'I know you're primed to think in genetic terms, but don't forget environment. Hudson's got your genes, but he's also grown up with you as a father, and . . . well . . . some of your traits . . . overlap with the diagnostic criteria.'

I had the information I needed.

'Sit down — finish your coffee,' said Claudia. 'I won't say any more about autism. But Hudson's been hard work for Rosie, hasn't he?'

'I presume all children are hard work.'

'It's just that last time we spoke, you mentioned that your sex life dropped off when Hudson was four or five.'

'Correct. We wanted another child, and the single most common reason for infertility is insufficient frequency of sex. I pointed this out to Rosie on numerous occasions.'

'I wonder if that might be the reason. Subconsciously. That she didn't really want another child, when one was difficult enough. And she had the chance of getting back to work.'

'She never mentioned it.'

'People don't always mention their motivations. They don't always know them. That's why I have a job.'

★   ★   ★

Laszlo was at his desk. I found a seat and worked at my laptop until he removed his ear defenders and stood up to take a break. Our conversation was brief, focused and direct. There was no other way to have a conversation with Laszlo.

'What happened to the goggles?' I asked.

'A failed experiment. Good for cycling in the rain, not so good for the computer screen.'

'Have you ever been tested for autism?'

'Your question is too imprecise.'

'Why?'

'I was tested for Asperger's syndrome, which at the time was not considered a subcategory of autism.'

'What was the result?'

'Positive. With a high level of confidence.'

'Has the effect of the diagnosis been positive or negative?'

'Positive. If I'm criticised for some behaviour, I say, 'I have Asperger's.' ' He tapped his bicycle helmet. 'There is no need to demonstrate any relationship between the diagnosis and the behaviour. Then they leave me alone. Except Frances. She says, 'You're not Asperger's; you're Laszlo Hevesi.' Which is true, but Asperger's is a good approximation for the working environment.'

'Do you think it would be a good idea for an eleven-year-old? To have an autism diagnosis?'

'It depends if they want to be left alone. If so, maybe yes. If not, I have no opinion. How is the cancer work going?'

'I'm having difficulty learning the data-analysis software.'

'Tell me if you need help. Scientists have to help each other.'

★　★　★

'Why have you chosen to call me at this time?'

Isaac Esler's standard phone greeting is a joke, related to his profession of psychiatrist, but it works just as well to treat his jokes as serious statements.

'I chose to call because we're having some problems with Hudson. I selected the time because we would both be awake.' It was 7.30 p.m. in New York.

'Well, Don, you know that I can't offer you professional advice, not over the phone, not without seeing Hudson and because of our social relationship. I'd say, see someone locally, but . . . there's so much incompetence. You don't want him shot full of dexmethamphetamine on the strength of a fifty-minute consult with a junior Australian clinician who thinks Freud is a way to serve rice.'

As always, Isaac argued himself out of his ethical statement, and we talked for two hours and seven minutes. His wife, Judy, brought dinner to the phone. He was oddly interested in Hudson's relationship with Blanche.

'As we know, the *cause célèbre* of the anti-vax movement is the supposed association of vaccination with autism. Which in turn is demonised, and I use that word deliberately, because I'd argue that a religious analogy is appropriate here. And this young woman, brought up to believe this, has formed a relationship with a young man who, at least according to what she's probably heard at school, may be autistic. How old are they now?'

'Hudson's eleven.'

'Hmm. I'd love to meet her. And the mother.'

'What about Hudson?'

'Difficult to explore until you tell me what it is you're holding back.'

'On what subject?'

'What's happening in your life. Or happened.'

'Numerous things . . . '

'Start with, 'Coincidentally' or 'In a surprising parallel to what's happening with Hudson'.'

85

'Coincidentally, my own experiences at school . . .' A better answer presented itself. 'It's been suggested, by the university, that I also seek a diagnosis.'

Isaac's next question was predictable: 'Do you think it's possible that these two things could be related?'

'Definitely not. They're independent. The school has no knowledge — '

'But the teacher met you while you were considering your own diagnosis? And then suggested that Hudson get one?'

'I didn't mention my situation to the teacher.'

'Don, you should know by now not to limit yourself to the overt.'

As it was late, we agreed that I should not have a separate conversation with Judy, not even to point out the advantages of a cordless phone. As usual, Isaac had offered fascinating insights that I — as yet — had no idea how to translate into action.

★ ★ ★

I raised the Hudson problem with George and Dave on our weekly Boys' Night Out. The name given to our Skype discussions was misleading in all respects: we were no longer boys (George was seventy-six); it was 7 a.m. in Melbourne (though late evening in New York); we were all 'in' at our homes.

'The school has requested that Hudson be assessed for autism,' I said when George's and Dave's avatars appeared on the screen.

'And good morning to you too, Don,' said

86

George. 'How's the weather, how's Rosie, how's your dad doing? And I'm fine too, thanks, just a little bored. Thinking about going back to England. Or I could migrate to Australia. I gather there's a shortage of drummers, judging from the music you lot are producing. What about you, Dave?'

'No change. Sonia's still pushing to do a secondment at one of the branches. She won't get a promotion till she's done it and the last thing I need right now is to relocate. Fulvio's got colic and he's waking up every hour. The antidepressants don't seem to be doing anything except playing hell with my weight. But tell us what's happening with Hudson. Take my mind off my own life.'

'All right,' said George, 'Hudson first, but we're not finished with you.'

'I can tell you what Sonia would say,' said Dave.

'Excellent,' I said. 'That will save a separate call.'

'I'll be straight with you because you're you. She thinks you both work too hard and you're missing out on watching him grow up. She thought Rosie did the right thing going part-time, but this isn't a good time for you to be studying as well as working. She'd say, 'If Hudson's having problems, I'm not surprised.''

'Take that,' said George.

'Sorry,' said Dave. 'Truth is, Sonia would happily change places with you and Rosie. Work part-time, be with Zina and Fulvio while I did overtime to save for college, play with the kids on weekends.'

'What do *you* think, Dave?' said George. 'You have any issues like this with Zina?'

'Totally different. She's a girl: when I was at school there were kids like Hudson, but all boys.'

George and I were silent while we waited for Dave to continue. Interrupting Dave led to loss of information.

'I've always been a big guy. Even at school. But nobody said anything until one day, this one time, this kid calls me Fat Boy. And after that it was always Fat Boy. Right through high school. I knew even back then that if I dropped the weight, the name would stick. And sometimes, when I'm trying to stop myself eating a burger, I think, what the hell, whatever I do I'll still be Fat Boy.'

'You got the analogy, Don?' said George.

'Of course.' I was far better at analogies than I had once been. 'Obesity equates with autism. Correct?'

'Correct,' said Dave. 'Give a dog a bad name.'

'What dog?'

'Just an expression. The dog was me. What about you, George?'

'If we're talking about names, when I went to school in London, they called me a git, because I was from the North and I wasn't big enough to do anything about it. It's not exactly an affectionate term. I didn't do so well with studies or sport or anything. And there was this bastard who was always having a go at me. Put me in hospital once, and they still didn't do anything.

'But then, because of one thing, which was playing the drums, I'm a rock star, and I couldn't have given a stuff what they thought. Them, in their crappy little jobs, taxi drivers and plumbers and bloody solicitor's clerks, and I'm up on the stage doing what they can only dream about, the best job in the world, all the birds and drugs you wanted . . . '

'So,' I said, 'your advice is the same as Phil's: tolerate school because things may be better later in life?'

Now that I said it myself, it sounded like a terrible philosophy for an eleven-year-old with six and a half years of schooling remaining. Calculated as a percentage of the time he had lived so far, it was the equivalent of me accepting unhappiness now because life would improve after the age of eighty-one.

'I suppose that's it,' said George. 'I just had to get through school. But I'll tell you, if I knew then what I know now . . . '

Dave said something, but I didn't notice. George had given me the solution to the problem. To all the problems.

11

If I knew then what I know now. While I was at university, and even later, I would lie in bed creating fantasies of what I could have done at school. Knowing what I knew now, a further thirty years later, those fantasies, had they become reality, would only have made things worse.

They largely involved my presenting better arguments — unassailable arguments — against the things that I didn't like: unreasonable rules; aesthetic, religious and political positions presented as fact; favouritism and discrimination. It was unlikely that the teachers would have bowed to my superior logic: *We admit it — Donald Tillman is right. We will abolish the hair-length specification, remove God from the school prayer and make Donald head boy.*

In terms of being accepted at school, it would have been better to fantasise about being the cricket captain. Blair Lindley, who held that position, as well as that of head boy, had 'gone on' to represent the state on two occasions, and was now a respected wealth-management consultant. My mother had provided this information.

I had not even been appointed a prefect, despite being the top student academically, and had 'gone on' to be a scientist participating in the search for cancer cures. Both career paths were predictable from our childhood interests and achievements. The school had made it clear which was more valued. This was the sort of argument I had imagined making in a speech to the assembly.

But now I had a chance to do something more practical — to share what I'd learned with Hudson. Because, after starting with some of the personality traits that Hudson had apparently inherited or learned, and consequently experiencing similar problems at school, becoming clinically depressed in my early years at university and feeling isolated until meeting Rosie at thirty-nine, I had *come through*. I had the world's best life. Hudson could have that, too. By knowing what I wish I'd known when I was his age.

George's insight was critical to finding the solution to my five problems. But multiple people had contributed.

Phil: *Keep the psychologists out of it.*

Claudia: *The school cannot be relied upon for psychological expertise.*

Dave: *Do not allow Hudson to be labelled.*

Laszlo: *A label is likely to result in social isolation.*

'Rabbit' Warren: *Hudson requires life skills.*

My father: *Who's going to teach him to ride a bike?*

Isaac Esler: *Hudson's life has parallels with your own.*

Allannah: *You and Hudson are peas in a pod.*

Liz the Activist: *The socially marginalised need to support each other.*

Sonia: *You need to spend more time with your son.*

Margot the Autism Mum: *Twenty-five hours a week. We did whatever was needed.*

And Rosie, of course: *Welcome to what women have been doing forever.*

★ ★ ★

'I'm quitting my job to devote maximum time to preparing Hudson for high school.'

'You're what? Don, no, we can't afford . . . you can't . . . '

I had anticipated this reaction, or some version of it that amounted to *this is not a good idea*, and had taken the day off to deal with the details that were likely to concern Rosie. We had eaten dinner and Hudson was now reading in bed. Rosie shut the hall door to prevent him hearing our conversation.

'I believe I've considered all reasonable objections,' I said.

'Of course you have . . . '

'I may be mistaken. Hence, I propose that we prepare cocktails, and by the time we have consumed them, I guarantee we will have reached agreement.'

'And you guarantee that how?'

'Either I will have dealt with all your objections, or I will have failed to do so, in which case the proposal is abandoned.'

'You haven't made any commitments yet?'

'Of course not. I needed to consult you.' I had learned a lot since the New York Relocation Surprise.

'All right. I'll have a Last Word.'

92

I was familiar with Rosie's cocktail preferences and had prepared accordingly.

I retrieved the lime juice from the fridge and ice cubes from the freezer, and placed two jiggers, two cocktail shakers and two glasses on the table. Then I produced the olive jars I had put aside.

'You've pre-squeezed the limes?' said Rosie.

'Correct. And the jars are labelled. Gin, Maraschino, Green Chartreuse. We have a set each.'

'Okay, it's a liquor comparison,' she said.

Rosie was accustomed to cocktail experiments, although we had not performed one since returning from New York. We also competed for speed, and Rosie generally won.

But tonight, for the first time in a situation which did not involve some kind of accident, I poured my glass first.

'Hey,' said Rosie. 'If it's warm, you don't win.'

I passed her my glass and she tasted.

'Okay, it's cold. I thought you hadn't shaken enough.' She sipped again. 'Wow, this is good, *really* good.' She tasted her own. 'And mine's crap . . . maybe just in comparison.'

'Any questions?' I asked.

'Obviously, what did you put in it?'

'I meant on the Hudson Project. Which is higher priority than the cocktail experiment.'

'How about you lay it out for me? You plan to quit your job and spend time with Hudson . . .'

'Correct.'

'You'd pick him up from school on the days that I do now?'

'Phil's days also. I would be available every day.'

'So I could go back to work full-time . . . '

'Is it too late to resume the chief-investigator role?'

'Stefan thinks it's his. He'll go ballistic. But . . . Hudson's at school most of the day. Maybe you could just go part-time.'

'My current job requires more than a full-time effort. If the person doing the job is me.'

'You're still thinking about Laszlo?'

'Laszlo is far better qualified. I will recommend he replace me.'

'Is that why — '

'It's a positive side effect. Also, no disciplinary hearing. Time to visit my father. Possibly resume martial-arts training.'

'Don, this is all wonderful — and I'd love you to spend more time with Hudson, and with me, and with your mum and dad, but you know we need your salary.' The house purchase had consumed most of our savings.

She sipped her cocktail. 'I guess we could move Hudson to the public school. I just — '

'Not necessary. The financial problem is solved. I'm opening a bar.'

Preparing to establish a small business that would replace my university salary had taken up most of the morning. My first cocktail-making experience had been at a medical-school reunion, where Rosie and I had discovered that we enjoyed joint activities, leading ultimately to marriage and the creation of Hudson. At the end of that night, the manager, a friendly and competent person named Amghad, had offered me a partnership in a prospective cocktail-making business. 'I'm in no hurry,' he'd said.

* * *

'I thought you might call me one day,' said Amghad. 'Maybe a bit sooner. Where have you been?'

'Primarily New York City.'

'Makes sense. Every serious cocktail guy ends up there sometime. I don't need to tell you that cocktails are back. You were ahead of your time — knowing the book backwards, tailoring the cocktail to the customer. Now everyone's done that and it's bacon-infused bourbon and giant ice cubes.'

'Scientifically unsound. The ice-cube theory. The reduced dilution is achieved at the expense of chilling.'

'I'm not telling you anything. You probably know I've got a few places now, but, like I said, the game has changed. Crowded market. I'm interested, but it's got to be something different. A killer concept.'

* * *

Rosie sipped the cocktail I had made. 'Don, working some shifts in a cocktail bar makes sense. But *opening* a bar? You'd be swapping one full-time job for another.'

'With different working hours. I'll be able to perform the Hudson activities while you're at work. School delivery, school pick-up, meal preparation in advance if necessary. Personal tuition, obviously. My total workload will be less due to elimination of the study. Also, once the bar is a success, I can reduce my hours.'

'*If* it's a success. I mean, a bar is a business, and — '

'I've engaged an experienced business partner and developed the necessary killer concept.'

'Which is?'

'Is your cocktail satisfactory?'

'It's the best Last Word I've ever had. Really strong. Not too sweet. I'm guessing you used overproof gin.'

'Incorrect. My liquor was the same as yours but stored in the freezer. I lowered the temperature to minimum. Virtually zero absorption of ice, hence no dilution. Subjectively less sweet due to chilling of the tastebuds.'

'Neat idea. A bit tricky to do in a bar.'

'It's totally feasible. But to optimise, all liquor should be cooled to just above its freezing point, which differs depending on alcohol content. Hence the need for a customised refrigeration system. Which requires a refrigeration expert.'

'Dave.'

'Correct.'

'Can he do it from New York?'

'No. He will be coming to Melbourne as refrigeration consultant. Which will give him income and a purpose in life, plus the support of his closest friend to encourage him to commence a rehabilitation program before he returns to New York. All problems solved.'

Rosie emptied her glass. 'You left some in the shaker, didn't you, and you were going to hold off until I agreed, right?'

'Correct.'

'You're good to pour. I said when I married you that I was expecting constant craziness, so I'd be letting us both down if I said no. We're a professor of genetics and a mental-health researcher and we're going to open a cocktail bar and fly in a refrigeration engineer from New York. Of course we are.'

I divided the remaining Last Word between the two glasses. There was only a small amount. 'There's enough juice left to make a margarita,' I said.

'You know how long it is since we made cocktails together?' said Rosie. 'You've been so busy with your job and the study, you've had no time for Hudson — at least until this autism thing came up. I thought we'd lost you.'

She drank the remains of the Last Word. 'Maybe this bar will work, maybe it won't, but something had to change. You've made the right call.'

As I calculated the quantities of tequila and Cointreau required to complement the thirty-five millilitres of surplus lime juice, I reviewed Rosie's words. I had almost missed the biggest problem of all.

12

My first action was to advise Professor Lawrence.

'I'm glad you called me before doing anything,' she said. 'Nobody should throw away a senior academic position without — '

'I've already — '

'Hear me out, Don. I'm going to suggest you take leave of absence. Without pay — that'll satisfy the lynch mob and build some sympathy. If you choose to return at some stage, the heat will have gone out of this and your complainant will probably have other things on her plate. Between you and I . . . '

'You and me.'

'You can spare me the grammar lesson.'

'Apologies. It's a habit from educating my eleven-year-old child.'

'Between you and *me*, this isn't the only issue she has running. She'll have moved on. Memories will have faded. With the exception of yours, of course.'

'Excellent solution.'

'I'll talk to the chair of the disciplinary committee this afternoon, but you can assume you won't be going to work tomorrow.'

★   ★   ★

I advised Amghad of my killer concept and he seemed enthusiastic.

'Cocktail science. It's been done, but the freezer thing may be new. Keep thinking about it.'

'I also have a possible location.'

My initial thought had been the University Club, which currently focused on wine. But Professor Lawrence thought that a disgraced academic serving cocktails might not be a 'good look'.

I described the laboratory being vacated by Dang Minh's genetics-research company. It was located in an inner suburb but not close to other bars, hence less competition. The décor would be consistent with the science theme and it might be possible to purchase and modify the refrigeration equipment.

'You know these guys, right? The current tenants?' said Amghad.

'We've had two meetings. They were extremely friendly.'

'Maybe you talk to them. If we go ahead, I'll negotiate the financials. But, like I said, we've got a way to go yet.'

'Also, I'll need a refrigeration expert.'

'Least of our problems.'

'The requirements are very specific. I know a refrigeration engineer — '

'And you want to send some business his way?'

'Correct. The costs — '

'Details. We'll deal with them when we've got the concept.'

★ ★ ★

I had not consulted Dave about his role, and he was opposed to it. Totally, irrevocably opposed.

'What do you think Sonia would say? I leave her holding the baby while I travel halfway around the world to hang out with my buddy? In a bar?'

'It would only be a few weeks. Sonia could take some time off. Due to you having an income. And we could talk about what you do next. Having a job is essential for sanity.'

'Man, I so appreciate you trying, and you're great with technical solutions, but there are people involved here. I can hardly walk. I'll probably never work again. If I came, that'd be the end for Sonia and me. *The end.* You don't know Sonia.'

Sonia called me back nineteen minutes later.

'Oh God, Don, I don't know how to thank you. Thank you, thank you, *thank you.*'

It was obvious that she was crying. This was not unusual for Sonia, in situations of both positive and negative emotions, so it was difficult to ascertain what she was thanking me for. Perhaps Dave was right, and I had given her an excuse to leave him. I asked for clarification.

'What do you think I'm thanking you for, Don? For giving Dave a job, some work, any work. If you could see him — he's gotten so big and we don't do anything together anymore ... And now we've got something to look forward to, something to do together: I've always wanted to see Australia.'

'You're coming?'

'Yes, yes, my company has an office in

Melbourne — they've got branches everywhere — and they've been pushing so hard for me to do a secondment, but Dave kept pushing back. Don't ever tell him, but I was close to taking the kids to Italy and leaving him behind. You're maybe the only person who could have persuaded him. You've answered my prayers, Don. Do they have Catholic schools in Melbourne?'

★ ★ ★

My assessment that Minh was on the edge of being clinically manic was reinforced when I phoned to enquire about leasing the premises. She was *ecstatic*. She owned the building and had not sold the refrigeration equipment. She *loved* what I planned to do with it. But I needed to allow her staff to drink *for free*. Every night.

I was stunned. I doubted it would be feasible or legal. Or wise for the owner of a research organisation to encourage their staff to drink.

She laughed. 'Just kidding. But I want you to know we look after our people. Maybe I'll cut a deal with your business guy. Maybe just me drinking for free. Maybe just mojitos. You're going to be making mojitos, right? That may be part of the deal. And when you're bored with running the bar, you're going to come work with us — I could add that in, too.'

'I don't think — '

'Chill. That's what you should call it. *Chill.*'

★ ★ ★

I had expected my boss, Diana, to be relieved that I was departing, given my incompetence. To my amazement, she was not.

'Don, you've been a huge asset to the project. I can't believe you'd think otherwise. You're a professor, and I thought you'd just be overseeing things, offering guidance, adding a little cachet, but you've dug right into the detail . . . '

'It was the only way to understand the work.'

'Well, you've exceeded all our expectations. But this racism thing . . . I understand what you're doing.'

I recommended Laszlo as my replacement, pointing out that his initial rejection had been based on interview performance, which research has confirmed is an unreliable method of assessment. After approximately half an hour, Diana terminated the discussion and I assumed I had convinced her. I shared the good news with Laszlo, but he was not prepared to rely on my assessment of another person's intentions.

'You and me, Don, we are not good at this. We will wait and see.'

But while we were talking, Diana called him with the job offer. And Professor Lawrence called me. The proposal that I take a year's unpaid leave had been accepted. The committee thanked me for my understanding and co-operation, and trusted there would be a speedy resolution satisfactory to all parties. According to Professor Lawrence, this was code for them agreeing that the problem, if ignored long enough, would disappear.

Things were moving fast. And my schedule was clear to proceed with the Hudson Project.

13

On the first evening in my new role, I had planned to create an action list for the Hudson Project, but unscheduled events intervened.

Dinner had to be delayed because Rosie was late: *Won't be too long* then *Hopefully home by 7* then *Start without me.* Hudson was understandably annoyed with the disruption, then with the change to the Wednesday meal. He had internalised the Standardised Meal System and expected it to be followed.

Unfortunately, the low-temperature-alcohol experiment had necessitated making room in the freezer, and I now needed to use up the pasta sauce which I had taken out and omitted to return. The memory lapse was possibly a result of the consumption of low-temperature alcohol.

'I'm going to have less time to read after dinner,' said Hudson.

'You had extra time before dinner. Exactly the same amount as you're now missing after dinner.'

'I don't read between school and dinner. I do homework.'

'Didn't you finish your homework? With the extra time?'

'I did some of tomorrow's. It was *homework* time. Now my whole week is messed up.' He pushed his plate to one side. 'This is totally wrong.'

I agreed, but not to the extent that I was going to deny myself nourishment.

'Aren't you going to ask, 'How was school?'' said Hudson.

'Your mother normally asks the question, so me asking it would be a violation of ritual.'

'Ask me. Do something normal.'

'How was school?'

'Fine.'

'If a terrorist had entered the classroom and shot everyone except you, because you threw yourself through a glass window and escaped by stealing a car, would that still be the answer?'

Hudson laughed briefly. *Autistic people often do not get jokes.* 'You would have heard it on the news. Also, I can't drive. I think the windows are some sort of super-strong glass and if they weren't, I would have cut myself and you'd see it.'

'How was your day between the hours of 9 a.m. and 3.30 p.m.?' I asked, thinking that a break from ritual might elicit a non-standard answer.

'Fine.' Hudson found an orecchietta which had not been in contact with the sauce and ate it. 'Actually, terrible. Like every day.'

'Can you provide more details?'

'I hate the teacher, I hate the other kids — except one — they won't let me do math — *maths* — the way I want to, which *works . . .* '

'What's wrong with Mr Warren?'

'Everything.'

'Can you provide an example?'

'He won't let us stay in the classroom at

recess. Can I be excused? Please?'

'First I need to share some information. Positive information. Commencing today, I'm going to be available after school every day to assist you in overcoming these problems.'

'What? What about Mum? What about Grandpa?'

'Your mother will be at work. Her job has escalated. And Grandpa won't be required. I will replace both in the after-school-care role.'

'You never asked me. You've changed everything without asking me. Like you did when you decided to leave New York and come to this place. This totally crappy place.'

Hudson swept his dinner across the table and onto the floor and began yelling, initially at me, but then more generally. I could guess, from personal experience, how he felt. At first, completely out of control, then aware that what he was doing was irrational, but locked into continuing, like a petrol pump with the trigger stuck.

What would I have wanted an adult to do to assist? I needed to give him a reason to stop, which meant removing the cause of the problem — the change in parenting protocol, which I had presented in an unnecessarily inflexible manner.

'The change is negotiable,' I said, raising my voice over his. I decided to repeat it. Hudson was screaming incoherently, and I was shouting the mantra, and Hudson's dinner was still spread across the table and floor when Rosie walked in.

Some of Hudson's anger seemed to dissipate. Rosie held up one hand and put the other on top horizontally — the time-out signal — and he ran towards his room.

'Jesus,' said Rosie. 'This is Day One.'

* * *

'If you think you and Hudson have had a bad day, let me tell you about mine,' said Rosie when we eventually sat down to freshly cooked pasta and reheated sauce.

She had spoken to Hudson and reported that he was less angry but still unhappy. I suggested we tackle the work debriefing first, since it might affect the Hudson situation.

'I'm assuming that Judas has failed to honour his promise, which would mean that you would be available for after-school care . . . '

'Wait till you've heard the story. Basically, Judas said it was too late. The funding proposal is due Friday — not enough time to change, according to him. I called bullshit. It's just names against roles. And he wouldn't budge. Said I could complain all I liked, but he's the boss, and he had to make the call about whether we had enough time.'

'Incredibly unreasonable. Management roles seem to encourage irrationality, even in scientists.'

'So,' said Rosie, 'the submission's online. I edited it to change the names and roles. Took me till 5.00 p.m.'

'Did you tell him?'

'Of course I did. After I'd done it. What was he going to say? I'd proved him wrong. So he

106

started looking for other ways to lock me out. And when he ran out of ways, you know what he said to me?'

'Obviously, no.'

'He said, 'I thought your son was having difficulties. Doesn't he need you at home?' Like Hudson had only one parent. And you weren't even in the frame, because . . . you know why because. So, you know how Hudson was when I came in? That was me. Approximately.'

'You had a meltdown?'

'I was in control, so, by your definition, no.'

'You've been fired?'

'No, I've got the job. At least my name's on the submission. It's still got to get funded. But — '

'The rest is irrelevant. Incredible. You should be happy.'

'I am. But still angry.' She laughed.

'Excellent. Now we can address the Hudson issue.'

★ ★ ★

Hudson was, said Rosie, prepared to discuss the arrangement. If I had, at eleven, behaved as Hudson had, my father would have told me that I had forfeited any right to input. Perhaps his goal was to deter future meltdowns, but if I could have prevented them, I would have already done so.

Rosie thought I should be the one to talk to Hudson, particularly given my new role. Then she told me how high the stakes were. 'If he needs me to be there for him, I'll be there.' To increase the degree of difficulty, she added, 'You can't tell him I'd lose the chief-investigator role. It'd be emotional blackmail.'

When I completed the *strengths* section on the performance-review form that was never submitted, there was zero chance I would have responded: *Negotiating with a justifiably angry and emotionally unstable eleven-year-old to separate him from time with his mother while not revealing that his preferred outcome would cost her the job she had travelled across the world to take.*

⋆   ⋆   ⋆

I spent the next day, before collecting Hudson from school, considering my approach.

'Where's Mum?' he said as he entered the Porsche. 'There's a big scrape on the car.'

'Gatepost,' I said. 'The door is still functional. Your mother is at work. She is required to do some incredibly important research — hence is not able to finish until approximately 5.30 p.m., Mondays to Fridays inclusive.'

'You both think her work's more important than me?'

'At a global level, yes. If it saves at least two lives, which is likely, then rationally it's more important. But your mother and I place a huge weighting on your welfare because you're our son. Fortunately, you have two parents, and I can function as backup. I can perform all tasks that your mother performs.'

108

I could see that Hudson was searching his mind for a counter-example. He must have failed, because he changed the subject.

'What sort of work is she doing? It's still mental health, right?'

'True, but a change of focus.' I gave him a summary of bipolar disorder, and the difference between clinical and patient-assessed outcomes.

'The drugs stop them committing suicide?'

'That's one possible outcome. They reduce depression. But they also reduce manic behaviour: they slow the patients down, which the patients don't always like. Which can also lead to them assessing their lives as less worthy of living.'

'The drugs make them easier to control, right?' I assumed he had been listening to Rosie, but he elaborated. 'Dov's on drugs. It's sort of zombified him.'

'Who's Dov?'

'The kid at school with autism.'

★   ★   ★

There were several outcomes of the conversation I had with Hudson while he was trapped in the Porsche. The first was learning that trapping him in the Porsche was an excellent approach to conversation: few alternative activities, minimal interruptions and no eye contact due to the driving task.

The second, and most important, was that he accepted the change to Rosie's working hours, subject to his participation in developing a new schedule for himself. My arguments of parental competence and the importance of improving — and possibly saving — the lives of people with bipolar disorder had apparently been persuasive.

The third was a mental note to learn more about Dov, the autistic boy, who was apparently being prescribed medication for his condition. My immediate reaction had been relief that we had not sought a diagnosis for Hudson: I felt certain that whatever problems he was having were not amenable to pharmaceutical solutions, but it would be difficult to argue with a psychiatrist whose opinion differed.

The fourth outcome was an agreement to visit my parents, subject to the dog being locked up.

When my mother called, as scheduled, on Sunday and asked when she would see us, I was able to give a non-standard response. She was pleased, but defensive about the dog, which was 'only a puppy', 'excited to see Hudson' and 'just being friendly'. Hudson needed to get used to animals or he would grow up like me, scared of cats. This was untrue: there is a difference between 'scared of' and 'does not enjoy contact with' — despite the reactions to having an unwilling animal thrown onto your lap being similar.

'Just tie the bloody dog up,' said my father in the background. 'And I need to speak to Don, privately.' I heard him take the phone from my mother.

'Hi, Dad, how are you?'

'You're the cancer scientist. Dying. I need you to do something for me — or get Rosie to.'

14

Rosie elected to avoid the trip to my parents' home in Shepparton, which would have involved discomfort for one of us, due to the dimensions of the Porsche's rear seat. She was pleased with my progress in de-escalating the Hudson situation: 'I think you just spending time with him, engaging with him, has given him some reassurance.'

I re-engaged as soon as we were underway. 'Have you considered the new schedule?'

'Yes.'

'Do you have any suggestions?'

'Yes.'

'What are they?'

'I want to get up at 5.20 a.m. on school days.'

'Why?'

'It's a good time to talk to George in New York.'

'You're in contact with George?'

'Of course. He's my friend. He's supposed to be your friend too, but he says you don't call anymore.'

Since Dave had started planning his trip to Melbourne, he and I had been in touch directly and the Boys' Nights Out had been deferred.

'What do you talk about?'

'Stuff. He *really* hated school. There was this kid who used to beat him up. George had to go to hospital once. But when George was famous,

111

the kid who wasn't a kid anymore called him and asked for free concert tickets, and George told him to go . . . to go away.'

'Presumably you don't talk to George every school day. There must be another reason.'

'I'll read.'

'But you'll have to go to bed earlier to make up.'

'Probably.'

'So, why do you want to do it?'

'If I've got something good to do before I go to school, I'll feel like getting up.'

'I wasn't aware of the problem. But it's an excellent solution.'

'And I want to go to Grandpa's after school Tuesdays and Thursdays. Like I do now.'

'Don't you get bored? Sitting around at a gym?'

'I need the time for homework. It's a good place to read. I should see Grandpa regularly. Before he dies.'

'But I want to teach you skills. To assist in making school more pleasant. With ongoing benefits.'

'Like?'

'Improving physical co-ordination. Acquiring friends. Avoiding being annoyed by others.'

'What do you mean 'annoyed by others'?'

'Mr Warren advised that you became angry because another student' — I remembered the word — 'niggled you.'

'What's *niggled*?'

'I don't know. Whatever it was that made you angry.'

'There's a kid who plays with my hair. It's

annoying, but . . . Did you ask him to do something?'

'No. I thought I should consult with you first. Do you want me to talk to him?'

'Definitely not.'

'Would you like some advice on tactics?'

'You're going to tell me to ignore him, right?'

That's what my mother would have said: *He's only doing it because you react. Just ignore him.* I knew it wouldn't work. In my case, being poked caused me considerable distress and the poker zero. It was obvious who would crack first.

My father would have recommended violence, or at least the threat of it. *Front him in the playground. Tell him to stop or you'll sort him out. You're big enough and you know how to do it.* If I had made and carried out such a threat, I would have been in serious trouble.

This was all hypothetical. I had never told my parents about the kid who used to poke me, because I knew what their answers would have been. It was time to share my adult knowledge with Hudson.

'Obviously, if you had a good relationship with him, he wouldn't want to damage it by annoying you.'

'You're saying I should make friends with him.'

'Correct. And you contribute to the second goal of increasing your number of friends. Friendships are largely random. I used to think that I was only compatible with a small proportion of people. In fact, most people are interesting.'

'He's interesting to his friends. He's the class clown. That's why he does what he does. He

113

thinks it's funny. I don't, so we're not
. . . compatible.'

⋆   ⋆   ⋆

In Shepparton, we visited the family hardware
shop, which continued to operate under my
brother Trevor's management. It would have
been economically non-viable if my parents had
not owned the building and stock, and provided
Trevor with free accommodation and meals.
When we arrived, he was occupied with a
customer, but I was able to procure the stud
finder and electronic distance measurer that I
had come for before proceeding to our parents'
home.

My father answered the door and looked
terrible. His facial skin was grey, and he had lost
weight since I had last seen him. I was surprised
that he was able to stand, and, in fact, he sat
down almost immediately in the chair that had
been reserved for his use all of my life.

'Light a fire, will you, Don,' he said. 'It's
freezing in here.'

Hudson and I collected kindling from the shed
and I threw it in with some paper. My father's
selection and installation of the stove had been
sufficiently well researched that there was no
need to waste effort setting the fire properly.

'That's not how you set a fire,' said my father.
'You ever set a fire, Hudson?'

'Not really.'

'Well, that's not how you do it.'

My father got out of his chair and

demonstrated the correct method. I sat in my own designated chair and reminded myself — several times — that it was an excellent bonding moment between grandfather and grandson, and that Hudson was learning a useful skill. A *life* skill.

When my mother left the room to make instant coffee, my father, still building the fire, asked, 'Well, what did you find out?'

'Continuing chemotherapy will improve your twelve-month survival rate by approximately twenty-five per cent.'

'Twenty-five per cent of bugger-all is still bugger-all.'

'Correct. Bugger-all in this case is approximately fifteen per cent.'

'You're going to die?' said Hudson.

'Everyone is. I'm eighty-six and I've got cancer, so it's not going to be long. You'd better see me again before I go, in case there's some advice I need to give you that I've forgotten.'

He turned to me. 'Don, tell your mother you've done your homework and there's *zero* value in the chemotherapy.'

'Dad said it was twenty-five per cent,' said Hudson.

'He did,' said my father, 'but he's not going to tell your grandmother that, or she'll make me keep doing it. I wouldn't wish it on my worst enemy. Now I'm going to bed to listen to Beethoven.'

★ ★ ★

'Why did you lie to Nan?' asked Hudson as we drove past Tillman Hardware for the second time in an hour. 'If Pa doesn't want to take the drugs, she can't make him, right? There's no law?'

'I didn't lie. I corrected for the fact that humans have a poor intuitive understanding of probability and statistics. Your grandmother would say, 'We should take any chance, no matter how slim,' without properly weighing the negative aspects. The most likely outcome is that Pa would suffer with no benefit.'

'Why is Nan always so sad?' *People with autism are poor at recognising others' emotions.*

'Because Pa is ill.' It was the logical answer, but it was possible that my mother had been sad for sixteen years — since my sister died. It was not something I had noticed.

★   ★   ★

The following day, Sunday, I rode to the cycle shop and purchased training wheels for my bike, which I estimated Hudson was now tall enough to ride. In New York, he had resisted learning and I was able to relate to his problem — precisely. My father had successfully taught my older sister and younger brother to ride, but I had failed to learn, due to multiple falls and fear of further injury.

I *knew* the solution, but my father did not want me to be seen with 'sissy' training wheels. I did not learn to ride until several years later and was excluded from numerous activities in the intervening period.

Hudson and I had negotiated a physical-skills session for Sunday afternoons and I requested his assistance to install the wheels.

'Training wheels? No way, Dad. They're for little kids.'

'Currently your bike-riding skills are at little-kid standard.'

'If someone sees me — '

'Obviously, I've considered the embarrassment factor. We will be practising at a remote location. Pass me the ratchet.'

Hudson looked around and I realised that he would not know what a ratchet was. Years of enforced labour in the hardware shop had given me an encyclopaedic knowledge of tools and their applications. I retrieved the ratchet from its case and demonstrated its use, along with the relative advantages of socket, open, ring and adjustable spanners.

With the first training wheel installed, I suggested that Hudson fit its counterpart on the opposite side, but he had not been watching with that in mind. I fitted the second wheel myself, instructing him to observe with the objective of learning: we would need to perform the task multiple times as the bike alternated between training mode for Hudson and transport for me.

We drove to a park in the opposite direction from the school, with the roof down to accommodate the bike.

'Is this sufficiently distant?' I said.

Hudson nodded, we unloaded the bike, he rode with the training wheels without incident, we returned home and Hudson resumed reading his book, all within the one-hundred-and-twenty-minute slot. Things were going well.

15

Compiling a detailed list of goals and activities for Hudson proved more difficult than I had expected. *If I knew then what I know now* had prompted thoughts of social rituals and physical competencies, but few specifics.

We had made a good start on physical skills with the bike riding. Next in importance was ball catching, which Rabbit had mentioned specifically. I was well qualified to teach it, having overcome a severe deficit of natural ability.

Appropriate dress was important. Even with a school uniform, there were subtle differences in deployment that Hudson needed to know, unless he wanted to be the class clown. Being the class clown provided some protection and positive interaction, but it was not as good as being accepted in the normal way. In any case, that position was apparently already filled in Hudson's class.

I would need to keep up the mathematics tuition, which I had incorporated into our dinner routine. Mathematics is excellent training for rational thinking, arguably life's most important skill.

What else? Times had changed. My knowledge of BASIC and transistors and how to fix a broken cassette tape was obsolete. Motor vehicles and electronic appliances were too complex or inaccessible or uneconomic for amateur repairers.

Hudson would never need to read a street directory or roll a cigarette.

One of my teachers had presented Rudyard Kipling's poem 'If as a specification for manhood, with its claim that a fully configured male should be willing not only to gamble but to wager his entire pile of winnings on a single event with a fifty per cent probability of success. Then and now, Kipling seemed to be describing a personality fault that would warrant professional intervention. Rosie would not have responded to such recklessness on my part by complimenting me on my manliness.

I checked my notes from the discussion with Rabbit Warren and added *team sports, tact, playing in a group,* and *dealing with anger and conflict.*

★   ★   ★

By the time I collected Hudson from school, I had a draft list which was daunting, considering the time available for working on it. Hudson immediately introduced a complicating factor.

'Can I go to Blanche's place and you pick me up afterwards? It's okay with her mum.' Blanche was standing beside him.

'We have ninety minutes scheduled for — '

'I can do it later, instead of reading. Wait.'

He indicated that we should move away from Blanche to speak privately.

'You said 'acquiring friends' was one of our goals. That's what I'm doing. So, this should count instead of whatever we were going to do.'

'Blanche is already your friend.'

'Aaargh.'

I could understand Hudson's reaction. It was important to maintain existing friendships — using tact and conflict-resolution skills — as well as finding new ones. And there was something I needed to give to Allannah, though I would need to go home to get it.

'How are you planning to travel to Blanche's?'

'She's getting the tram because her mum has to work. Can I borrow your myki?'

'I'll give you a ride.'

★ ★ ★

'Cool car,' said Blanche from the back seat. 'Does the roof come down?'

'It's winter,' I said.

Hudson actuated the roof mechanism and we travelled to Blanche's, via our home, in extreme discomfort.

Blanche's residence was an organic-food and unsubstantiated-therapies business: Thornbury Natural Living. Allannah was behind the counter in the shop, and Blanche's brother was playing on the floor.

'Don't bother your father,' said Allannah to Blanche.

'Der,' said Blanche, and she and Hudson proceeded up the stairs.

'I have the information and equipment you requested,' I said to Allannah.

She looked surprised, then said, 'Would you like a tea? Or a coffee? I drink herbal, but I can make an instant coffee.'

'Herbal, please. I don't drink caffeine after 3 p.m.'

While she prepared the infusion, I unpacked the items I had brought.

'Cheek scraper for DNA collection, plus zip-lock bag. You scrape the inside of Blanche's cheek with it. In fact, it's better if she does it herself.' Hudson would not have permitted another person to scrape his inner cheek.

'Also, a letter specifying the test required and indicating you've consulted with a geneticist, which is me, to be signed by you. You need to add your full name, contact information and credit-card details. Then, mail it to the laboratory in the accompanying envelope with the sample. There's a document explaining how to interpret the results.'

'You've gone to so much trouble.'

'There would have been more trouble if you or the laboratory made an error due to poor instructions.'

'Well, again, thank you. I'm really sorry, but . . . It's Don, isn't it? Blanche wasn't sure.'

'Correct.'

'Do you want to wait till Hudson and Blanche are finished? She needs to start her homework in an hour or so.'

★　★　★

'Of course. I've got my computer. I can sit somewhere and work.'

'You've got stuff to do?'

'In fact, no. It was an automatic response, due

to being constantly overloaded in the past.'

'But not anymore?'

I outlined my situation. The explanation consumed the full hour and Allannah listened without interrupting.

Hudson and Blanche returned. 'Can Hudson stay a bit longer? We can do our homework together.'

Allannah looked at me and I nodded. The parents-after-school discussion was a new social situation for me, and I felt that I was handling it competently. With the extra time, I could do even better: 'Any questions?' I asked.

Allannah laughed. 'About what? No. You're so . . . articulate. Just like Hudson. Or I guess Hudson is like you. Blanche really likes him. He's got her into science and space travel and now it's all she talks about.'

'You indicated last time we met that you were interested in discussing the science of vaccination.'

'I did? Don't bother. You'll get frustrated with me. Or angry.'

'Frustration is a possibility. But you seem rational to me. Rational people, if they have all the information and the brainpower to process it, should reach similar conclusions. But science is so complex that most of us are forced to rely on authorities. The theory that pharmaceutical companies would cover up side effects to promote vaccines is plausible.'

'Don't you get into trouble for having views like that?'

'I said it was plausible. I don't think it's true.

In any case, the postulated side effects of vaccines are minimal compared with the impact of diphtheria or rubella or measles.'

'But Blanche will be okay because of . . . herd immunity . . . right? She won't get anything and she's safe from any side effects.'

Allannah must have noticed my silence. 'If you think vaccines are safe, then nobody's telling you not to have your kids vaccinated. But, I mean, we were never meant to inject stuff into our bodies.'

'*Meant* implies some sort of higher purpose or deity. Are you religious?'

'Not traditionally . . . I get what you're saying. I should let you and Hudson go. But thanks again for the laboratory stuff.'

★ ★ ★

'Is there any change to the situation with the class clown?' I asked Hudson while he was trapped in the Porsche.

'Mr Warren caught him doing it again and said he'd move me to another desk. I said he should move Jasper — that's his name — but he said it had to be me. And I didn't want to move.'

'Why not?'

'I like where I sit. Then Mr Warren said if it wasn't bothering me that much, I could stay where I was and so could Jasper. I told him it *was* bothering me, but I *really* like where I sit.'

'Do you want me to talk to Mr Warren about it?'

I knew the answer already, but I also knew that Rosie would want to know whether I'd asked.

★   ★   ★

I called Amghad to ask him to negotiate the rental of the lab, but he wanted to meet with me first. He specified a coffee shop less than a kilometre from our home. The owner was cleaning up and Amghad ordered beers.

'You're wondering why we're drinking beer in a coffee shop?' he said.

I nodded, although alcohol was a better choice than coffee at 4.33 p.m.

'It closed half an hour ago and it'll be empty until 7.00 a.m. Wasted real estate, wasted liquor licence. In a couple of weeks that's going to change: it'll be my newest bar. Same name, same décor. A few coffee-based cocktails, to play to the theme. Neat idea?'

I nodded, though I was unlikely to use its services. The street had numerous bars, but Rosie and I could produce better drinks at home in a more pleasant environment and at lower cost.

'Don, I've been thinking about your idea. The more I think about it, the more I think it's not going to fly. The science-lab thing has been done. I'm not saying it's a bad idea, but we'd need something more.'

'Like pretending to be a coffee shop?'

'This project's a no-brainer. The space was available; it's a busy street. With yours, the lab's upstairs, off the main strips . . . it needs a bigger concept.'

'You're withdrawing your offer?'

'I don't want to lose money and I don't want you to either. I talked to your lady at the lab.

125

Smart operator. She said she tried to hire you. Told me a bit about your day job. You're a dark horse, all right.'

'It's no longer my day job.'

'So, you find another one. In the same game.'

'Unfortunately, I can't work during the day. How long do I have to create an alternative concept?'

'Your lady said she'd keep the rental offer open until something else comes along, but, like I said, it'll need to be something special.'

★　★　★

I had long ago learned that withholding information from Rosie was unwise. The reduction in her stress levels was more than offset by the increase when she detected deceit.

'The bar project appears doomed, Dave is arriving on Tuesday expecting me to have work for him and Blanche's parents are still objecting to her being vaccinated.'

'Don, do I get to put my bag down? Have you and Hudson eaten?'

'You don't need permission to put your bag down. We agreed to wait for you. I texted the information.'

'Sorry, phone was flat. Just give me two . . . ten . . . minutes to get changed and we can talk over dinner. I've spent all day trying to get permission to hire an admin person so I don't have to do what I spent all day doing. And in the middle of it, fucking Judas asks me to make coffee.'

126

'I'll brief you on the problems before you get changed. Then you can incubate your solutions while we eat.'

'I heard you already. No killer concept. The rest follows, except the stuff about what's-her-name — your new-age flake. If you want to take that on, that's fine, but I don't need to be involved.'

Rosie's mood improved during dinner. We were playing a mathematical game every night and I was also offering occasional lessons on social skills, which Rosie elaborated on.

Me: When someone sends you an email conveying information, you should reply, even if no reply seems logically necessary.

Rosie: You just have to say *thanks* or *got it*. Is that what you mean, Don?

Me: Correct.

Hudson: But *got it* is information. So, the other person has to reply and then . . .

Me: Excellent point. Normally they don't reply again after you give the unnecessary response. So, there's a limit of one.

Rosie: How can you guys make something so simple so complex?

Me: It's the opposite. We're establishing simple rules to replace imprecise and error-prone intuitive decisions.

Hudson: Anyway, I only use email for school. Mostly the emails go out to the whole class. It'd be seriously weird to write *got it*.

Rosie: You're probably right.

Hudson: Okay, I'll ignore what Dad said.

Rosie and I waited until he had gone to bed,

earlier thanks to the new schedule, to revisit the bar problem.

'People — marketing experts — spend months coming up with so-called killer concepts,' said Rosie. 'And a lot of the time they don't work. Don't beat yourself up.'

'It's possible I considered myself more competent than marketing people.'

'Academics always think they can do any job better, until they try it. Including designing a bar.'

'If I'm incompetent to design a bar, we have a major problem.'

Rosie sat back in her chair and looked at the ceiling. 'I can go part-time again. Give up the chief-investigator role. You can take the job with the genetics-editing company or look for another academic job. Or see if you can go back to the old one.'

'We could move Hudson to the public school. You suggested that.'

'I know,' said Rosie. 'But every time he moves it takes him ages to settle. Whatever's wrong with the current school, we've no reason to think the alternative would be any better. And he *is* starting to settle. You've been doing well with him.'

Except that was about to end. And we hadn't even discussed Dave.

16

Five weeks and two days after our initial telephone conversation, Dave arrived at Melbourne airport, along with Sonia, Zina and the baby, Fulvio.

I had swapped cars with Phil, after he had noted the cosmetic damage to the Porsche and made negative comments about Rosie's driving. I was now using his vastly more practical Toyota four-wheel-drive. It seated seven people; the air-conditioning, heating and sound systems functioned reliably; and it was far less likely to suffer mechanical failure.

Dave's weight had increased substantially and I estimated his BMI at forty-five — morbidly obese. He was walking with the aid of a metal crutch, while Sonia pushed a luggage cart, and Zina, who was approximately eight weeks older than Hudson, guided a baby vehicle containing her brother.

I knew better than to comment explicitly on Dave's appearance, and raised the problem indirectly. 'Greetings, Dave. You should modify your diet and begin an exercise program. Immediately.' Sonia was nodding violently.

'I've let it go too far,' he said. 'I didn't want to say it on the phone, but I don't think I can help you with your bar thing. I'm just here while Sonia works, and I have to look after the kids . . . '

'Gym sessions begin tonight. To assist in recovery from jet lag.'

'Listen to Don,' said Sonia. 'He's talking sense.'

* * *

I had a well-equipped gym available at zero cost due to my father-in-law being the owner. Phil had met Dave when he visited us in New York and now appeared less shocked than I had expected by Dave's appearance.

'I'm no doctor but I'd think if you dropped the kilos you might not need the crutch. What do the doctors say?'

'What you said. More or less.' Dave looked embarrassed. 'I enjoy my food.'

'You don't look like you're enjoying anything much at the moment. It's a habit and you'll have to break it. You only need one rule: don't eat junk.'

'That'd do it,' said Dave. 'But man, it's not easy to just turn it off.'

'Distract yourself. Do something. You won't eat when you're working hard. You're a drinker?'

Dave nodded.

'That's junk too. Same rule. If you want to lose weight, stay off the booze. If you want to stay off the booze, keep busy.' Phil was looking at me.

* * *

I took advantage of driving time to provide Hudson with further guidance on social interaction. I was finding it difficult to describe desirable behaviours at an appropriate level of generality: they were either too situation-specific, hence unlikely to be of use on a daily basis, or too general, hence difficult for Hudson to interpret. *If someone tells you that their dog has died, the appropriate response is to say you're sorry to hear that and ask about their feelings rather than to demand details of the circumstances* was probably too specific, as dog deaths were likely to be infrequent. But *When someone has experienced a loss, express sympathy and focus on their emotions* would lead to an inappropriate response to 'I can't find my eraser.'

The bike-riding lessons had stalled following removal of the training wheels. Hudson had been riding confidently, and I had judged him ready to proceed to the next stage. He disagreed — and was right.

With the supplementary wheels gone, his confidence disappeared, and he faced the traditional problem of learning to ride a bike: stability increases with speed, but so does fear of falling. He failed to pedal hard enough, then fell and grazed his knee. After that, he began making excuses to avoid practice. It was disappointing, particularly because it provided evidence that my father may have been right in refusing to buy me training wheels.

★   ★   ★

Amghad and Rosie were also right: my best chance of a well-paid job was with Minh. It occurred to me that she might consider

131

employing me on a non-standard-hours basis, which would allow me to continue with the Hudson Project.

I called her, but she only wanted to talk about the bar. 'I *love* your idea. I'll be your best customer.'

'Worst customer if you weren't paying.'

'But I have so many friends. Don, you have to do this thing. If you've lost your business partner, maybe I can come in.'

It was a generous offer, but I trusted Amghad. I did not want Minh to lose her money as a result of relying on my business judgement.

Minh refused to be dissuaded. 'Meet me at the old lab. Seven p.m. We can brainstorm ideas. And you can make me a mojito.'

I brought mojito ingredients, glasses and Dave with me. Minh was already inside, with her own liquor, lime juice, mint, sugar, soda and glasses. She laughed, and I introduced Dave.

'Now you're here,' she said to Dave, 'you can tell us how to make Don's chilling idea work. Technically.'

The lab was actually two large rooms. The refrigeration units were still in place.

I outlined the requirement. 'All liquor would need to be kept minimally above freezing point, which for most spirits is minus twenty-six degrees Celsius but for fortified wines such as vermouth is minus seven. Prosecco, champagne for mixing: minus five, hence we could share space with the fortified wines. Table wine is served at traditional recommended temperatures. Non-alcoholic mixers obviously freeze at zero degrees. Minus thirty-two for overproof spirits and liqueurs.'

Dave walked over to the biggest refrigeration unit, examined the control panel and turned a dial. 'Minus twenty-six. I'm done here. If your buddy had paid for my flight, you might not have wanted him to see that.'

Minh put her bottle of rum in the freezer and laughed. 'I like you. Mojito time.'

I made two conventional mojitos, using ice, while we waited for the rum to chill, and Dave found a beer in one of the other fridges.

'So, you need a big idea for the bar, a game-changer?' said Minh.

'Correct. But I know zero about marketing.'

'What sort of bars do you like to drink at? Where do you go yourself?'

'We drink at home. It's cheaper and not noisy.'

'Forget the money for a minute. You don't like noisy bars. That's a disruptive thought, because we associate bars with noise. The popular ones, anyway.'

'It's possible the unpopular bars are quiet due to being unpopular,' I said.

'Hard to say. But deliberately quiet — that could be a thing.'

'We could put up a sign: *Quiet, please*,' said Dave. 'Call it The Library.'

'Go on,' said Minh.

'I'm joking,' said Dave. 'My perfect bar would have a few good craft beers and wall-to-wall baseball. And a time-out room for Don.'

I had enjoyed watching baseball in New York bars with Dave and George, but the sensory input sometimes became overwhelming and I would need to escape temporarily, usually to the street.

'If you had multiple games playing, the obvious solution would be earphones, with channel selection,' I said. 'It's common in gyms. Earphones would also reduce ambient noise, and possibly eliminate the need for time-outs.'

'Keep going. Give me your perfect bar, Don,' said Minh.

'High-quality cocktails.'

'Naturally,' said Minh.

'Not 'naturally'. Cocktail standards vary enormously. Customers pay for premium spirits but then the bartender uses poor-quality juice, or the cocktail is not made according to the official recipe or is insufficiently cold or too diluted.'

'Which is what the cooling system is about, right? What else?'

'Minimal waiting time. Eliminate the requirement to stand at the bar trying to balance the risk of unwanted physical contact and impolite behaviour with the need to attract attention and be served in the correct sequence. While being excluded from interaction with the people you are *supposed* to be socialising with. And paying for the drinks.'

'I'm with you there,' said Dave. 'I buy a round and it's three top-shelf margaritas, two glasses of Napa Valley Special Reserve 1999 under nitrogen, and all I want is a beer. The guy who invents a way of everyone paying for their own drinks without making me look like a tight-wad . . . '

'So, the requirement,' said Minh, 'is a quiet bar . . . '

'No music,' I said.

'People can choose their own music. Or none. Earphones, like you said. Everybody orders from their tables — with an app, individually — straight to their credit card.'

'Might as well just sit by themselves and use Facebook,' said Dave.

'Exactly,' said Minh. 'I guess a lot of people will want to do that. Good Wi-Fi, obviously. One room for conversation, one for solo stuff. Maybe the solo room should be the bigger one. What do you think, Don?'

I thought about it. A bar with standardised high-quality drinks, where everything worked efficiently, without the need to wave for attention, perform social rituals with staff, negotiate drink orders and bills, calculate tips, check change: no interaction at all, except with your drinking companions. Such company being optional. A variety of entertainment and informative content on big screens, but no superfluous noise or lighting or decoration. World's best bar.

'Do you want to let your friend back in on the deal?' said Minh.

★ ★ ★

After I had made a low-temperature mojito with Minh's rum, and she had pronounced it superior to the first (probably a result of the higher-quality rum or psychological factors, as liquor chilling had minimal impact in long drinks), she left Dave and me to lock up.

'Since the refrigeration task is trivial, and you don't have another job, I recommend you assist at the bar. Obviously in exchange for payment. I can provide training and you'll have a valuable transportable competency.'

'Buddy, I really appreciate you trying, but I'm spending all day looking after a baby, and then I've got to get Zina from school and fix her something to eat and make sure she does her homework. All I want to do in the evenings is have a burger and a beer, and sleep.'

'A burger? Who's doing the cooking?'

'We're still settling in. I've been getting take-out.'

'Have you been attending the gym?'

'Still finding my way around.'

'But — '

'So, that's a no on the gym. Buddy, I've got nothing left in the tank.'

'You're in a loop. Lack of stimulation leading to lassitude and weight gain, leading to — '

'Don, like I said — '

There was one certain method to motivate Dave. It was brutal, but there seemed no other way.

'If you fail to break the slob cycle, Sonia may leave you.'

Dave sipped his beer. 'I'm figuring that's what's gonna happen.'

17

Hudson and I drove to Shepparton again, this time with Rosie. My father was confined to bed and had ceased chemotherapy, which meant that he was now no longer 'fighting cancer' but 'dying of cancer'.

He was asleep when we arrived, and my mother made us tea.

'Are you going to cut off a finger or something when he dies?' asked Hudson.

'*Hudson*,' said Rosie, but my mother smiled. 'Why would we want to do that?'

'For the DNA. So we could clone him. And we'd get him back.'

'Except he'd be a baby,' I said.

'That'd be so weird,' said Hudson. 'Pa coming back as a baby and we'd watch it grow and . . . '

'That's enough, both of you,' said Rosie.

'It's okay,' said my mother. 'I had three of them asking me questions like that.'

'Did you keep any of Dad's sister?' said Hudson.

My mother got up and went to the kitchen.

Rosie was visibly angry. 'I told you to stop. But you kept going. And now you've upset your grandma.'

Hudson burst into tears, and then my mother came out and hugged him, which added to his distress.

'I'm not in any pain, thanks to science,' said my father. 'How's the bike riding going?' he asked Hudson, who had benefited from a time-out period in the garden.

'Badly.'

'Training wheels?'

'Uh-huh. It's easy with them on.'

'Tell your father to forget the training wheels.' I was in the same room and thus able to hear directly, so 'tell your father' made no sense. I guessed he was losing some cognitive function. 'Your dad always wanted training wheels but ask him how he actually learned.'

Incredibly, because I had learned to ride a bike eventually, I did not know the answer. I had memories of practising, but not of any breakthrough that had overcome the falling problem.

'If he hasn't remembered by the next time I see you, I'll tell you. But don't leave it too long.' He pointed to me. 'Next time you come down, bring me a CD of Beethoven's Opus 125 — the Ninth Symphony. The Karl Bohm 1980 version. Can you remember that?'

I looked at the rack of CDs. 'I thought Mum had bought them all for you.'

'She bought the von Karajan version. The 1977 box set. I'd like to hear someone else have a go at the Ninth. But don't tell your mother or she'll be upset.'

'I can download it,' said Hudson.

'Thank you, but I'm too old for things I can't

138

hold in my hand.' He pointed to me. 'Don't leave it too long.'

★   ★   ★

I spent some time trying to recall how I had learned to ride, and found it disturbing that I had lost or suppressed the memory. Finally, I enlisted the help of Claudia.

'Why is it bothering you?' she asked. 'You were how old when you learned to ride?'

'Eleven. Just after I started high school. I remember because I had to walk to school for the first part of the year.'

'Forty years ago. You must have forgotten a lot of things from that time.'

'First, I have a good memory. Second, learning to ride a bike is a significant achievement and I remember the approximate timing. Third, I remember failing to learn, falling off, when I was eight.'

'But, again, why does it matter to you?'

'I need to teach Hudson, and I want to remember the technique. Since he is also encountering difficulties.'

'You can't assume the same approach will work . . . ' She laughed. 'It probably will. You may just have forgotten. Not everything has a deep-seated psychological cause. But you think this does, don't you?'

'Possibly.'

'Well, I could send you to a hypnotist, or tell you that it'll probably come back to you now that you've started digging, but there's an easier way. Of course, the reason you haven't taken it may have its own deep-seated psychological cause.'

'You're being obscure.'

'Ask your father.'

★ ★ ★

I had not planned to attend the school swimming carnival. Hudson had a medical certificate exempting him from water sports due to a phobia of having his head underwater. It may have been hereditary: I had a strong dislike of submersion and Rosie also failed to conform to the Australian stereotype of enjoying having eyes and nostrils inundated with seawater.

But Hudson had invited both of us to attend, perhaps to avoid drawing attention to his non-participation. Rosie had commitments at work, so I arrived alone at the Aquatic Centre, which the school had hired for the event. I was surprised to find Phil there.

'School sports: got to fly the flag,' he said. 'Hudson tells me they've found something for him to do.'

Of course. There would be a requirement for marshals, judges and record-keepers, roles that would offer experience in organisation, observation and documentation for future scientists. It was important that parents support these intellectual endeavours as well as the physical performances.

Phil and I talked as the younger children competed. For a while Hudson held a rope which served as a finish line for swimmers who were not required to attempt the full fifty-metre length.

The Years Five and Six events commenced. One boy had entered a high proportion of the races and was winning all of them. He was in Blue House and an adult male immediately behind us was supporting that team with an enthusiasm that seemed excessive for children's sport. Blanche was also in Blue House; she finished next to last in a backstroke event, but received loud applause, presumably because of her disability, which was not swimming-related.

'Pay attention,' said Phil, and pulled a video camera from his bag. It was the medley relay: each of four swimmers performing a different stroke. 'The key is the butterfly leg, because not many primary-school kids can swim fifty metres of butterfly. If Blue House gets the big guy to swim it, they should win, but I bet they use him for the freestyle leg.'

It was illuminating to have an expert explain the tactics. But then the Green team walked to the starting end of the pool, and I saw a tall child with an unmistakable loping gait. Hudson was in a swimming costume and wearing small goggles, like an Olympic competitor. His long hair was tucked inside a swimming cap. I was stunned.

Two swimmers from each of the four teams walked to the far end of the pool. Hudson stayed where he was and the remaining swimmer from his team entered the water for the backstroke lap.

'Thought so,' said Phil, and pointed out the

141

Blue House champion, who was walking to the other end. 'The big kid will swim the freestyle leg.'

I was looking at Hudson. Someone called his name and he waved awkwardly, and then I heard his name chanted, followed by laughter. He was being mocked.

The race started, and by the time the swimmers had changed over and the breaststroke exponents were in the pool, there was a substantial gap between the leader and Hudson's teammate in last place.

The Blue House swimmer beside Hudson was first into the water and it quickly became obvious that he was incompetent at the butterfly stroke. The second had the same problem, as did the third. Phil was right — the technique was too difficult for primary-school students. The school had made an astute decision in Hudson's interest. Since no student could swim the butterfly stroke, he could compete without embarrassment. But he was terrified of water.

Hudson's teammate touched the wall and Hudson dived into the water — unbelievably *dived into the water* — and suddenly he was swimming the butterfly stroke, effectively, arms operating in synchrony, his head clearing the water to enable breathing, moving swiftly as the other swimmers struggled to maintain any momentum.

Phil was cheering loudly as Hudson overtook them and opened a lead. The crowd was also shouting his name, now in a positive way.

For many years I had ignored sport, but Dave

had encouraged an interest in baseball and I had slowly acquired the ability to engage emotionally with the outcome of a contest that had no direct bearing on my life. It was apparently transferable to a school swimming event. I was yelling too. It was hard to believe the person I was cheering for was my son. *People with autism often have poor physical co-ordination.*

The big kid was waiting for his turn, jumping on the spot and shouting at his teammate who had paused to tread water. Hudson had slowed noticeably but still had a substantial lead when he touched. The final swimmer for Green House was halfway down the pool before the champion dived in.

He almost made up the distance: he was an excellent swimmer and trying hard, but Phil's tactical assessment had been correct. Hudson's teammate held on to win by approximately two metres.

'Fuck,' said Blue House Fan, behind us. It seemed an inappropriate comment for a primary-school competition, but I was still trying to work out how Hudson had not only overcome his fear of water but gained competence in a difficult stroke. He must have needed his swimming costume laundered. Had Rosie been keeping a secret from me? If so, why wasn't she here?

I watched as Hudson's team hugged each other and Hudson pulled away.

'Something wrong with him,' said Blue House Fan, presumably to his neighbour.

I had an urge to respond but fortunately, the

neighbour had an appropriate answer. 'Nothing wrong with his swimming.'

There was one more race — the girls' hundred-metres freestyle — before the champion reappeared for the equivalent boys' race, the final event on the program. He stepped up and received a round of applause. Then Hudson walked out to an even bigger round of applause and cheering. He was slightly taller than Big Kid, but not nearly as strongly built.

'Payback time,' said the voice behind us.

'Get a life,' said Phil, and I heard the sound of breath blown out between pursed lips, but then the race started. Big Kid surfaced from his dive well ahead of Hudson, and quickly increased his lead.

'Give it time,' said Phil. 'The champ's swum a lot of races and that medley took it out of him. Hudson left him with just enough of a chance to make him go all out.'

'Deliberately? Hudson slowed down to encourage him to think that he could win?'

'Let's just say Hudson paced himself intelligently,' said Phil.

At the turn, Big Kid was still in front, but slowing. Hudson began narrowing the lead. Trying to judge the rate of gap-narrowing against the distance remaining was too difficult, and I joined the entire crowd in standing and making noise as they touched the wall together — *almost* together. The two judges, both children, walked from opposite sides of the pool, conducted a short conversation and raised Hudson's hand, as if he had won a boxing match.

'Bullshit.' The voice from behind again.

Phil turned around and I deliberately did not. People became passionate at sporting events, and it was better to avoid confrontation.

'Settle down, mate,' said Phil. 'It's primary-school sports.'

'You ever play sport?'

'I've played sport.'

'I was a professional kickboxer,' said Blue House Fan.

'And I played on the half-forward flank for Hawthorn. So, your point is?'

'If you knew sport, you'd know the weird kid didn't win. They gave it to him.'

'You call it as you see it. But don't go saying kids you don't know are weird.'

'I'll say whatever I like.'

'You do that, mate. Talk to yourself. We've got a winner to congratulate.'

Phil got up quickly and I followed him. He began laughing. 'He was hoping I'd have a go. Might have detracted a bit from Hudson's moment of triumph to have his dad and his coach carted off in a divvy van.'

Phil put his arm around my shoulders and I was too busy processing what he'd said to object.

'It's you? You're his coach? He hates water.'

'*You* hate water. You're as bad as Rosie. What chance did he have? We've got a swimming coach at the gym — you might have noticed a pool there? She's great with kids. And adults who can't swim, in case you're ever interested.'

Phil removed his arm. 'He trains every time he's there. He may be a talker, but he can keep a

145

secret. VIP member; we even wash his togs.'

'He's competent?'

'You saw. Not as good as the kid he beat, but that's what you have a coach for. Tactics. The big kid blew himself out. Hudson went two for two and left them wondering.'

18

After the swimming carnival, Phil joined us for dinner, and we played his videos for Rosie with commentary from the three of us. Hudson was extremely pleased with the results and the contribution made by Phil's advice. The atmosphere resembled that of a New York sports bar after a Yankees victory, obviously adjusted for the smaller number of people.

That thought prompted me to invite Dave over and we replayed the videos for him.

'Who's the big kid?' Dave asked Hudson.

'His name's Blake. He's okay. He was crying afterwards because he has to get up at 4.30 every morning to train and his dad expects him to win everything.'

'Did you know how close he was?'

'I could see him, but I couldn't go any faster.'

'You opened your eyes underwater?' I said.

'That's what the goggles are for. But I can do it without them if I have to.'

'We're very proud of you,' said Rosie.

I raised my glass of beer. 'World's greatest junior swimmer.'

Hudson laughed. 'You're more excited than when I came top in maths in New York. That's pretty weird for you.'

After Hudson had gone to bed, Phil told the Blue House Fan story. 'I was in the line at the kiosk afterward, and he came over and it was: 'No offence, buddy; didn't know he was with you; chill out.' Dickhead.'

'You know how I feel about violence,' said Rosie, 'but I'm sort of sorry he didn't get physical. He'd have picked the wrong guys.'

I was pleased with Rosie's confidence in me, but Blue House Fan's voice had reminded me of a category of martial-arts practitioner that did not fit the popular stereotype of humble, conflict-averse disciple. I would not necessarily have defeated him. Also, I was out of practice. Before going to bed, I reinstated karate and aikido classes in my schedule.

★   ★   ★

On the next visit to Shepparton, my father, who was continuing to deteriorate, took Hudson aside and privately explained his theory of learning to ride a bike. Hudson shared it with me, but only after we arrived home. To my surprise, the recommended procedure turned out to be totally different from the way my father had attempted to teach me.

'Both my feet have to be able to touch the ground,' said Hudson, sitting on my bike.

'It's not possible to adjust the seat that low.'

'You'll have to buy me a smaller bike. Or borrow one.'

The bike shop was prepared to lend us a second-hand cycle, but it lacked a crossbar — a girls' bike.

'Perfect for learning,' said the bike-shop guy.

148

'Pa said a girls' bike is fine,' said Hudson. 'Actually, better.'

Incredible.

We put it in the back of Phil's Toyota and took it to the park.

Hudson's approach, as dictated by my father, was to walk the bike with his feet on the ground, and, when he had mastered that, advance to propelling it with both feet, at which point he was travelling short distances unsupported. As I watched his tall, thin body on the bike without a crossbar, my memory returned.

This was how my sister had taught me to ride, after dinking me miles from our home so that we would be out of sight of anyone who might have seen me riding a girls' bike — an even more shameful display of sissiness than using training wheels.

★   ★   ★

The bar project was progressing. Minh had negotiated a percentage of the business in place of rent, and I would initially work for reduced remuneration to pay for my own share. Amghad was enthusiastic about the concept, which Minh had conveyed to him in person, and the liquor-licence application was being processed.

There was already a bar named Chill in Melbourne and we reverted to Dave's original proposal: The Library. There were obvious advantages in our customers being able to say, 'I'm going to The Library,' but I also hoped that it would convey a feeling of sanctuary and emotional calm.

149

★ ★ ★

In keeping with the conventions of social reciprocity, Blanche visited our home as Hudson's guest after school. I was interested to know how his swimming achievements had affected his social status. I was not optimistic: success at martial arts had done little to improve mine. If anything, it had added to the reasons to classify me as weird. Once the label has been applied, even conventional behaviour and achievements are seen as weird, since they are not expected of a weird person.

I asked the question with Blanche present, in the hope of obtaining an independent opinion. 'Has your social status improved as a result of the swimming victories?'

Blanche laughed. 'Everyone was pretty amazed — but, you know, other stuff happens.'

'Any progress on the class clown?' I should probably not have asked that question in front of Blanche. However, Hudson gave no indication of being embarrassed.

'I did what you said. Asked him if he wanted to be my friend. It didn't work.'

I realised that my advice had been incomplete. While social media was built on the concept of asking someone to be your friend, it was, for no logical reason, not considered appropriate to do so in real life.

Our conversation was interrupted by a loud bang: a pigeon had flown into the glass door and was now on the ground. I went outside and established that the collision had been fatal:

birds cannot afford to carry much natural armour due to the flying requirement.

When I returned with a shovel, Blanche was bent down examining the bird.

'Dad dissects animals — mice,' said Hudson. This had once been true, but it had been a long time since I had done the work personally.

I expected Blanche to say 'gross' or give some other indication of revulsion. Instead she said, 'Could you dissect this one? So we can see inside it?'

'Gross,' said Hudson.

'Animals should be properly prepared for dissection,' I said. 'And there are specialised instruments which I don't have available at home. Also — '

'Are you sure you can't do this one?' said Blanche.

'Why are you so interested?'

'I might end up blind, so I want to see as many things as I can first.'

Blanche's argument was compelling, but before we commenced, I needed to deal with Hudson's response. Most people found dissection unpleasant, yet it was important to be able to perform unpleasant tasks. Changing nappies, cleaning up vomit and hugging relatives were *life skills*.

For me (and, it appeared, Hudson) contact with animals, alive or dead, was in the unpleasant-task category, but I had overcome the problem to the extent necessary to function professionally and socially. Hudson needed to learn to do the same.

'How did the swimming teacher persuade you to overcome your dislike of submersion?' I asked him.

'Easy. First, I had to splash my face with water, then put just my nose in, then my face, then . . . '

I let him finish the explanation, but I had seen the pattern of gradual increase in exposure — under personal control. We had not tried the technique with him, primarily because my father had employed it with me without success. Possibly Hudson had been demonstrating nothing more than natural resistance rather than an inherited phobia. Or the dynamics between Hudson and the swimming teacher may have been different from those between me and my father.

It took me only a few minutes to position my laptop computer as a camera in the kitchen. Hudson configured his own computer as a monitor in his bedroom. I donned a pair of the surgical gloves I used for house cleaning and commenced the dissection using a razor blade, a freshly sharpened kitchen knife and several bowls.

It was many years since I had dissected a bird, but animals share common organs, and I took the opportunity to explain similarities and differences with human anatomy. Hudson watched remotely for a few minutes, then joined us, but did not come close and refused to conduct any of the dissection himself. In contrast, Blanche seemed extremely interested.

'Pigeons are really intelligent, right?' she said

as I scooped out the brain. 'Like, one of the smartest birds.'

'It depends how you define intelligence. Pigeons are good at learning when they're motivated by rewards, but seagulls have worked out for themselves that if they follow the furrows in a field, they'll find insects. Both survive in the urban environment, but neither species has learned to recognise windows.'

When we had finished, and I had demonstrated the cleanup and disinfection protocol, I commented on Blanche's enthusiasm.

'Are there blind scientists?' she asked.

'Of course. Some tasks require sight, but almost anything physical can be delegated. Science may also be able to prevent blindness in the first place.'

After Blanche had left, Hudson was annoyed. 'You told her that science might be able to stop blindness. She *knows* that, but her parents won't take her to a doctor. There's a law but the police won't do anything unless she's basically dying.'

'How do you know?'

'Internet, obviously. And a teacher at her old school tried. Which is partly why she got moved. There's only one way. You have to persuade her mum. She's your friend.'

I was doing my best.

★ ★ ★

There were three items on the Hudson-life-skills list that were relatively straightforward but of disproportionately high importance: greetings, ball catching and sex education.

I had once purchased a book by Eric Berne: *What Do You Say After You Say Hello?* The title was misleading, but if it had been accurate, the material would have been too advanced for me. I could not even get the initial greeting correct, because people do not generally commence a conversation by saying 'Hello'. It sounds odd and I was conscious of sounding odd no matter what formulation I used.

I had settled on the deliberately quirky formulation of 'Greetings!' which was consistent with being the class clown and a person whose nickname was that of a *Star Trek* character. Looking back, surely 'Hi, John' (or, obviously, the name of the person being addressed) would have sufficed both as greeting and response. However, what worked in a country school forty years ago might not work today. I called Claudia on her home phone.

'Claudia Barrow.'

'Greetings.'

She laughed. 'No need to ask who's calling.'

'Coincidentally, that's what I need to discuss. Can I speak to Eugenie?'

Claudia and Gene's daughter was studying engineering. Claudia handed her the phone while I was in the middle of pointing out the advantages of having two parents living in the house.

'Hey, Don. I think last time I spoke to you I was about nine. You were having a baby . . . Remember you helped me through a really bad time?'

'No.'

154

'At school. They used to call me Calculon. And you said something that helped.'

'What was it?'

'Can't remember. Something about other kids being jealous of smart people. I think it was more that it was you, rather than my parents. They were probably saying the same thing, but who listens to their parents? Anyway, I get to thank you at last. So, thank you.'

'Excellent. But the baby you referred to is now eleven and named Hudson and I need to know the correct form of greeting for him to use.'

I explained the problem and we settled on 'Hey, Eugenie' (substituting, obviously, the name of the person being addressed) with an optional raising of one hand as if commencing a 'high five' but without that level of energy and maybe better not to do the action at all if he's not completely relaxed about it. He should be careful not to display too much enthusiasm, even if he is extremely happy to see the person. It was okay to use the greeting with teachers, probably with an attenuated hand movement and not too loudly.

She asked: 'When do I get to meet Hudson? He sounds cool.'

'His problem is the exact opposite. Lack of coolness.'

'Lack of coolness can be pretty cool.'

19

Hudson was now riding independently and Rosie insisted that I phone my father to thank him for his help.

'He'll appreciate it.'

'He'll just grunt and say something critical.'

'Let's see.'

I called him with the phone in speaker mode so Rosie could hear, and thanked him for his help.

He grunted. 'Someone had to tell him how to do it. Don't know who's going to do that when I'm gone.'

'There you go,' said Rosie. 'I told you he'd appreciate it.'

★　★　★

Ball catching was the second of the three items on my high-impact, modest-effort list. When I was eight, my parents had forced me to join the local cub-scout pack. The only aspect that appealed was the accumulation of badges, but before I could earn any, I needed my 'bronze boomerang', which required that I complete a prescribed set of tasks, including catching a ball from a set distance with a specified success rate.

After *months* of preparation, I took the test, but failed by one catch. The leader insisted on a waiting period of four weeks before I could retry, and at that point I persuaded my parents to let me replace the pack meetings with aikido lessons. However, I continued the ball-catching practice and began to enjoy the achievement in its own right.

'Throw me the keys,' I could say to Rosie, and snatch them from the air with one hand as though I had always been able to do it, like the rest of the human race. I could give Hudson that same satisfaction.

I attempted to introduce the subject in a casual, round-about way.

'Feel like a game of catch?' I asked.

'You think I can't catch a ball?' said Hudson. 'You want to show me how, right?'

I shouldn't have bothered with the oblique approach. Hudson and I were both comfortable communicating directly.

'It's an essential life competency,' I said.

'What's going to happen if I never learn?'

'It's a skill common to numerous sports. Hence you would be unable to play those sports.'

'Good. If they won't let me read a book, I can score or something. Or select teams. Which I'm good at.'

'Sport was invented so we could practise skills that might be needed in critical situations. Actually, throwing is more important than catching. Humans are amazingly good at throwing — better than any other animal. How might that be useful?'

'Hunting. Killing animals with rocks. I don't need — '

'Correct. Animals are so scared of humans'

ability to throw that if you are threatened by a dog, then just pretending to pick up a rock is likely to discourage it. Even in the absence of a rock.'

'Seriously?'

'You're suggesting I'm making a joke?'

'No, Dad.' Hudson laughed. Was there a legitimate underlying joke in our conversation or was he laughing inappropriately?

'I'll do it if we can use a tennis ball.'

'Of course. What would be the alternative?'

'Mr Warren makes us use a cricket ball. Which hurts. If you throw it hard. Which he does.'

We didn't own an example of either ball type.

'I think there's one on the roof,' said Hudson. 'The kids next door came looking for it and Mum wouldn't let them go up.'

I got the medium extension ladder and the roof-hook kit from the shed and removed the Tillman Hardware packaging. 'Do you know how to use a ladder safely?' I asked.

Hudson did not. By the time we had completed the ladder-safety briefing and the roof-safety briefing, fitted the hook, climbed onto the roof, cleared the gutter, reinstated a loose tile and located the ball, we had only three minutes left of scheduled Hudson Project time.

'Looks like we'll have to do it some other day,' said Hudson.

'We have time for a quick assessment. To establish the baseline competency.'

Rabbit had been correct. Hudson's skill level was not only low, but obviously so, a major problem for the school playground. He stood with his hands wide apart and his mouth open. I recognised the stance and the response it had provoked in our Shepparton backyard when I was a child.

'You're not going to catch the ball in your mouth,' I said, before remembering what had followed. Hudson closed his mouth and stood waiting for further instructions. Nothing in his expression indicated humiliation, but no interpretation was necessary. Memory sufficed.

'Sorry,' I said. 'Whether your mouth is open or not is irrelevant to the catching process. I used to do the same thing, which is why I noticed and made a joke.'

'A dad joke.'

'A *grandad* joke.'

I walked up to Hudson and demonstrated the hands-close-together position, then threw the ball into his hands from approximately thirty centimetres. He caught it.

'Enough for one day. One-hundred-per-cent success rate. Now we increase the distance. Gradually.'

'Easy. We could use a cricket ball if you wanted.'

★   ★   ★

I gave considerable thought to the approach to sex education. I knew from my schooldays — and later — that sexual ignorance was a serious social disadvantage.

As a teenager, I had been given the relevant facts, primarily by other children and often in the context of jokes, but had somehow failed to absorb them, and was left confused and disgusted.

In retrospect, the problem was information overload: the mechanics of sex were presented in conjunction with nudity of older persons of both sexes, foetal development, birth and some of the most controversial moral issues in the adult world, all in language more carefully regulated than for any other topic.

If I had been taught my times tables while being forced to look at images of naked adults, with interruptions about the methods of preventing conception and the life-shattering results of failing to do so by someone who was manifestly uncomfortable with the task, it is unlikely that I would have learned to multiply.

My most useful sex education had occurred in the high-school playground when two dogs had engaged in mating until a teacher had intervened with a bucket of water. Somehow, many of us had sat through an entire educational film without 'getting it' but the dog demonstration addressed the basic mechanical questions, although obviously not the issues of informed consent, gender identity and sexual orientation which I imagined would now be further cluttering the biology lesson. Hudson would not understand these subtleties if he did not know what they were referring to — like learning traffic safety in a village without vehicles or roads.

With modern technology, I was able to improve on the dog incident. Using videos from the internet, I assembled a collage of animal mating, from redback spiders to Tasmanian devils. I knew better than to do anything in the realm of sex without consulting Rosie, and replayed it to her that evening. Hudson's revised schedule, which entailed going to bed earlier to compensate for waking at 5.20 a.m., was giving us more time for discussion.

Rosie agreed that the video was 'as good a starting point as any'. I loaded it onto a memory stick and gave it to Hudson on our way to school.

'Animal mating: it's interesting and also funny,' I said.

'You want me to watch it?'

'Correct.'

'It's supposed to teach me something. What?'

'Sex education. But without the embarrassment of naked adult humans.'

He put the stick in his pocket without further discussion.

★   ★   ★

The three high-impact, modest-effort initiatives produced mixed results. Hudson had not reached a level of expertise in ball-catching that would allow him to contribute to a sporting contest. However, he had learned how to *not* catch a ball in the style of proficient catchers, who sometimes made errors. Failure no longer appeared inevitable.

I had not conveyed the greeting protocol to Hudson. It was important knowledge, but, after some reflection, I concluded that if my parents had offered it to me I would have considered

161

their behaviour odd.

The sex-education video exercise confirmed that schools' sensitivity to sexual topics had not declined since my childhood.

'Since it doesn't include humans, it isn't pornography,' I told the principal and Rabbit after being summoned to explain. Rosie had, over my protests, taken time off work to accompany me. ('I'm sure you can handle it, but when it's something official about Hudson, I just like to be there.')

'Come on — ' began Rabbit.

The principal interrupted: 'You're quite right. And you've found a way of starting what can be a difficult conversation for many parents. But we'd rather Hudson hadn't brought it to school.'

'Were other children upset by it?'

'I don't think *upset* is the right word,' said Rabbit. 'It's the parents. Nothing so far, but we've got some strange types. Diverse, as we say.'

Blanche's father and Blue House Fan.

'To be honest,' said the principal, 'we're not too concerned, but we need to say something, in case there's a complaint. I'm sure they can find it on the internet, or on TV for that matter. The polar bear breaking his . . . '

'Penis bone.'

'Thank you . . . might give a few of the high-school boys something to think about. But we do want to come back to what we've discussed before. Every time Hudson does something that's a little odd — '

'It reinforces your idea that he's autistic,' said Rosie.

162

'*Has autism*,' said the principal.

Rosie breathed in audibly, and I guessed she was about to argue the position of Liz the Activist, which was now our position, but which would inevitably provoke an off-topic argument. I deftly returned the conversation to the subject.

'The topic of this meeting was the sex video and we should confirm that we have resolved that before addressing other issues,' I said.

Rabbit laughed. 'Sorry, no offence, but it's uncanny. You and Hudson . . . '

Rosie completed the sentence for him: 'are two different people and we're here to talk about only one of them, right? I remember last time we had some issues about sport. And they contributed to the idea that he might *be autistic.* Has that changed?'

'Well, we were certainly surprised by his performance at the swimming carnival,' said Rabbit. 'Especially since he has a letter excusing him from swimming, which you might like to review. But swimming's an individual sport. He's not a team player. I'd guess he finds it hard to put himself in someone else's place.'

'You mean he lacks *empathy*,' said Rosie. 'I wonder what made you think of that?'

'Well, that's the word, and I think we all know that it goes with the territory.'

'So,' said the principal, 'have we thought any further about an assessment?'

'Yes,' said Rosie, 'and for the moment the answer is no. Is that all right with the school?'

'Well, we can only advise,' said the principal. 'Unless it escalates. I do have to say that if he becomes violent, and we hope that never happens, but without a diagnosis . . . If that should happen, everything changes.'

'I'm sure that would apply to any child,' said Rosie.

'Of course.'

'And I'm sure you'd be similarly concerned about verbal abuse.'

'Well, yes, as I said — '

'I mention it because it seems he's acquired a rather unpleasant nickname. *Nasty.* And whatever concerns you have about him, I don't think he's done anything to deserve that.'

'No,' said the principal. 'Not at all. I'll see what I can find out. And we're sorry these meetings are becoming a bit more regular than we'd all like.'

'It's a thing I've learned,' said Rabbit, 'and don't take this the wrong way. But every year, in the first class, I can spot three or four kids that I know are going to take the lion's share of my time. I'm not saying it's a bad thing.'

'The Pareto principle,' I said. 'The so-called eighty — twenty rule, which will occur with any normally distributed attribute, hence to be expected. I have a similar experience teaching at university. From the first lecture, I identify the small cohort who will ask for extreme guidance on assignments and challenge assessments.'

'Bit different at primary school, Don,' said Rabbit.

'I don't think Don was trying to tell you anything, Neil,' said Rosie. 'He was just being empathetic.'

20

'Are you sure you haven't missed something? Spiced cranberry bitters or pencil sharpeners?'

'None of the cocktails on the proposed list require cranberry bitters, spiced or unspiced. No pencils — '

'I was joking,' said Amghad. 'This is the most comprehensive spec anyone's ever given me. I could give it to the fit-out company as it stands. Actually, I'll write a summary first, in case they see the size of it and think they're quoting for a refit of the Dubai Hilton.'

'You're happy with the design?'

Amghad waved his hand to indicate the empty lab. 'A bit Soviet for me, but we can change that if it doesn't work. Unisex toilets: same thing. I don't know much about sound damping, but it looks like you've done your research.'

'Did you read the specification for the app?'

'The ordering system? I'm leaving the computer stuff to you.'

★   ★   ★

Allannah was now collecting Blanche from school following an eyesight-related incident on the tram and subsequent verbal abuse by another passenger. Twice a week one of us would host the other's child. Allannah *thanked* me for the animal-sex video. She had found the subject difficult to raise — and, *exactly as intended*, it had provided background information and prompted Blanche to ask her mother some important questions.

Allannah had not seen it herself, so I brought my computer and we watched it in her shop.

'I guess as a scientist you don't get awkward about these things,' she said as we watched the bonobo orgy.

'All conversations with children are potentially awkward,' I said, remembering that I had not found a way of communicating the greeting protocol to Hudson. I explained the problem to Allannah.

'Leave it to me,' she said. 'And Blanche. I think getting greetings right is a pretty small price to pay for expert help with sex education. And I think she'll appreciate the advice herself. She can be a bit unsure about that sort of thing too, but it never occurred to me that I could do anything about it.'

When Rosie arrived home the following evening, Hudson emerged from his bedroom, raised his hand and said, 'Hey.' After he had gone to bed, Rosie said, 'He seemed in a good mood. I think he's becoming a bit more comfortable in himself.'

It seemed like an ideal time to review progress. Rosie was aware of the bike-riding, ball-catching and sex-education initiatives, although the impact of the last of these on Hudson had yet to be assessed.

'However,' I said, 'it seems to have encouraged Blanche to talk to her mother about the subject.'

'I hadn't realised that helping Blanche's

mother was part of the project.'

I sensed criticism. I explained that, in return, Blanche had assisted with the greetings protocol which had, according to Rosie's assessment, resulted in Hudson's improved mood and internal comfort.

'You never told me you were working on that.'

'It was slightly embarrassing.'

Rosie laughed. 'I guess you guys can have a few secrets between you. As long as that's all you're keeping from me.'

*   *   *

I had prepared further material on vaccination for my next visit to Allannah's, but, on our arrival, Blanche fetched a shoebox and asked if she could visit our home instead. The shoebox turned out to contain a large dead rat, fortunately not yet malodorous.

'Can we dissect it?' asked Blanche. 'It's only been dead since yesterday. I haven't touched it — I wrapped it in a tea towel and put it in the fridge.'

'Where did it come from?' I asked.

'The kitchen. I probably should have put it in the wash afterwards, right?'

'Correct. But my question was imprecise. I was asking about the rat rather than the tea towel.'

'Dad set a trap. To protect the quinoa.'

'I assumed your parents would be opposed to killing animals.' It was an assumption based on a stereotype, but I guessed that statistics would support it.

'It's almost impossible to grow and store grain without killing animals. Like rats in the fields. Or bugs. My dad says all animals have souls, so it's no worse to kill a rat than a bug or a cow.'

Despite numerous visits to Blanche's, I had never met her father, the homeopath, who worked upstairs. His choice of profession suggested extreme gullibility, but I had learned that people with irrational beliefs in one domain could be sensible and reliable in others. The animal-soul logic — easily adapted into reason-ableness by replacing 'soul' with 'central nervous system' — made sense and I was looking forward to using it in arguments with vegans.

'You're not vegetarian, then?' I asked.

'We are, but because of health. We eat fish, though. Sometimes. Not whale, obviously.'

'Whales aren't fish,' said Hudson. 'But you'd get a huge amount of food for one soul.'

I dissected the rat. Blanche undertook some of the task under my supervision, with Hudson holding her magnifying glass.

'Brilliant work,' I said to Blanche as we disinfected our hands. 'You definitely should consider becoming a scientist. Would you like to see a video of how to dissect a larger animal?'

'Blanche has to go home,' said Hudson.

Afterwards, Rosie was surprised by Blanche's continued interest in dissection.

'She's a weird kid,' she said. 'In lots of ways.'

'But also Hudson's best friend.'

Rosie laughed. 'The two things may not be unrelated.'

★　★　★

Rosie accompanied us on the next visit to my parents' in Phil's Toyota.

My father's condition appeared unchanged, but my mother advised that, according to the doctor, he was 'getting very near the end'.

All three of us went into his room and my father sent Rosie and me out.

Hudson exited a few minutes later.

'What were you talking about?' Rosie asked.

'The difference between *effect* and *affect*,' he said. *Effect*'s usually a noun and *affect*'s usually a verb, but there are some important exceptions. Do I have an odd *affect*?'

'Possibly. It's hard for me to tell because I'm used to you.'

'It wasn't a question. I was giving you an example of *affect* as a noun.'

Hudson continued his explanation while my mother and Rosie made tea. It was good to have a discussion in which hard, unambiguous information was exchanged.

'Pa wants me to remember him every time I see *affect* or *effect* used incorrectly.'

'You won't have to make any effort. It will happen automatically.'

'He also wanted to know if you brought the CD. I think you'll be in huge trouble if you forgot.'

I had purchased the recording. My father and I seldom failed to communicate requirements and specifications.

'Look in the rack,' said my father quietly,

169

indicating the compact-disc collection.

'For what?'

'This one. The Ninth Symphony. It's not there. Not even the von Karajan version. It's the last symphony he wrote, and your mother's hung onto it because she's got it into her head that after I've heard everything, I'll fall off my twig. So, now I've listened to every piece Beethoven wrote — everything that survived, a good number of them more than once — except this. Put it on and let's see what happens.'

'Do you want me to tell Mum?'

'No, I don't. Not now.' He waved his hand to indicate the recordings again. 'Fifty-six when he died. And all of this. Do you know how he died?'

'No.' It didn't seem like information that would ever be useful, but obviously it would have been now in impressing my father.

'He was on his death bed, and there was a flash of lightning and a clap of thunder and he sat bolt upright. And that was the moment he expired. According to the biography. Not that you can believe these things.'

My father and I listened in silence for the hour and nineteen minutes. The choral section was familiar, and it seemed like a suitable prelude to a Beethoven-like death. When the display on the CD player indicated that the music was finished, my father was still alive.

'So much for superstition,' he said. 'You can tell your mother she was wrong. She ought to know I wouldn't leave a project unfinished. Put on Opus 27, No. 2. Not the most complex piece but I've only been listening to classical music for a few months. If I'd had more time I'd have had a go at Mozart. He's supposed to be on much the same level.'

I found the CD — the *Moonlight Sonata* — and gave it to him to verify.

'Put it on and go and make me a cocktail.'

'You want a cocktail?'

'Do I have to say it twice? You're the famous New York barman and you've never made me one. Do the best you can with what you can find in the cupboard. Make one for yourself and Rosie and your mother, too. Cocktails — who'd have thought you'd have that bent?' He handed me the disc. 'You know, I was worried about you, but in the end, you've surprised me.'

I put on the *Moonlight Sonata* and Rosie and I made Boston sours, the best option with the limited selection of ingredients, and by the time we had made syrup, squeezed the lemons, separated the eggs, poured the whisky and shaken it all with ice, the music was still playing, but my father had died.

* * *

Driving back to Melbourne, much later than planned, due to the need to notify relatives, arrange for the removal of the body and provide emotional support for my mother, Rosie suggested we stop in the town for pizza.

'We're supposed to be having dinner at home,' said Hudson.

'We needed to get away,' said Rosie. 'Your grandmother didn't want to eat, and we couldn't

171

ask her to cook. But I'm starving.'

Food was definitely necessary. We had finished by drinking the sours, my brother Trevor arriving in time to consume the spare one, and my mother had seemed emotionally stable.

'You said we'd eat at home,' said Hudson. 'I've been looking forward to it all day.'

Sunday was the only day on which I cooked separate meals: some variety of red fish for Rosie and meat for Hudson and me. There was a chicken in the refrigerator which was intended to yield sandwiches for Monday and Wednesday. Any disruption was irritating but, on this occasion, Rosie was right.

'Unfortunately, there is insufficient time to drive home and cook and eat without causing lack of sleep and probably indigestion.'

Rosie had stopped the car outside the pizza restaurant. 'And it's a school day tomorrow,' she said.

'I got up late. I can go to bed late.'

'Your dad and I need to eat. We're getting pizza. You like pizza.'

'Not on Sunday nights. I can skip reading in the morning and get up late.'

'If you can change the morning routine, you can change tonight's.'

'It's been a terrible day. Pa died. I want to go home and eat the chicken.'

'It's been a terrible day for all of us. For Grandma, for . . . '

It was obvious that either the argument would continue indefinitely, or Rosie would back down. I was certain Hudson would not change his

172

mind. And I found myself speaking words that seemed to come from some other part of my brain.

'That's enough. Your mother and I are going inside and getting pizza. You can stay in the car if you want to, or you can come in and either eat or not eat. If you want to get something from the fridge when you get home, that's up to you. But we're not going to be held hostage by this behaviour.'

Rosie looked stunned.

I got out of the car and walked into the restaurant. Rosie followed, and Hudson stayed in the car. Rosie ordered a small pizza for Hudson and took it out. I did not check whether he ate it: he was asleep on the ride home and Rosie was silent as I drove. I was remembering times where I had been as inflexible as Hudson, involuntarily locked into an unreasonable position. And I remembered — apparently — how my father had dealt with it. On the day that he died, my subconscious had delivered me a reminder that something of him had survived.

21

It is recognised — and supported by research — that humans do not generally enjoy public speaking, due to the fear of making some mistake that will be noticed by others. Even as an academic working with familiar material, I had encountered problems.

Social occasions are even more perilous. I had done my best to persuade my mother that someone else should deliver my father's eulogy, but she had a compelling counter-argument: 'I suppose I'll have to ask your uncle Frank.'

Uncle Frank had delivered an insulting speech in the guise of humour at my twenty-first birthday and had apparently remained alive since then, although his wife, my aunty Merle, had died while we were in New York. He must now be at least eighty-five, and I suspected any change would be in the negative direction. In the absence of anything hilarious to say about my father, he might use the occasion as an excuse to make jokes about me.

I had four days to prepare my speech, and suspended the Hudson Project and development of the app for The Library. The latter had, until my father's death, been occupying almost all of the spare space in my schedule. Now I found myself unable to code. Although my brain did not seem to have a specific emotion that I could call 'grieving', my thoughts had been dominated

— overwhelmed — by memories of my childhood and my final moments with my father.

'We grieve in different ways,' said Rosie. 'I think you're so ... cerebral ... that you translate your shock into thinking rather than feeling. If that makes sense.'

It did. 'But it's making the eulogy incredibly difficult to write.'

'Don, you only need to say a few words, maybe tell a couple of stories. You're getting way too knotted up about this.' It was 4.58 a.m. and I had disturbed Rosie as I got out of bed to record an idea that might have disappeared if I resumed sleeping.

She sat up. 'Hudson will be up in twenty minutes anyway.'

We made coffee and Rosie sourced a pen and paper.

'Best story about your dad?'

'He didn't do anything noteworthy.'

'What about the soundproof crib he built for Hudson? That's a great story. Generous, smart, a bit quirky.'

'You think my father was quirky?'

'Do I think the Pope's a Catholic? Of course he was quirky. What about the way all the nuts and bolts are organised in the hardware shop?'

'I started that. Forty years ago.'

'That's a great story too, then. What about listening to all of Beethoven, and dying when he got to the end? You have to finish with that.'

'The funeral attendees will know those things already.'

'You're not informing them — you're

reminding them. Now, what about something he taught you?'

'He found me frustrating to teach. He used to say, 'With all that knowledge of yours' — because I got good marks at school — 'why can't you . . . ?' I was incompetent at numerous physical tasks, which was annoying in the context of assisting in a hardware shop.'

'Really? Your dad expected that being intelligent would make you good at mechanical things?'

'Not exactly. He would have said I lacked common sense. He was probably right. I did some incredibly stupid things.'

'Like Hudson putting the maple syrup in the tools drawer back in New York?'

'Correct. I said some stupid things too — to customers and suppliers. I even knew they were stupid at the time — immediately afterwards.'

'But you got there, right? Your dad persisted. That's got to be a huge positive you can say about him. Maybe you've got some sort of self-deprecating story about screwing up and him teaching you . . . '

'You could ask Uncle Frank. He would have numerous examples.'

'Hey, don't get tetchy. Without your dad, you'd have turned out differently. And you've turned out okay. Better than okay. So, you owe him. I do too.'

★   ★   ★

'When I was six, the other kids had Lego and Meccano sets. But my father made me the world's best construction set, assembled from commercial hardware items.'

Rosie's suggested approach to the eulogy was going well. My voice had, to my surprise and discomfort, been affected by emotion as I started, but it was now under control. The Mechanics' Institute Hall was almost full: my father had been well known in the community and had continued to assist my brother in the shop until recently. And to my surprise, several people who had met my father on only a few occasions, or not at all, had travelled to Shepparton: Phil, Claudia ('I'm here for all of the Barrow family'), Dave and Sonia, Laszlo and Frances the Occasional Smoker, and, amazingly, Amghad and Minh, and Simon Lefebvre. Judas. 'At least he can see I'm taking the day off for something other than Hudson,' said Rosie. He was sitting beside Claudia, who had dumped him for infidelity and coined his insulting nickname. Unfathomable.

The construction set had, I now remembered, been jointly used with two other boys on numerous occasions, so my father had indirectly facilitated some social interaction. My own interest had been more in collecting and organising the components, which were aug-mented on birthdays and at Christmas, than in actual construction.

I finished with the story of the Beethoven project, then returned to my seat between Rosie and my mother, who was, understandably, crying. My primary emotion was relief: I felt that I had done an acceptable job.

Then: disaster. The celebrant announced that another relative would be saying 'a few words'. I had not seen him for years, and he was now physically decrepit, in a wheelchair. With the help of his daughter — my cousin Lynda — he succeeded in pulling himself to his feet to address the crowd.

'Who is he?' asked Hudson, leaning over Rosie.

'Your great-uncle Frank,' I said. 'Grandma's brother. He's very old and has Alzheimer's disease. Ignore anything he says.'

'Jim wasn't exactly a people person,' said Uncle Frank, and, inexplicably, the audience laughed. Perhaps they were giving the response he had historically sought, out of kindness to an old man.

'My family weren't too sure about it when Adele said she was going to marry him. We thought he was a bit of a boffin. Turned out we were right.' More laughter. 'Couldn't get him to join the masons. I said to him, 'All you need is a belief in a supreme architect, and the desire to spend time having a drink and a yarn with your fellow man,' and he said, 'Nought out of two, Franklin.''

Judging by the response of the audience, it appeared that Uncle Frank had succeeded in making fun of my father after all, although I would have given much the same answer to the masonic-lodge offer.

'I used to give him a bit of a hard time, all in fun, and he'd take it seriously. He used to correct me if I got my nouns and verbs wrong. But when we fixed up the masonic hall, he donated everything we needed, and he was there every minute he didn't have to be in the shop, making sure we didn't stuff it up. Jim didn't like anyone stuffing up.'

Uncle Frank stopped and wiped his eyes with a handkerchief. My mother, who had joined in the laughter at Uncle Frank's earlier comments, was now crying again.

'Some of you here know that I came close to stuffing up, many years ago now, and it was Jim who set me straight. He had a very clear sense of right and wrong. If I didn't know before, I knew then that my sister had seen further and deeper than we had.

'He wouldn't see his kids stuffing up either. I'm sure they didn't always like it, but all of them, even Michelle who we lost far too young, had their . . . challenges . . . and he wasn't going to see any of them go out into the world and get knocked around like he did . . . That's another story.'

Lynda pulled at his arm, but he continued. 'I know how proud he was of Trevor keeping the business going, and of Don who just gave such a wonderful speech. And young Hudson. He loved his grandson. And . . . '

Uncle Frank's speech had slowed. Now he was looking around the room, and it was apparent that he had lost his concentration.

'I just can't tell you how much Jim did for Merle and I.'

'Merle and *me*.' Hudson's voice was loud in the hall, and within seconds of him speaking, I could see that he was embarrassed.

Then there was a huge round of laughter and applause, and Lynda used the opportunity to help Uncle Frank back into his wheelchair. Hudson and I were possibly the only ones not laughing. I knew — as the audience surely also realised — that the relevance of his interjection had been accidental, and in a year or two such behaviour would no longer be cute.

It was appropriate at a funeral of a family member, but I was surprised to find that I was crying. Uncle Frank had been right: my father had given high priority to teaching me the skills I needed for school and adult life. And I hadn't liked him for it.

22

The wake was at the family home. Judas congratulated me on my speech and encouraged me to return to work.

'I'd say front the committee. Get the African woman to support you. They won't be game to take her on, you'll get off, and you'll be doing a public service for the rest of us.' He laughed.

'I'm required to look after our son during the day. If I went back to work, Rosie would have to return to part-time. Your advice is against your own interests.'

Judas laughed again. 'That's me, always looking out for the other guy. But, Don, I want you to know that I can see Rosie's struggling with the work — life balance. If at any time . . . '

'I thought the project was on schedule. And the pilot's producing interesting results.'

'That's true. But it must be tough for her finding the time.'

★ ★ ★

Hudson went to bed in the room that had once been my sister's, after we had persuaded my mother that he did not require the comfort of the dog sleeping with him. Rosie had expected he would be troubled by the change in routine, but I had briefed him in advance, emphasising that he would be required to take two days off school.

There was some Scotch left over, and my brother Trevor suggested that Rosie and I make sours again. It was a cheap brand — one I would never consider ordering for The Library. But with lemons from the tree in the garden, and Rosie's cocktail-making expertise, the result was as good as the Yellow Spot Irish whiskey version.

My mother wanted us to exchange stories about my father, though she provided the majority of them.

'Remember when you let that little disabled boy win the karate tournament? Your father was so proud of you.'

It was amazing that she could fit so many errors into such a short statement. It was aikido, not karate, and only a single bout in an early round rather than the entire tournament. The boy was neither unusually little nor disabled, but merely awkward. And, unknown to my mother, I had earlier done a terrible thing: I had deliberately tripped him at school, participating in the sort of bullying more frequently directed at me.

I had not been caught, but my self-inflicted punishment had been more severe than any the school would have prescribed. I had been obsessed for weeks with thoughts of what I had done and what it indicated about my character. When the boy's parents enrolled him in self-defence classes for the same reason that my parents had enrolled me, I assisted him and formed a plan to compensate for my actions.

My mother would not have known those details, but she had got one *major* thing wrong.

'Dad wasn't proud of me. He criticised me for losing.'

'Donald, he did not. He wouldn't have, and I remember it anyway.'

'I remember it too. He went on and on about — '

My mother laughed. 'He was teasing you. You took things so literally. He wasn't silly. He saw exactly what you did, and he was very proud of you. He always has been. Of all of you.'

Trevor coughed. 'Any of that cold remedy left?'

I refilled his glass from the shaker. Trevor drank most of it in one gulp, then put it down firmly. 'Well, everybody, I always promised myself I'd do something on this day, so I hope it's not going to upset anyone. But I'm almost fifty now and I think you should all know that I'm gay.'

Incredible. It was consistent with his never having had a female partner, but nor, to my knowledge, had he had a male partner. He had suggested in the past that *I* might be gay and had implied that this was a negative, an attitude consistent with my view of him as a redneck.

My mother laughed. 'Well, of course you are, Trevor. Your father and I have known that for a long time.'

I interpreted Trevor's reaction as 'flabbergasted'. It was several seconds before he spoke. 'Why didn't . . . '

'It's not the sort of thing you talk about, is it? And we didn't think you'd be comfortable with us knowing. But your father didn't have any

183

issue with it. As long as you didn't flaunt it, of course.'

★　★　★

I had hoped that my sleep would be less disturbed now that I had completed the public-speaking task. Although Trevor's revelation was surprising, it was unlikely to have any impact on my life. But I needed to review the Hudson Project.

The parallels with my own upbringing were obvious. My father would probably have assessed that I appreciated his help, but my co-operation was motivated by my desire for his approval. I guessed that Hudson felt the same way, and that the pizza incident had been a manifestation of his underlying dissatisfaction with me. I was pleased with my analysis but unhappy with the conclusion.

In the morning, Rosie said, 'You're planning to teach Hudson something today?'

'No, he'd normally be at school. Hence, no plans.'

'Good. We should do something he'd like to do,' said Rosie.

'Excellent idea.'

Hudson's response was instant. 'Is Clunes on the way home?'

'Why Clunes?'

'It's the capital of second-hand bookshops. But you should have told me, and I would have brought some books to trade.'

I checked the GPS: 'We can go via home and collect the books.'

'What?' said Rosie. 'We're not driving home from Shepparton then driving to Clunes and back. It's miles.'

'Kilometres. One hundred and forty from Northcote. I'll take Hudson. You can put in some extra time at work with no possibility of being needed at home.'

★ ★ ★

We arrived in Clunes at 3.12 p.m. On the journey, Hudson spoke in detail about the books he was seeking. At his age I had read exclusively non-fiction and had been under pressure from school to broaden my reading. Hudson's specialisation was different, but the principal had made an equivalent recommendation.

We conducted a tour of the bookshops. Hudson talked knowledgeably and at length with the booksellers and provided them with specific requests, as well as selling the books he had brought with him and purchasing others. In these interactions with adults, I detected zero social inappropriateness. I made use of the time by borrowing a book from the shelves at each shop and time-sharing reading with some floor exercises.

At the final bookshop, I offered to buy Hudson any book that did not have a theme of space travel. He had a quick conversation with the proprietor, and selected a large, illustrated book of twentieth-century fashion. An incredible choice.

I said nothing and made the purchase.

'The problem is the conflict between developing Hudson's life skills and maintaining a positive father — son relationship,' I told Rosie that evening.

Rosie was not convinced. 'If he is rebelling a bit, well, he's eleven, he's on the verge of puberty, he's still dealing with moving here from New York, he's got some issues at school, his grand-father's just died, he's developed a relationship with Phil . . . It could be anything.'

'Agreed. But I think it's the coaching.'

I had continued to reflect on my feelings about my father trying to mould me into something that he considered desirable. He was, in retro-spect, largely right, but emotionally — meaning irrationally — I had resented it. If Hudson was in the same position, I would be wasting my time trying to convince him of the value of the skills I was teaching him. I had learned, reluctantly and over many years, that rational argument seldom overcame irrational resistance.

'What about the swimming?' said Rosie. 'He got over a huge psychological hurdle. And the bike riding's coming along, isn't it?'

Rosie was right. Hudson was teachable. I had a flash of insight. 'Phil taught him swimming. Or the coach at the gym did. Lucy taught him to snowboard. My father gave him the instructions for bike riding. Blanche taught him the greetings protocol.'

'That's what I'm saying. He's learned heaps.'

'From other people. The problem is me.

186

Because I'm his father.'

Rosie laughed. 'You're probably right. To some degree, anyway. Isaac would give you a lecture about oedipal jealousy. I guess that's why we have schools.'

'And grandparents,' I said.

But schools and grandparents were demonstrably insufficient in this case. The solution was clear. The Hudson Project would need to be outsourced.

23

Outsourcing the Hudson Project solved two problems — my lack of expertise in several domains, and the need to free up time to code the ordering app for The Library, which had fallen behind following my father's death.

After considerable thought, I settled on three multi-skilled mentors.

'Have you asked Hudson?' said Rosie, before I had even named the team.

'I thought I should check with you first.' It was a neat answer, but I did not anticipate any objections. There would be no increase in Hudson's total time allocation.

'Phil will be in charge of physical development and sport,' I said.

'So far, no surprises. I hope you're not going to get Gene to coach him on relationships with girls.'

'Obviously not,' I said. 'But both of his children will contribute. Eugenie for mathematics and social skills, and Carl for personal presentation.'

'Carl's gay, isn't he?'

'Correct. Gay men are famous for their expertise in style and etiquette, even for straight people.'

'Whoa. Stereotype alert.'

'I selected him because he owns a male-clothing shop.'

'Why didn't you say that?'

'I would have, but you wanted to talk about his sexual orientation.'

'It's still sounding like an episode of *Queer Eye for the Straight Guy*.'

'You're assuming Hudson is straight. If not, Carl will provide a positive role model as an alternative to Trevor, who has spent his life living a lie.' I had not mentioned the fashion book.

'It's like *The Italian Job*,' said Rosie. 'I hope you're not planning to get the team together and give them all a pep talk before you send them off.'

I had not planned to do so, but the idea seemed good, except that Rosie had just rejected it.

⋆   ⋆   ⋆

Hudson was easily persuaded to undertake mathematics coaching. He had become accustomed to success and was frustrated that he had dropped back.

'I haven't tutored a primary-school kid before, but let's see how it goes,' said Eugenie when I called. 'And the social stuff — I needed someone like me back then, so I'm sort of paying it forward.'

At Rosie's suggestion, I did not mention Phil's expanded role directly to Hudson but simply asked him to assist with the physical-skills items on my list, to which I added Australian Rules football. It seemed foolish not to take advantage of having a relative who was an expert in that sport.

'He's the school hundred-metre swimming champion,' said Phil. 'When I was playing for Hawthorn, teenage girls walking around with my number on their shirts, nobody asked me whether I was any good at tiddlywinks.'

Phil was making no sense. His success had come from football. I pointed this out.

'If he wants to spend his childhood kicking a ball back and forth so he can play two seasons of top-level football and end up spending more on knee surgery and dental bills than he ever earned playing the game, I'm your man. But I'll ask him first.'

'He doesn't have to be good,' I said. 'Just not embarrassing.'

'Embarrassing to who?'

It was a good question, except for the grammar. I had no evidence that Hudson was embarrassed or even concerned that he lacked football skills. But one day he would be sent into a game and it was important that his performance did not become legendary in the wrong way.

★ ★ ★

The visit to Carl's shop was interesting, firstly because Hudson was *not* interested. Rosie attempted to persuade him.

'Dad's going to buy you clothes. New stuff. Whatever you want as long as it's not too expensive and looks okay.'

'I hate clothes shopping. I've got clothes. I don't care about clothes.'

'What about the book? The fashion book?' I had intended to defer discussion on the subject, but Hudson's statement that he didn't care about clothes was so contrary to his purchase that the words came out of my mouth before my mind could block them.

'I sold it. You said I could have any book in the shop, so I picked the most expensive.'

I abandoned the idea of purchasing clothes. Hudson would probably sell them on eBay.

'We have a ninety-minute slot scheduled. I allocate it to visiting Carl, who is an expert in personal presentation. You can acquire the knowledge and choose whether or not to use it.'

★   ★   ★

Carl's business was in a city lane. I had minimal difficulty recognising him, as I had seen him five years earlier when he stayed with us in New York. Also, he was the only person in the shop.

He stepped out from behind the counter and we exchanged greetings according to the tradition established when he was an adolescent: he attempted to punch me, and I blocked the punch, locked his arm and levered him to the floor. It was probably the first time Hudson had seen me deploying my martial-arts expertise. A man looking in from the entrance walked away quickly.

I released Carl, and he stood up. 'Oh dear,' he said. 'I feel like a dentist saying, 'Why did you leave it so long?''

Hudson was wearing his school uniform. It

seemed inappropriate for Carl to be so critical of an eleven-year-old, particularly when we had chosen to seek help. Then he pointed to me — specifically, the place where my T-shirt was tucked into my trousers.

'We came to evaluate Hudson,' I said.

'Quite, but I can't have you walking out of here looking like that. For a while you were looking quite spiffy. Who's been dressing you? What are these — expired running shoes?'

Hudson began laughing (*autistic people don't get jokes*) and I realised that Carl was exaggerating his manner to achieve a comedic effect as well as reducing the pressure on Hudson by directing his attention to me. Very neat.

I explained that in New York I had undertaken a shopping expedition with Rosie and purchased clothes that she found acceptable. I had subsequently bought multiple examples of the shirts, trousers, sweaters, shoes, underwear and socks, in a range of colours. Most had eventually worn out, and the shirts and trousers I had retained had shrunk since our arrival in Australia, presumably because of the change in laundry equipment. When I attempted to restock, I was unable to locate identical items.

'That's called fashion,' said Carl. 'Time to update, but, frankly, what I have here is not really you. But let's have a little play.'

Carl enlisted Hudson as his assistant in fetching clothes and in evaluating the results as I tried them on, a tedious and annoying process, especially as some of the selections were patently unsuitable.

192

'Don't you have other customers?' I asked.

Carl waved his hand to indicate what was obvious: we were alone in the shop.

'How do you make any money?'

'We have a modest number of loyal patrons who are happy to pay a price for quality. Now, Hudson, I think we're agreed on the jeans, the three shirts, the tees and the black knit. And the belt.'

Carl turned to Hudson. 'I understand you were looking for sartorial advice.'

'Sure.'

Amazing. Not that Hudson knew the meaning of 'sartorial' but that he was interested in the advice.

'Backpack on one strap, not both. And loosen it off.'

'It'll be harder to walk with.'

'That's the choice you make. Fashion isn't always comfortable. If you want to blend in, look average without being really cool, then long pants when you're allowed to wear them, hair a lot shorter, tie just a little bit loose. Probably wear socks.'

I hadn't noticed that Hudson was not wearing socks.

'What if I wanted to be really cool?'

'You have to find your own look. The sockless thing could work for you. In the end you've got to be yourself, but it helps to know how other people are going to see you.'

24

'Don!' Eugenie hugged me and when I pulled away said, 'C'mon, you used to ride me around on your shoulders.'

I had arranged to meet her at the University Club because it was largely patronised by older faculty and she would stand out. She rendered my strategy unnecessary by recognising me first and joining Hudson and me in the courtyard.

'You must be Hudson. Relax, I'm not going to hug you.'

'You must be Calculon.'

'You don't get to call me Calculon until you can do . . . What year are you in?'

'Six.'

'Simultaneous linear equations. Until then I'm Ms Barrow.' She laughed. 'You can call me Eugenie if you know what nine times seven is.'

'Sixty-three.'

'Two hundred and forty-three divided by three.'

'Eighty-one.'

'Nice work. Sixteen thousand, seven hundred and sixty-seven divided by two hundred and forty-three?'

'Um, too hard.'

'Too hard for anyone except a maths freak.'

I was about to announce the answer, but Eugenie gave me the stop-sign signal.

'I'd have thought you'd be top of Year Six with

what you can do in your head.'

'That's not what we're doing. We have to show our working.'

'Ever written a computer program?'

'Not really.'

'Want to learn?'

'I guess so.'

'That's how you learn to do stuff step by step. And it's a good skill to have anyway. Okay with you, Don?'

I nodded, but it seemed strange that someone else would teach Hudson computer programming. Coding the app for The Library was currently my major activity.

'Now,' said Eugenie to Hudson, 'give me a minute to talk to your dad to sort out the money.'

I had been right about the benefits of engaging Eugenie. She had already identified a custom I had overlooked.

*   *   *

Hudson was still socialising with Blanche. When he visited the shop, I would stay and discuss science with Allannah. Humans instinctively trust personal experience over research, and Allannah's position reflected her husband's apparent success in treating Blanche and his other patients.

Blanche was at little risk personally from her parents' anti-vaccination position. But her eyesight was being left untreated.

'How long till you get Blanche's mum to let her see a doctor about her eyes?' Hudson asked as we drove home.

'Possibly forever. Her parents have made a joint decision and I doubt I can persuade a homeopath.'

'I have a plan. We say we're going to our place after school, but you take us to an eye doctor.' *Autistic people are poor at deception.*

'Have you discussed it with Blanche?'

'Of course. That's how we came up with the idea.'

'It's probably illegal to take a child to a doctor without her parents' permission.'

'We researched it. If you get caught, you probably won't go to gaol. Anyway, we can just drive her there and she can go in by herself.'

'Rationally, it seems the obvious thing to do. Which is frequently a trap in situations involving humans. We should seek input from your mother.'

Rosie was not immediately supportive of Hudson and Blanche's plan, even after we reassured her that the legal risk was minimal. I had done my own checking.

'I get that. I doubt we'll be prosecuted for taking a kid with medical problems to a doctor, given she's asked to go and I'm a doctor too. But we're overriding her parents' wishes. Which they've made crystal clear.'

'What about Blanche's wishes?' said Hudson. 'She doesn't want to go blind. If you don't take her, I will.'

'Slow down,' said Rosie. 'We'd be very unhappy if you did something like that without discussing it — '

'That's what I'm *doing*.'

'*And* . . . most doctors wouldn't take an appointment with an eleven-year-old without

196

their parents being involved. She'd need a referral. *If* we do it, I'll need to organise it.'

'So, are you going to help?'

'Hudson . . .'

'What's wrong with letting an eye doctor see her?'

Rosie looked at me, eyebrows raised, head nodding.

'How would you feel, Don, if someone took Hudson to a doctor without your permission? A doctor who was perfectly respectable, but whose methods you disagreed with?'

'Psychiatry is less evidence-based than physical medicine.'

'What's this got to do with psychiatry?' said Hudson.

'That's the sort of doctor your father is suspicious about,' said Rosie. 'He had some bad experiences when he was younger.'

'You had to see a shrink?' said Hudson.

I realised I was embarrassed about admitting it, which was ridiculous. Hudson knew about my knee injury.

'I had depression,' I said. 'Incited by social isolation. It's one of the reasons I want you to have friends.'

'That's incredible. You have great friends.'

'Now,' I said. 'They've taken a long time to accumulate.'

Rosie was right. I would not want anyone to submit Hudson to an autism assessment without my knowledge. But what if Hudson wanted one? And Blanche's situation was different in another important way.

'There's a risk in psychiatric intervention. But almost zero risk in having eyes assessed.'

'What if Blanche were deaf?' said Rosie. 'A lot of people see deafness as a difference, not a disability.'

'Mum, *Blanche doesn't want to go blind and she doesn't have anyone else to help her.*'

Ultimately, Rosie accepted that as the overriding argument, as it had been before she introduced the complications.

She used her network to identify an ophthalmologist who specialised in problems associated with albinism.

'She didn't seem particularly worried,' said Rosie. 'And she's seen Blanche before, five years ago. Apparently the school reported her to Protective Services and they intervened. Parents were *not* happy — she wanted to be sure we got that message.'

★　★　★

We scheduled the medical visit for a Thursday afternoon. Hudson and Blanche exchanged their school uniforms for anonymous clothes, I put on a beanie to disguise my own appearance and we parked half a kilometre from the clinic.

When Blanche returned from her appointment, she seemed happy with the outcome: extremely happy.

'I'm not going to go blind,' she said. 'Ever.'

'What if someone stabs you in the eyes?' said Hudson. 'Or if you stare at the sun?'

'I mean, not from my albinism. When you're a

baby, it can get better for a while, then it stays the same forever.'

Gary's homeopathic treatment was working exactly as science would have predicted.

'Can she make it any better?' asked Hudson.

'Nup. But I'm used to being like this.' She smiled: the world's biggest smile. 'This is how I am.'

★ ★ ★

Dave called me on a Saturday with an unexpected request. 'I guess you don't have a saw?'

'Your guess is wrong. What kind of saw?'

'If I could have any kind, a nine-inch circular. But — '

'I have one of those. Mounted on a bench, but detachable.'

Dave wanted to make some wooden blocks for Fulvio.

'I have Phil's Toyota. We can buy the materials and transport the saw.'

'You should bring Hudson. Men's stuff.'

'You should bring Zina. Humans' stuff.'

'She wouldn't be interested. She's a girly girl.'

Hudson was not interested either, due to reading a novel.

Dave and I visited a timber yard, and Dave, after knowing me for thirteen years, was surprised that I was able to advise on the choice of wood. He was more surprised when I took him to the shed to collect the saw.

'Holy shit, Don. This is the best home

workshop I've ever seen. And everything so neat.'

'Due to lack of use.' I had been progressively assembling equipment from the family hardware store, but had little time to employ it.

'You've got a lathe. A damn good lathe.'

'This model is rated as the best domestic option.'

'Um, do you think I could make the blocks here? It'll only take an hour or two.'

'Do you have a design?'

'Square blocks. Couple different sizes. Maybe some way of holding them together.'

'We need additional input. Young-person input. I'll get Hudson.'

★　★　★

Dave didn't create any blocks that afternoon, but the three of us made considerable progress in designing a wood-based construction set for Fulvio. Hudson and I continued the conversation over dinner. Later, he asked if he could phone Dave, and they spoke for some time.

The following day, Dave visited again, and we created prototype blocks and pegs. I commented on his competence.

'When I was Hudson's age, I wanted to be a cabinetmaker,' he said. 'But my dad said it was a dying trade.'

He completed turning a peg on the lathe. 'This is good therapy. Keeps the hands busy.'

'I don't like the pegs,' said Hudson. 'You'll get gaps between the blocks. And they'll be difficult for a little kid. Could you make some kind of groove, so they don't slip, and we can just stack them?'

Dave activated the router and created two grooves in the prototype block.

Hudson examined it. 'It has to fit with every other size of block. How old is Fulvio?'

'Six months. It'll be a while before he can do anything fancy with them.'

★ ★ ★

I had completed coding of the ordering app for the bar and gave it to Hudson to test.

'Ten dollars if you can break it,' I said.

'Meaning if it does something it's not supposed to?'

'Or if it fails to do something it's supposed to do.'

'Do you think I'll be able to? Break it?'

'No.'

'Then you can make it a hundred dollars. So I'll try really hard to break it, which is good for you.'

'Twenty.'

After I had briefed Hudson on the application, it took him thirty-six minutes to earn his twenty dollars.

'Obviously easier to break than I predicted,' I said. 'Two dollars per error in future.'

By the time we were ready for an on-site trial, the premises had been refitted, the refrigeration equipment was functioning, and the bar was installed and provisioned. Hudson had earned a further eighteen dollars.

Our test team consisted of me, Hudson, Blanche, who had been given permission to join us for dinner, and Laszlo, whom I had invited because of his Asperger's syndrome. Aspies were renowned for their aptitude as testers.

Rosie, Minh and Amghad worked the bar, then joined us to review the app's performance.

'It accepted my order for a margarita,' said Blanche. 'But I registered as allergic to oranges.'

Hudson typed at his laptop then announced, 'There's no orange juice in a margarita.'

'It's in the Cointreau,' said Blanche, pointing to her tablet.

'I selected a channel but there are no televisions,' said Laszlo. 'This will be an expensive error to fix.'

'Not installed yet,' I said. 'Ultimately, all walls will be covered with screens.'

'I've held off on that,' said Amghad. 'It doesn't seem to me that the people who come here are going to be sports fans.'

'Excellent point,' I said. 'I specified the bar, so it's likely to attract people like me. My interest in baseball is an anomaly resulting from my friendship with Dave.'

'Maybe show science programs,' said Rosie.

'*Star Trek*,' said Hudson. 'Original series on one screen, rotate the others on another screen; *Star Wars*, just the good ones; *Battlestar Galactica* . . . '

'Hey,' said Minh. 'I love it. Wall to wall sci-fi.'

'It's called The Library,' said Hudson. 'Aren't we going to have any books?'

'Cheaper than screens,' said Amghad.

'You can rent mine,' said Hudson.

'*Borrow*,' said Rosie.

'Non-fiction science books also,' I said. 'Not everyone reads science fiction.'

While Amghad and Minh cleared up, I ordered pizza.

Hudson had begun describing the plot of a novel he was reading and stopped. 'What's a slide rule?'

A slide rule? They were obsolete by the time I was old enough to operate a calculator. I knew of them in the same way as Hudson: from reading science fiction.

'When was this book written?' I asked.

'Last century. Maybe nineteen-sixty-something.'

'Funny,' said Rosie. 'The moon landing happened back then, before I was born. Phil thought he'd go there one day, and if not, then I would, and now Hudson . . . '

'Space travel has barely moved,' I said, 'but computers have progressed incredibly.'

'And genetics,' said Blanche.

'Correct. When I was studying, the idea of rectifying genetic abnormalities in living people was considered ludicrous. And now . . . '

'I'm definitely going to be a geneticist,' said Blanche.

'It's only *crewed* space travel that hasn't progressed so much,' said Hudson.

25

Eugenie reported that Hudson was making excellent progress in learning to code, using the Library application as a case study. However, she did not think Hudson had exceptional mathematical skills.

'Good, but he's not a maths genius.'

'He was top of his class in New York,' I said.

'I believe you. I said, 'not a genius'. I don't think that's what he wants to do anyway.'

'Do you have any career preferences?' I asked Hudson as we drove home.

'What would you like me to be?' asked Hudson.

It was a strange question, and I subtly applied the psychiatrists' trick. 'What is it that you think I would like you to be, and why do you ask?'

'You sound like a psychologist. I guess you'd like me to be a geneticist. Like Blanche.'

'It's the world's best job. In my opinion, obviously, since I chose it.'

'But you're not doing it now. So you must be less happy.'

'Actually, the project I was working on was not very stimulating.' I realised it only as the words came out of my mouth. 'It would be more exciting to be working on genome editing, but it's difficult to change.'

★ ★ ★

Dave had become obsessed with block-making. After refining the design with Hudson, he had transported the tools to his residence. The stock was now in excess of what could conceivably be required for one child's construction project.

His initial explanation was unconvincing. 'If I'm not around, because Sonia's finished with me, or I have a heart attack or stroke, this will be something for Fulvio to remember me by.'

'Surely the remembrance is not proportional to the quantity. You can stop now.'

'Why?'

'You're using time that could be allocated to other activities, the materials are costing money and eventually you'll have to store or dispose of the blocks.'

'I get that. But I'm not eating junk.' Dave showed me his belt. It was clear from the notches that he had lost weight. I had not noticed because he was still obese. Morbidly obese. But less morbidly obese.

'Maybe you could sell the blocks,' I said.

'Hudson's working on it.'

⋆　⋆　⋆

One Wednesday, I arrived at Allannah's shop. As soon as Hudson and Blanche left the service area, she pulled an opened envelope from a drawer and gave it to me. It was the lab report I had requested on Blanche's DNA. The results were unambiguous, but Allannah was apparently unsure.

'Does it say what I think it says?' she asked.

'How can I tell? I don't know what you think it says.'

'But you understand what it says?'

'Correct.'

'Don, please just tell me. In English. *What does it say?*'

'Blanche does not have the form of albinism that is associated with reduced lifespan.'

'Meaning she's not going to die young? Right?'

Obviously, the test results were no protection against car accidents, drug overdoses or, in Blanche's case, whooping cough, tetanus and polio, but I presumed Allannah realised this.

'The result is good news.'

Allannah flung her arms around me. I do not enjoy physical contact, even with friends, and particularly not unanticipated physical contact. She could not have been expected to know this, but we are encouraged not to feed a person peanuts without first checking for an allergy. It would be reasonable if social conventions incorporated a similar sensitivity.

I pulled away, knocking over a stand of vitamin supplements.

'I'm sorry,' said Allannah. 'I was just — '

She was interrupted by a male voice from the top of the stairs. 'Allannah. I need you up here. *Now.*' The tone was at odds with my mental picture of Gary the homeopath as misguided but gentle.

Allannah picked up Blanche's brother and pointed to a beam where a CCTV camera was mounted. 'You'd better call Hudson and go,' she said. 'I'll be okay.'

Later, reviewing the conversation, I noted the implication that I might have thought she would *not* be okay. But for the moment, I was processing my reaction to her husband. Though he had said only a few words, I felt an immediate primitive response, as I had when Blue House Fan criticised Hudson at the swimming carnival. It took me a few moments to realise that it was the same voice.

⋆　⋆　⋆

I shared my discovery with Rosie, omitting unnecessary detail. She was not happy.

'This guy . . . Are you sure Hudson's safe there?'

'I'm a poor judge of character. Dangerous people are often superficially pleasant; presumably many superficially unpleasant people are not dangerous. He apologised to Phil at the swimming event. Blanche is also Hudson's only friend — '

'I know that.' Rosie was sounding annoyed.

'I recommend we interrogate Hudson about his experiences.'

'And add our adult judgement.'

⋆　⋆　⋆

'What are Blanche's parents like?' Rosie asked Hudson as we ate breakfast.

'Ask Dad. He's the one who's always talking to her mum.'

'Right.' Rosie looked at me. 'I could have

found out all about her without bothering Hudson.'

'Correct.'

'So, what's she like?'

'Slim, extremely attractive, a number of anti-science views which I'm working on changing.'

'I wasn't really interested in what she looks like, but . . . What about the father? Is he slim and attractive too?'

'I've never seen him,' I said.

'He's mainly in his room,' said Hudson. 'He comes out sometimes, obviously. He's not slim, more chunky. I can't tell if he's attractive, but I don't think so. He's pretty bald.'

'Is he nice?' said Rosie.

'He's okay to me. He was a little weird the first time: he was a bit obsessed with the swimming race. But then he congratulated me.'

I argued that on the balance of evidence, and taking into account the relative risks and benefits, Hudson should be allowed to continue visiting Blanche after school. Rosie argued, based on the same information, that we should remain alert for signs of trouble and insist on all four parents meeting if he wanted to stay there longer or participate in excursions involving Blanche's father. We agreed to implement all the proposals.

★   ★   ★

I saw Allannah the next day when I collected Hudson from school.

'I don't think it's a good idea for you to stay while Hudson visits,' she said.

'Your husband objected to you . . . touching me?'

'He wasn't happy. I guess most husbands wouldn't be. You seemed pretty unhappy, too. I'm really sorry.'

'No apology required. I was surprised. I'm likely to be surprised anytime somebody does that to me, so I would advise against it in future.'

'It wasn't because you don't like me?'

'Obviously I like you. Otherwise, I would have made an excuse to avoid conversations.'

She smiled. 'But I can't give you a hug now to say thank you? Now that you're prepared?'

'No need. The thank-you message has been successfully delivered. Have you told Blanche? About the diagnosis?'

'I told her on the way to school. She's very happy, but I'm sure she'll want to thank you herself.'

'What about your husband? Is he also happy? Presumably he has some belief in science. Or he wouldn't trust the security camera to deliver an accurate image.'

Allannah laughed. 'That's technology, not the medical industry. We're not Amish.'

'But you believe the test results? Blanche's genetic test?'

'I do. Thank you again. But Gary would have gone troppo if I'd told him.'

'He appears highly susceptible to anger.'

'Only when he's protecting his family. He'd have seen it as me not trusting him to do that. I had to make up a reason for hugging you, so I told him that you were having another baby. I hope that's not too weird.'

'Incredibly clever.'

'You think so?' She laughed. 'And . . . if I get here ten minutes early to pick up Blanche, and you do too, we can still talk.'

26

'Get out there on email, social media. Invite all your friends,' said Amghad. 'We're off the street, so customers aren't going to find us by accident.' He wanted the bar to be full on opening night to create an impression of popularity for the two journalists who had accepted his invitation to attend.

I didn't need social media to invite all my Melbourne friends. I told Carl (not available, working) and Eugenie (sorry, you should have told me earlier). Claudia had a conference in Sydney. Dave and Sonia were committed to a school function for Zina. Phil would be taking care of Hudson. Which left Laszlo. He agreed to contribute, despite having the same objections to crowded bars as I did.

Opening was at 6.30 p.m., and one of the journalists, named Sylvie, arrived exactly on time. She was outnumbered by Amghad, Rosie, Minh and three casual staff.

'Can you make me a margarita?' Sylvie asked me.

'Of course. But I recommend using the app.'

Amghad was shaking his head. The bar's first drink would be ordered in the conventional manner, bypassing our most important 'point of difference'.

'Salt?' I asked.

'No, thanks. And thanks for asking.'

I pulled the liquor from the twenty-five-degrees-below-zero freezer, and the lime juice and water from the fridge.

'Pre-squeezed?' said Sylvie.

'Correct. Aged for four hours to allow enzymatic bittering, resulting in a more complex flavour.'

'I guess we'll see.'

I poured the ingredients into the shaker.

'Blood Orange Cointreau?' said Sylvie.

'Eighteen per cent of the orange-liqueur component. Optional if you prefer the conventional form.'

'Your call. But a house margarita is my benchmark.'

'Excellent approach to evaluation,' I said.

'What's that?' said Sylvie, pointing to the water flask.

'Water.'

'You're watering down my benchmark drink? In front of me?'

'Correct. I'm adding the optimum amount. Conventional margaritas are diluted by the melting of ice, but the dilution is dependent on the temperature of the ingredients, the quantity and size of the ice units, and the shaking time and intensity. Hence uncontrolled. This one is precisely controlled, so if it's too strong or weak we can vary it and record your preference in the database.'

I handed the shaker to Rosie.

'No ice?' said Sylvie.

'Correct.'

Rosie agitated the shaker to mix the citrus and

the liquor, and poured the drink.

We all watched as Sylvie tasted it.

'Shit,' she said. 'Excuse me, but this wasn't what I was expecting.'

'You don't approve? I can — '

'It's excellent. What tequila did you use?'

'The tequila is a basic hundred-per-cent agave silver. The taste is more influenced by the limes. It's cheaper to buy high-quality key limes than prestigious tequila.'

'Well, you had me fooled. Better make me a Negroni and tell me about this thing at the university. If you don't mind.'

I told her the story of the Genetics Lecture Outrage and she appeared sympathetic. She wanted a photo at the bar, and we posed with Rosie in front and Minh and Amghad either side of me.

'Put your arms around them,' said Sylvie. I complied. I couldn't risk a bad review because of an aversion to doing something that was generally considered easy.

When she had left, Amghad looked around the bar. Still zero customers. 'Don't know. She loved the drinks and that's a big deal for her, but . . . '

'Relax,' said Minh. 'We always knew this was going to be a word-of-mouth thing. Give it time.'

'I can't remember seeing you so stressed,' said Rosie.

'I wasn't stressed,' I said.

'What was Sylvie's BMI?'

I had no idea.

Then a single customer walked in. For a moment I thought, from his costume, that he must be a homeless person. Then I recognised Laszlo.

'Laszlo is here,' he said. 'And he has brought two friends.' He reopened the door at the top of the stairs to let in his partner, Frances the Occasional Smoker, and another woman. Laszlo made some signal to Frances and she said, 'I am here. And I have brought two friends.' She opened the door and summoned a man and a woman.

People continued to enter, and Laszlo continued to conduct their introductions in what was obviously a geometric progression.

I had a moment of fear. 'Did you limit the number of iterations?'

'Of course. The total will be one hundred and twenty-seven.'

It was a challenging test, with so many arriving at once and the systems being designed for seated customers. Amghad solved the problem with trays of drinks offered at zero cost.

Laszlo's friends and friends of friends and friends of friends of friends drank, talked, browsed the bookshelves and watched *Star Trek*. Several people from Minh's company arrived. It was noisier than I had hoped it would be but much quieter than a typical bar, especially considering the number of customers.

I found Laszlo finishing a drink. 'Excellent lemon juice.'

'You're drinking lemon juice?'

'I have Asperger's,' he said. 'So I drink fruit juice. But I am also Hungarian. So I have some vodka in it.'

'I'll order you another. Free.'

'No. You are running a business and I am making a small contribution, as you asked.'

Brendan, the second journalist, arrived at 9.13 p.m. He was in his mid-fifties and over-weight — BMI approximately thirty-two.

This time, I made a more forceful effort to demonstrate the advantages of online ordering. Brendan began entering details, but it was apparent he had a short concentration span.

'I haven't got time to read terms and conditions.'

'Just hit *OK*,' said Rosie.

'Allergies?' said Brendan. 'What's that about?'

'Do you have any?' I asked.

'None that affect my drinking.'

'Select *Nil*. Then you can submit your credit-card details.'

'Forget it. Just make me an Old Fashioned. Can you do that, or do you need to know my Medicare number?'

Amghad nodded violently.

I made Brendan an Old Fashioned, then a second, while I explained the design of the bar and the advantages of the app. He took his third drink into the crowd and began a conversation with Laszlo, which continued until he returned to the bar to order 'one for the road'. He was the last to leave, at 10.34 p.m.

'Older crowd, finish early,' said Amghad. 'But we've done well.'

★ ★ ★

Amghad argued that 'all publicity is good publicity'. On that basis, the articles that Sylvie and Brendan wrote were 'good publicity'. On any other basis, I would have evaluated them as 'bad publicity'.

Sylvie's article was published eight days later in the newspaper that had defended my professional conduct. Her thesis was that 'the smartest man in Melbourne' was using his skills to make 'possibly the best margarita you'll find anywhere', but that it would be better if my talents were employed in curing cancer. The remainder of the article criticised the university and the complainant, and was illustrated with the picture Sylvie had taken of us, captioned: *Accused racist Prof. Don Tillman and wife Rosie with business partners Amghad Karim and Dang Minh. Mr Karim was born in Egypt and Dr Dang is Vietnamese.*

Professor Lawrence phoned to say that she hoped the bar was prospering, as the review had 'stirred the pot'. It was not, to the extent that I was able to run it without assistance. Most nights we had only two customers — a male couple in their twenties who read books and consumed soft drinks.

Brendan's article appeared in an online 'lifestyle' publication a week later. It was entirely negative, with the possible exception of his mention of a 'special' Old Fashioned, and was titled *The Place to Drink if You're Not the Full Bottle*.

On the second reading, I understood what Brendan was saying: he considered people who preferred non-intrusive surroundings and enjoyed science fiction to be 'nerds', 'on the spectrum', and 'the kids at school who always did their homework'. All of these terms, even the last, were employed in a negative sense. It was apparent he considered that Minh and I both fell into that category, though he had barely spoken to Minh.

My immediate thought was to confront him to correct his misunderstandings about the bar and the people whom it was intended to attract. Amghad dissuaded me.

'He just came up with an angle and ran with it. It may not even be what he thinks.'

I scheduled an extra workout at the dojo, and, as my anger dissipated, I realised that it was largely due to my own misunderstanding of the category of people that Brendan had vilified. I had thought they would want to drink in my bar.

27

It was Minh who drew my attention to a 'tweet storm' related to Brendan's article. A Twitter user identified as @TazzaTheGeek had suggested that Brendan be fired. The tweet had been widely circulated and commented on by sci-fi fans and people who identified as autistic. There appeared to be some overlap between the two groups.

Tazza the Geek had suggested that the autism community show its solidarity by patronising The Library. Amghad believed that advertising on social media was ineffective, so I did not expect any results.

At 8.06 p.m. that evening, I called Rosie. 'Come in immediately. We have customers. Thirty-seven.'

'Call Minh.'

'She's on her way. But it's incredibly exciting.'

'Someone has to look after Hudson.'

'Bring him. With his book and his sleeping bag.'

Rosie arrived with Hudson and also Dave. 'Rosie said you were desperate,' he said. 'You look like you're doing okay.'

Rosie directed him to the order screen.

A problem immediately became apparent. A significant percentage of customers were not prepared to use the app.

'I don't know what temperature and dilution

factor I want: can you just make me a normal Cosmopolitan?' said a woman in a grey tracksuit.

'No problem,' said Rosie, before I could object.

'You think we could be losing custom because of the app?' she said to me as she made the drink.

'It's our most important feature.'

'What about the décor and the refrigeration and — '

'We tested it thoroughly for user-friendliness.'

'You, Hudson, Blanche and . . . '

'Laszlo. Expert testers.'

Rosie laughed. 'But not exactly average bar patrons.'

Hudson had been listening.

'Do we have a marker pen?' he asked me.

'Yes.'

'Where?'

'Top-left drawer.'

He fetched a red marker. 'Write on my head: *App Help*.'

'Don . . . ' said Rosie, but I was already writing.

About an hour later, Rosie drew my attention to Hudson, who was engaged in conversation at the bookshelves with a male of approximately forty, estimated BMI thirty-two.

'He's been talking to that guy too long.'

'I was thinking the same thing,' said Dave.

'Is there some problem with him?'

'Just a bit creepy, if you know what I mean,' said Dave.

The customer was partly bald, with his remaining hair longer than average, a beard and glasses. He was wearing a heavy-metal T-shirt, slacks and running shoes. Carl had criticised me for wearing running shoes with formal trousers, but the combination was popular this evening.

'Stereotypical science-fiction fan. Or scientist,' I said.

'Or creep,' said Dave. 'Not saying he is. But he's what people think a creep looks like. And he's hanging out with an eleven-year-old.'

Before we could take any action, one of our two regular customers, the tall thin male with glasses, long hair and an insubstantial beard, approached Hudson. His companion, who was shorter with dark curly hair, joined them and the older customer moved away.

After a few minutes, the taller male came to the bar and spoke to Rosie.

'Excuse me, but are you Hudson's mother? Rosie?'

Rosie confirmed her identity.

'I'm Merlin. I thought you might be worried about us hanging with Hudson. There was a guy talking to him and we thought he was a bit creepy, so we stepped in, and then I thought you might think the same about us.'

'Well, thanks for making yourself known. He's only eleven. He's still at primary school.'

'We know. But he's got both his parents looking out for him. Which is more than most kids have. Anyway, I think you know my friend Tazza's mother. Katerina.'

Rosie smiled, hugely. 'Tell Anast . . . Tazza to come over. I haven't seen him since he was eight.'

'He's a bit shy. But I thought someone should let you know who Hudson was talking to.'

Rosie explained the connections. Katerina was the school friend with the autistic son who was 'doing well'. But I recognised the name: Tazza the Geek, who had called for Brendan the Offensive Journalist to be fired and thus generated the bar's most successful night.

Hudson needed the sleeping bag. Before he went to sleep in what had once been Minh's office, he said, 'Can I come again tomorrow? I can go to bed late and wake up at the old time. We need to fix the app.'

'You can fix the app at home,' I said.

'Der,' said Hudson. 'I need to find out what people want it to do. You can't specify software without user input.'

There was no point in upgrading the app if the improvement in custom was not sustained. I explained that to Hudson.

'If we don't fix the app, it definitely won't be . . . sustained.'

★　★　★

The improvement was sustained: Brendan's article had mobilised a community of people who became habitual customers and recommended the bar to their friends.

'I don't mind doing this when it's for us,' said Rosie one evening as she loaded glasses into the bar's dishwasher. 'But we had a couple of people from the Mental Health Foundation in today, and while Stefan was setting up the projector, do you know what Judas said?'

'He asked you to get the coffee?'

'Have I told you this already?'

'There was a previous occasion, and history is an excellent predictor of future behaviour.'

'Well, that's what he did. 'Rosie, maybe a pot of coffee for everyone?''

It seemed a sensible division of labour, given Stefan was busy and Judas was presumably encouraging the visitors to fund the project, but I knew better than to point this out.

'Totally unreasonable,' I said. 'What did you say?'

'I said, 'Thank you, Simon, that would be great,' and the two women from the foundation saw what had happened, and as soon as he left the room to get the coffee, they burst out laughing. He must have heard but he didn't say anything afterwards. By the way, I'm assuming I'm getting paid for all this work I'm doing here.'

'Of course. Your hours will be contributing to paying off our share of the business.' The future tense was appropriate. I had seen Rosie's work as being part of her support for me personally. But when I mentioned it to Amghad and Minh, they insisted on backdating the credits. And criticised me for not asking earlier.

28

A week later, I had a call from the principal. She wanted to see me, and suggested I come alone. It was a 'very awkward matter' which she would rather not discuss on the phone.

Rosie insisted on attending. 'If they don't want me there, I should be.'

Rabbit was not present: only the principal.

'Professor Tillman, Dr Jarman,' she said. 'We all make mistakes sometimes, and I'm afraid a quite serious mistake has been made.'

'The autism diagnosis?' I said.

'I'm afraid it's not that. You remember telling us that Hudson had a rather unfortunate nickname?'

'Nasty?' said Rosie. 'That's what you're talking about?'

'I'm afraid that's not the nickname. You're not Jewish, are you?'

I shook my head.

'Well, that's something. But it's *Nazi*. They've been calling him Nazi, and we're obviously going to do what we can to put a stop to it. But . . . '

'Why Nazi?' said Rosie. 'You're not going to tell us he's done some horrible thing?'

'No. Just what he always does. It seems he corrected something that Mr Warren said, and Mr Warren, without thinking, called him a grammar Nazi.'

'No filter,' I said, without thinking.

The principal looked at me for a moment, then continued. 'The kids picked it up. Without the grammar part. Mr Warren's very embarrassed and apologetic. But . . . '

'How did you find out?' said Rosie.

'You asked me to follow up about the nickname. I know which children will give me an honest account of these things. And Mr Warren immediately owned up when I spoke to him.'

Informants. Confessions. Nazis. School had not changed much since I was a child.

'Frankly, if you insist, and I can understand you doing so, we will be obliged to take disciplinary action. In today's climate, we may even have to ask Mr Warren to leave. I'd be sorry . . . '

'Incredible,' I said. 'The expression — '

Rosie gave me the stop signal. 'Can Don and I have a few moments?' she said.

The principal looked unhappy. We stepped outside.

'You were going to let it go, weren't you?' said Rosie.

'Because of what happened to you with the Great — '

'The Genetics Lecture Outrage. Correct. He — '

'That's why they wanted you here without me. Mr Nice Guy. Mr Empathy. Mr White Male Solidarity.'

'Possibly. But — '

'You think it's okay to call Hudson a Nazi?'

'A *grammar* Nazi. It's a common expression. My father was one. There's a soup Nazi in *Seinfeld*.'

'Don, you got fired — suspended — for this

sort of thing. I'm not saying that should happen to Neil, but we should push back a bit.'

Rosie insisted that we purchase coffees and 'take our time'. 'Let her stew a bit.'

When we returned, I could see no signs that the principal had stewed. She was walking around outside her office, presumably reflecting on some problem.

'Thank you for coming back,' she said. 'I just want to reiterate that I'm truly sorry this has happened.'

'So are we,' said Rosie. 'You may be aware that after a lesser incident of this kind at the university, with adults, not schoolchildren, Don decided that the right thing was to step aside.'

'Yes . . . we were aware . . . I'd thought he might understand that we all make mistakes . . . '

'Correct,' I said. 'Rabbit said something totally inappropriate. We should consider the possibility that he's autistic.'

The last statement was not part of our good-cop — bad-cop plan, but I saw Rosie trying not to laugh.

'We should go into my office,' said the principal.

She directed us to the chairs in the corner rather than opposite her desk. 'I take your point,' she said. 'It's possible Neil's been hasty in pigeonholing Hudson . . . '

'You call a child a Nazi, his classmates pick it up, and then you report he's not popular,' said Rosie. 'And suggest a psychiatric intervention.'

'It didn't happen in that . . . How would you like us to respond?'

'It's the middle of the third term,' I said, as instructed by Rosie. 'Rather than disrupt anything, maybe we can defer any action until the end of the year. When we can take into account what happens between now and then.'

'We'll do everything we can about the nickname. But regardless, we'll have to move Hudson to another Year Six class.'

'Why?' I asked. 'He doesn't like change.'

'I understand that, but . . . well . . . change is a fact of life, isn't it, so maybe the move will help to build his resilience. But that's not the reason.'

Resilience, in my experience, was seldom the reason to do anything. It was only ever stated as a goal *after* some action that required it had occurred or been committed to.

'If at the end of the year you do decide to make a formal complaint, we need to have been seen to have taken some action. We can't leave him with a teacher who could be seen to have picked on him.'

'Not a good look,' I said.

'Fuck,' said Rosie when we had left. 'You know why she's moving him?'

'Not because of resilience, I assume.'

'She didn't want Hudson's teacher being beholden to us.'

'Which was your intention.'

'Correct.'

★　★　★

'You told them about the nickname. You promised you wouldn't, and then you did and

226

now I have to change classes.'

This was an excellent summary of what we had done. It was exactly what I had hated my parents doing and what I had worked hard to avoid doing with Hudson. I was looking forward to hearing Rosie's explanation for her behaviour.

'Don, you explain,' said Rosie. 'You were there.'

I tried to remember the circumstances. They involved human interactions for which there was no precise language — hence difficult to commit to memory. But I could remember one important thing.

'We were attempting to act in your interests. The nickname revelation was to achieve a higher-order goal.'

'What are you talking about?'

Rosie and I looked at each other.

'You're always talking to them. I know you are. What about?'

Rosie and I looked at each other again.

'Mr Warren thinks there's something wrong with me, doesn't he? Because I hate cricket and Harry Potter, and wear shorts, and I'm friends with a girl. And I know stuff he doesn't know. And . . . ' Hudson stood up. 'That's why you're making me do all this training. You want to change me.'

'The goal is to make school easier,' I said.

'You don't like me the way I am. If you did, you wouldn't want to change me.'

'We both love you,' said Rosie. 'Your father's trying to teach you stuff like all fathers do. Pa made him learn karate when he was seven. He didn't like it at first but now . . . You're happy to be riding the bike, aren't you?'

'I don't want to talk about it,' said Hudson. 'I'm feeling sick. I don't think I'll be able to go to school tomorrow.'

'That had to happen at some point,' said Rosie after Hudson had gone to his room. 'What do you want to do?'

'I have to go to work.'

When I reconfigured my schedule, I had failed to consider the need for extended discussion during the evening handover from me to Rosie. The requirement to be at the bar by 6.00 p.m. was fixed. And any attempt on Rosie's part to leave work early was likely to provoke a 'coded' response from Judas.

'Judas says, 'No problem, Rosie, we know you've got to look after Hudson. Whatever you're doing can wait till tomorrow.''

'Seems very accommodating.'

'It's not. If Stefan takes off early, nobody asks why; nobody makes any assumptions. But I'm a mum. So that has to be the reason.'

Fortunately, Rosie and I were able to converse at The Library, where the remote ordering system minimised the interruptions from customers. I suggested she come in.

'What about Hudson? He's supposedly sick. And I'm cooking tonight.' Two of the standard meals had proven unsuitable for reheating and Rosie had volunteered to cook on those nights.

'Which reminds me,' said Rosie. 'Another thing for you to teach your son. When I say, 'I'm going to hang out the washing; watch the rice,' that doesn't mean, 'Watch the rice boil dry and burn until the smoke alarm goes off.''

'Obviously, you were gone too long.'

'He only had to turn the burner off. *You* would have worked that out.'

'As a result of being an experienced cook and considerably older.'

It was entirely possible that I would have done the same as Hudson at his age, and my father would have given me his 'I can't understand how someone with all your brains didn't have enough common sense' lecture.

'I'll explain it to him to prevent a recurrence,' I said. 'Of that specific scenario.'

'Don't bother. I think he got the message.'

'But you asked me to teach him — '

'I was hoping you could convey some sort of general principle. But, no, I see the problem.'

'Good decision. We need to give priority to the current issue. Which, given our agreed division of labour, is my responsibility.'

'Which means?'

'I'll talk to him tomorrow. Instead of school.'

29

Rosie called the principal to advise that Hudson would take the day off to enable debriefing of the Nazi conversation and adjustment to the change of class.

'I think Bronwyn's a bit scared of me,' said Rosie.

It seemed a reasonable response to a designated bad cop.

'I'm assuming you're not actually ill, but require recovery and thinking time,' I said to Hudson after Rosie had left for work.

Hudson thought for a moment then nodded. 'That's okay?'

'Adults do the same thing. They take 'mental health days' which they register as sick leave. Because the system has insufficient options. But now we need to find a long-term solution.'

'I don't want to change classes.'

'We'll have to decide if that's a mandatory requirement or negotiable. If it's negotiable, we have more scope for innovative solutions.'

I made myself a coffee while Hudson considered the proposition.

'Negotiable,' he said.

'Excellent. The process for problem-solving is first to explain and explore the situation and objectives. We can ask questions and share information, but we can't propose solutions. Then we require an incubation period for subconscious problem-solving, during which we undertake some mundane activity. As we have only one day total, I recommend we allow three to four hours. Then we co-operate on finding solutions.'

'If we solve the problem by lunchtime, can we go book shopping in Clunes?'

'We won't. The incubation period is critical to generate the best possible solution.'

'Why not have the incubation period while we're driving and shopping?'

'Brilliant idea.'

We departed immediately, with a plan: explore problem on outbound journey; incubate while book trading; propose and evaluate solutions on inbound journey. As a bonus, travelling to Clunes was associated in our minds with recovery from a difficult time — my father's death and the Pizza Incident.

The original problem, which had seemed so severe that I had given up my job to address it, appeared to diminish in importance as I explained it to Hudson.

'Mr Warren is concerned that you don't have the social skills to cope at high school.'

'It'll be the same kids that are in my year now. We all go up together.'

'But you don't like school.'

'I won't like it any better if I can play football. I'd like it less, because I don't like playing football.'

'What if you have to — ?'

'Grandpa's showed me what to do if I have to play for some reason. Anyway, it doesn't matter what Mr Warren thinks, because I'm not going to be in his class anymore. So, problem solved.'

Hudson did not speak for the next fifty-seven minutes, except to read aloud occasional road signs and billboards, something I did myself when I was alone in the car. I used the time to reflect and realised that he was resisting being classified as intrinsically deficient — even if only in a small number of domains. It was more accurate to characterise his situation as *ill-prepared*.

'Have you read any science-fiction books where an unprepared person has to travel into space?' I asked.

'Heaps. Sometimes it's a kid.'

'And sometimes they have time to get some basic training? And that's part of the story. Correct?'

'Sometimes,' said Hudson.

'Can you provide an example?'

'Yes.' Hudson went silent, then laughed. 'That's what you'd say. You do it on purpose, right?'

'Correct.' It was an opportunity to say more, about how it was in line with what people expected of me, but under my control — but I needed to stay focused.

'Some of the Robert Heinlein books,' said Hudson. 'He wrote a lot for teenagers, so . . . *Time for the Stars*. You'd probably hate it, because of the science.'

'Telepathy. Perfectly acceptable to propose a single new discovery as a basis for the plot. The application of the special theory of relativity in the context of instantaneous communication is handled plausibly.'

'You've read it?'

'*Have Space Suit — Will Travel* is better, but *Time for the Stars* is a suitable example.'

'You said you didn't read science fiction.'

'Not now. I read it at a time when I was incredibly unhappy.'

'So you could imagine you were somewhere else?'

'Correct.'

'Why were you unhappy?'

'Lack of friends. But the point is that the boy who can communicate telepathically with his twin has to go into space, without the preparation that a conventional astronaut would have. There's only time to teach him the most important things — those necessary to survive in a hostile environment.'

Hudson laughed. 'High school.'

'Correct.' *Autistic people are poor at analogies.*

'His major strength is his telepathy skill, so they can't neglect that. Analogous to mathematics or coding for you. But that strength is of zero value if he makes some simple mistake and dies from oxygen starvation or failure to operate his weapon correctly against an alien.'

'I don't think I'll be killed at high school.'

'True. But you should relate *killed* to *unhappy*. If some skills that can be acquired in a few months can alleviate that . . . '

'You think you know what the skills are.'

'You should consider me the experienced

astronaut who almost died in space multiple times.'

'The clumsy astronaut.'

'Correct. It's better to learn from people who have had to work hard to achieve their skills, rather than the naturally talented.'

'The *old* astronaut. Things have changed. I don't think school is the same as when you went.'

'True. So, we should review the plan using what we both consider to be the required competencies. Presumably you want to continue swimming. And coding?'

'You said no solutions until the drive home.'

'I'm only seeking information.' I was beginning to feel that, as frequently happens, articulating the problem had been the most crucial step.

We spent two hours and twenty minutes in Clunes, shopping for books and eating fried chicken.

On the drive home, Hudson proposed several schedule changes, which appeared reasonable, but I had already explained that I would need to discuss them with Rosie before granting approval.

★   ★   ★

'Why Clunes?' said Rosie. 'You could have gone to Shepparton and seen your mother. You haven't seen her since the funeral.'

'Excellent idea, but unfortunately too late. Also, I spoke to her on Sunday.' The weekly telephone calls had continued uninterrupted after my father's death. 'And we needed to focus on the Hudson-unhappiness problem. Which we have solved. Subject to your approval.'

'Go on.'

'He wants to abandon the 5.20 a.m. pre-school reading. He'll call George on weekends.'

'So far, so good.'

'Obviously that allows him to stay up later. He wants to continue visits to Phil's and Eugenie's as currently scheduled.'

'I see what you're doing. Give me the bad news.'

'He wants to go to the bar every night. He wants to be paid for being the Library app helper and developer.'

'What's he going to eat? And that doesn't mean I agree — I'm just wondering.'

'Pizza.'

'No. Absolutely not. He's not eating pizza every night.'

'I was joking. He's happy to vary his diet but he wants to eat at the bar.'

'Because of my cooking?'

In preparing my presentation, I had decided not to include Hudson's views on this topic. I opened my hands in the Italian signal for *Who knows?*

'Of course he can't go to the bar every night.'

'What are your objections?'

'He's eleven.' Rosie paused. 'He had answers to all of this, didn't he?'

'Correct. It's a family business. He's legally allowed to work a limited number of hours. He will be with his father, hence supervised, and you can join us when convenient. He will do his homework before he goes. If he needs a time-out or there is a problematic situation, he can retreat to Minh's old office.'

'What's the purpose of all this? Besides him making money?'

'He will be practising application-specification skills which could provide the basis of a respectable and well-paid career.'

'He said that?'

'No, that's supplementary information from me. His argument is that he'll be getting personal-interaction practice in a traditional environment for socialising. And learning how people think, through the way they use the app. Which is his most significant need and the most difficult to teach.'

'The customers are all adults.'

'Who are more sophisticated socially, so he'll be in an advanced class. He said.'

'Have you looked at the people who come to the bar?'

'Diverse. Which is perfect. Also, I have a bonus outcome from our discussions. If you say, 'Observe this situation and if you detect a problem, take action to rectify it,' the rice incident is less likely to recur, in more general contexts.'

Rosie laughed. 'I guess it shouldn't all be on him to change.'

'Excellent principle. Is the proposal approved?'

'Four nights a week — max. I want some time at home with him, and he needs that too.'

'I expect he'll consider that acceptable.'

'Pleased to hear it. But how's he going to get to the bar?'

'He wants a myki, so he can catch the tram. Another important skill.'

'I'm not sure he's ready . . . '

Earlier in the year we had experimented with Hudson undertaking a short tram journey alone, and he had missed his stop. Finding him had involved trauma on his part and Rosie's.

'We reviewed the incident. Apparently, you provided vague references to landmarks, when tram stops are unambiguously identified by route and stop number. *I* would have had trouble finding my way with your instructions.'

'No argument there. I'm just thinking safety . . . '

'Melbourne is one of the world's safest cities. The probability of a child being a victim of violence on public transport is low but receives disproportionate media coverage. Like crocodile attacks. Hudson is more likely to be killed or maimed while — '

'I get it. I guess it's a good sign. He's beginning to chart his own life. Maybe that'll translate into him taking his own action at school, but . . . hold on. What about changing classes?'

I smiled. 'Accepted.' For no apparent reason, the issue seemed to have slipped from mandatory to optional to irrelevant.

'You know why?' said Rosie. 'He *wanted* to get away from Rabbit. Once he got everything he asked for, he didn't need the class change as a bargaining chip.'

30

Dave came into the bar a few times to assist me but found it difficult to be surrounded by people consuming liquor without joining them. Conversely, I had a rule of not drinking before or during working hours. My alcohol consumption had fallen substantially.

'I think I'll go home and make some blocks,' Dave said at the end of what became his final shift.

'It seems to be becoming an obsession,' I said. 'Possibly you should consult a psychiatrist.'

'Look,' he said. 'New pants. I'm down seventeen pounds. And . . . Hudson hasn't told you?'

'Told me what?'

'We made our first sale.'

Dave pulled out his phone and showed me the website.

WB^2. *World's Best Wooden Blocks. Handcrafted in Australia by David Bechler.*

'Hudson thought David sounded more artistic than Dave.'

'Surely there's some error with the price? They seem incredibly expensive.'

'Handcrafted.' Dave laughed. 'I thought so too, but then Hudson told me how his buddy Carl prices clothes, and I thought, what the hell, we can always drop it. But at least one person thinks they're worth what we're asking.'

I raised the WB^2 project on the drive to school. I had to wait for a wet day, as Hudson was now taking the tram by default.

'Who invented the brand name? World's Best Wooden Blocks?'

'Dave and I. You always say, 'world's best everything', so it's sort of yours, too.'

'What about the abbreviation?'

'Me. Dave's not exactly a mathematician.'

'It's incorrect. It should be $(WB)^2$. Both the W and the B are squared. Eugenie needs to improve her teaching.'

The last statement was a small joke, but Hudson didn't laugh.

★　★　★

Rosie and I celebrated our thirteenth wedding anniversary at the bar. It was the perfect venue — the result of a joint project to improve life for ourselves, our son and some of our friends, and, it appeared, for the increasing number of regular customers.

As I had on every anniversary, I gave Rosie a gift according to the published schedule: year thirteen was lace. Hence high-quality running shoes with laces.

'You need to exercise more,' I said. 'We're getting older and it's necessary to apply conscious effort to maintain health. Obviously, I'd like us both to live as long as possible so that our marriage can continue.'

Rosie laughed. 'Good save. And good present. I'd looked it up and I was expecting lacy . . . I don't know, but it wouldn't have been me.'

'The present is acceptable, then?'

'As always. I really do need to get to the gym. In between the bar and my real job and Hudson and doing the laundry. You know, when I tell people that you do this for me every year, they're envious. They say you're a great romantic. And you are.' She kissed me, unnoticed by Hudson and the customers, who were absorbed in television, books, computers and phones.

It was hard to think of myself as a romantic. Our wedding anniversary was diarised, and the themes for each year were publicly documented. And I would not have adopted the tradition without encouragement — *instruction*.

Rosie appeared to have read my mind. 'This was Gene's idea, wasn't it?'

'Originally. It's not a secret.'

'I know. But you owe him a lot. We owe him a lot.'

Rosie's statement was true, but still extraordinary. 'You hate Gene.'

'I don't *hate* anyone. I was pretty unhappy with some of the stuff he did. But he was your friend, and I tried not to stand in the way of that. I think you miss him.'

It was our wedding anniversary. My wife had made an extraordinary statement of concession. I owed it to her to be completely open in return.

'Possibly,' I said.

'Don, maybe you need to reach out to Gene. This business of trying to persuade Claudia and him to reconcile: you don't think you might be projecting a little?'

'Emotionally, possibly. But the situation between us is unchanged from eleven years ago. So, there's no rational reason.'

'What about you? Haven't you changed? Maybe he's changed. Don't tell me the situation hasn't changed. Your attitudes are part of it. Most of it.'

She pointed to Hudson, who was by the bookshelves, talking animatedly to Tazza and Merlin. 'He seems a lot happier. But you're not really happy, are you?'

Rosie, as always, had a better understanding of my emotional state than I did. I looked at the computer screen. 'I need to fill this order. Then I'll answer the question.'

As I mixed the cocktails, I tried to make sense of the negative feeling that Rosie had detected. It was true that Hudson's mood seemed to have improved, at least when he was at the bar. I doubted it extended to his time at school.

Although my overall memory of schooldays was of exclusion, there had been periods of happiness. I had enjoyed programming my computer, playing chess and much of the actual schoolwork. But by the age of twenty, I was suicidal, to the extent that I was briefly resident in a psychiatric hospital. Essentially, my problem had been social isolation. And Hudson still had only one friend, zero improvement since the beginning of the Hudson Project.

I finished making the cocktails and Cheng, one of the casual staff, picked up the tray.

'Analysis complete?' asked Rosie.

'Not really. But I'm concerned about . . . the issues that Rabbit raised.'

'Have you thought any more about the autism diagnosis? I don't know if you've noticed, but when he gets up in the morning, he does this repetitive tapping for maybe ten minutes.'

I nodded. I had chosen not to raise it with him in case of embarrassment. Or with Rosie, for what felt like the same reason. It was possible it had been going on for a long time, but we had only noticed it recently because Hudson was getting up later.

'I think he does it to get set for school,' said Rosie. 'It's called stimming . . . It's a characteristic of autism. You knew that?'

'No.'

'It's strange,' said Rosie. 'I was going to read up on autism, and then I thought, no, Don will know it chapter and verse before I've got started. But . . . nothing.'

'I did some research online, the day you interrupted me. I also studied Asperger's syndrome for a lecture thirteen years ago. And we went to the seminar. I reached a provisional conclusion that Hudson wasn't autistic, hence the information was not relevant.'

'Right,' said Rosie. 'But . . . you see him here with these guys.' She indicated the skinny male in his twenties that Hudson was talking to. 'I'd guess a lot of them are on the spectrum.'

'Possibly. I suspect they're a bad influence.'

'Wow. Big call. When I met you, you were a lot like that.'

'And unhappy.'

'I guess I'm saying that if he *is* on the spectrum, and you want him to have better social skills, make more friends, maybe we get him some assistance from people who do this every day. With a . . . scientific basis.'

I thought about Hudson's classmate, Dov: 'zombified'. And my twenty-year-old self, lost in a psychiatric hospital. *After* we had received professional help. Perhaps because of it.

I turned to the screen. 'Caipirinha at table twelve. No dilution.'

★ ★ ★

Minh was in the bar as often as Rosie and Hudson, despite not being required contractually to work at all. During the establishment stage, we were relying on casual staff, and she had designated herself induction officer.

'I want you to make me the best cocktail you've ever made. I don't care if it's something you invented yourself, or just a great martini. But the *best*. Right now. Then we're going to put it in the app with your name next to it. You're gonna go home tonight and say you've done the best work you've ever done. Or else, why are you alive? And why am I here?'

Amazingly, even after such hyperbole, the staff loved her.

One Friday night, Rosie, Hudson and I were closing up and our door team, Nick and Callie, came in to sign off. Minh had left a few minutes earlier.

Callie was laughing. 'Did Minh tell you what she did?'

'In what context?'

'About eight o'clock, there was a bit of a queue, and these three guys turned up just when she was coming in. There's a certain kind of guy who thinks the girls who come here are soft targets. Shits me, but what can you do?'

Nick continued. 'Minh walks up to them, and — like, Callie's right — she sees it, and she says, 'Sorry, but we've got a dress code.'

'And these guys are like . . . The punters in front of them are wearing . . . I don't have to tell you . . . And these guys in their tight pants and pointy shoes are like: *what the fuck?*

'Minh just points to the people in front of them and says, straight face, 'I think you can see the standard we expect.' You know what she's like. Five-foot nothing and she's totally owning these guys and they . . . slink off into the night.'

Everyone was laughing. Callie high-fived Rosie and Hudson did the same to me. It felt like we were doing something worthwhile.

31

At 8.51 on a Friday morning, the doorbell rang. It was Allannah, with Blanche's brother. I had not seen her for some time, due to Hudson travelling by tram to school and to Blanche's home. She was incredibly agitated, but I deduced that her dominant emotions were anger and disbelief.

'I can't tell you how angry I am. I can't believe what you did.'

'Is there some specific issue?' I guessed that the problem was Blanche's visit to the ophthalmologist, but it would be poor strategy to confess to that and then discover that I had done something else to upset her.

'You took my child for medical treatment — medical treatment she didn't need. Even the *doctor* said that, right? Without my permission; without my husband's permission. It's illegal, you know that? The school could kick Hudson out because of what you've done. Did you think about that?'

Allannah continued for some time, without adding significant further information. If she had been Hudson, I would have enforced a time-out, but this seemed tactless in an adult situation.

'Would you like an infusion?' I asked.

'What? What are you saying?'

'A herbal tea.'

'You're offering me herbal tea?'

'I can add boiling water to citrus peel and rosemary or thyme. While we work on solving the problem.'

'Have you been listening to anything I've said? Do you realise how much trouble you're in? You and Rosie?'

'Of course. So, I'm invested in finding a solution. Which is presumably your goal as well. We should begin by identifying any damage that needs to be rectified.'

Allannah came in, and I gave her son some of Dave's sample blocks to play with, showing him how they fitted together.

By the time I had completed the preparation of an orange peel and rosemary infusion, and given the orange segments to Blanche's brother, Allannah was crying.

'I don't know what to make of you. I've threatened to have you thrown out of the school; I've told you Gary could come around and . . . and you're giving us tea and blocks and being so calm' — she laughed — 'and I can't think of anything that needs to be fixed. Except me, I guess, for not taking her to the doctor myself.'

'So, zero action required?'

'You know, Gary says 'chill out' all the time, and you're just permanently chilled.'

'I presume he was unhappy about the ophthalmologist.'

'I haven't told him. Blanche only told me last night. I feel I have to keep her confidence. And there's something else. She wants to get immunised.'

246

'I haven't spoken to her directly about that.'

'No, but Hudson has. And you're encouraging her to be a scientist. Which you'll understand we have mixed feelings about.'

'Science is — '

'Don't bother. We have to accept that she's getting old enough to make her own decisions. And because she's not a baby, they spread the injections out, so no system shock, right?'

I considered my answer. 'Zero evidence of system shock in older children.'

'Better I sign the form than she has to ask someone else. And you know I let her have a phone. You persuaded me on that one, too.'

I did not think of it at the time, but when Hudson arrived home, I asked him, 'How did Blanche afford a phone?'

He had already left the kitchen and was on his way to his room before he responded. 'I bought it for her.'

★   ★   ★

In the bar that night, I briefed Rosie on the Allannah confrontation. She admitted that she would probably have reacted exactly as Allannah had expected me to — combatively. I suspected that Hudson's approach would be more like mine: rational and problem-focused . . . and effective. Yet Rabbit had cited 'dealing with conflict' as an area in which he considered Hudson deficient.

I also shared the information about Blanche's phone. I hoped Rosie would be able to explain the unease I felt about Hudson purchasing expensive objects for another eleven-year-old.

'Does that mean he has a phone of his own?' said Rosie.

'Why would you assume that?'

'Who is Blanche going to talk to on her phone?'

I walked over to Hudson, who was discussing the app with a customer.

'Do you own a phone?' I asked.

He nodded and resumed his conversation.

'How much money does he have?' Rosie asked.

'I don't know. He trades books; the bar pays him for helping with the app; he's been doing some work on Carl's website.'

'What about Dave? Did Dave pay him for helping with the blocks?'

'It's possible.'

'It's not like he'd tell us. He's getting a lot more secretive.'

'He's in danger of becoming an entrepreneur. A capitalist.'

'In *danger* of?'

★   ★   ★

I was no longer accompanying Hudson to and from school, nor to his appointments with Phil, Carl and Eugenie, as a result of his tram pass and apparent mastery of the public-transport system. In the bar, he was generally in conversation with customers — frequently Merlin and Tazza — or coding.

At home, he spent most of his time in his room. I explained to Rosie that this was normal for an eleven-year-old.

'You're using yourself as a reference,' she said. 'Bad science. When you were a kid, there was no internet. For all his supposed confidence in adult company, he's still very vulnerable. Perhaps because of it.'

'Agreed.'

'Do you think you could have a look at his computer? Just to see what he's been doing?'

Incredible. Rosie was asking me to deliberately invade the privacy of a family member. To commit cyber-crime. On the vaguest of suspicions. Fortunately, there was a practical impediment.

'It's likely he has a password. He's intelligent and he'll have used some complex string.'

'Don, he's eleven. He likes hanging out with older guys. Plenty of parents would have installed some sort of filter or would insist on having the password.'

'We could do that. It would be more honest.'

Rosie won the argument, despite my reminding her of the nickname incident, where we had disregarded Hudson's wishes due to good intentions.

The technical quality of computer security is generally excellent. The weakest point is the involvement of humans. I did not expect to find Hudson's password on a piece of paper stuck to the underside of his desk. But I only needed a minute to walk into his room as Rosie distracted him while he was logged on and copy his browsing history to a USB drive.

The results were mostly predictable for an eleven-year-old entrepreneur interested in science fiction. He contributed to a discussion group for sci-fi book collectors, had a PayPal account that I had authorised for book trading and interacted with various online sites for that purpose. There had been minimal recent activity — no surprise, as he had been focused on the Library app.

The unexpected discovery was a series of visits to sites devoted to autism, including a diagnostic questionnaire — a self-administered adult instrument rather than a version for use by parents.

'Can you tell what he scored?' asked Rosie.

'No. The URLs are for the public websites. They don't include his responses or the derived score.'

'So, do we discuss it with him?'

'I thought the idea was not to reveal our unethical activity and hence turn him against us. As we did with the nickname incident.'

'You agreed to it. Anyway, it seems he's a step ahead of us, so maybe this is the time to tell him what the school's been thinking.'

* * *

Hudson's move to Ms Waddington's class had proceeded without apparent trauma.

'She's okay,' said Hudson as the three of us drove to the bar.

'Also, you've escaped from the class clown,' I said.

'Yeah. Jasper was a little out of control. But there was a kid who started annoying me, and Ms Waddington gave him a detention just like that. Bang. He says he's going to get me.'

'Is the threat credible?'

Hudson laughed. 'He's not big and his friends aren't . . . dangerous. So, probably not.'

'You'll tell us if he does anything?' said Rosie. 'Anything nasty.'

'Uh-huh.'

'Any other benefits of the class change?' I asked.

'I'm allowed to use my computer to write. And she lets me sit behind the screen.'

'*Behind* the screen?'

'Not the computer screen. A different screen. It doesn't matter.'

'Go on,' said Rosie.

'We're almost there.'

'We can wait. Tell us about the screen,' said Rosie.

'It's just a big whiteboard at the back of the room. It blocks out the rest of the class, so you don't get distracted. It's not punishment or anything: you get to choose. You can still hear.'

'Brilliant idea,' I said. 'Who proposed it?'

'I think Ms Mingos, the teacher's aide. She comes in to help with Dov. The kid with autism.'

It was the obvious opportunity to raise the topic with Hudson but by the time Rosie had pointed this out, I had parked the car and Hudson had gone inside, where staff would be setting up for the evening.

32

'Aren't you due for a night off?' Amghad had come in for an 'informal review' but had spent most of the time talking with Minh.

'We agreed that I would work every night for the first three months.'

'Always best to set the bar high and then ease off. And you've had your whole family putting in. Anyway, give some of the staff a chance to shine. I hear you're a bit of a control freak.'

'You want me to — '

'All good. But let's call it five nights a week from here till the end of the three months. Minh's fine with it. And we won't be keeping score.'

★ ★ ★

'I plan on taking Sundays and Tuesdays off as statistically they have the least orders,' I said.

'Fewest orders,' said Hudson. He laughed. 'You did that on purpose.' It was our first family dinner at home since the bar had opened.

'How was school?'

'Fine.'

'Stop it, you two,' said Rosie. 'Tell me about this screen you were talking about the other day. Isn't ... Dov ... pretty annoying? And he's trying to have time out and now you're there.'

'Not really. He's only there so he doesn't get

hassled. I don't hassle him; he doesn't hassle me. He's actually okay — he's pretty funny.'

'Funny hilarious or funny weird?' I asked.

'Both.'

'Do you consider him a friend?'

'Maybe,' said Hudson. 'I mean, he's weird, but I'm getting more used to weird people. And he's pretty smart. Doesn't code, though. He's into cars. He knows everything about Grandpa's Porsche: like, *everything*. You can ask him any question.'

'So, if we consider him a friend, you have a total of two, correct?' I said. 'Including Blanche.'

'I've got lots of friends. Maybe more than you. I'm not . . . isolated.'

'Don't you two turn this into a competition,' said Rosie.

'It's not a competition — it's a game,' I said. 'Dave.'

'Dave,' said Hudson. 'He's my friend too. Ask him.'

'Carl.'

'Ditto. Ditto Eugenie. Ditto George.'

Hudson was right. He and George had spent time together in New York. But he had spent minimal time with our other older friends.

'Isaac and Judy Esler,' I said.

'Merlin and Tazza.'

'Hold it,' said Rosie. 'I'm going to change the rules. Only friends within two years of your own age.'

'Unreasonable,' I said. 'Obviously — '

Rosie gave me the *zip it* signal. 'Start again.'

'Blanche,' said Hudson.

I was in trouble already.

'Dave,' said Rosie and followed it with a firm nod. I was apparently supposed to lie about Dave's age.

'Dov.'

'Judy Esler,' said Rosie and gave me the same signal. Judy was at least ten years older than me, but Hudson might not be aware of that. It seemed that, having defined the rules, we were conspiring to cheat against him.

'Hey, two on one,' said Hudson.

'He already said Judy,' said Rosie. 'And Dave. Two all.'

Hudson appeared to be searching his mind for additional friends.

'The point I'm making,' said Rosie, 'is — '

'Nadia.'

'Who?' said Rosie.

'A girl in my class. She's a friend. I'm not making it up.'

Rosie told me later that Hudson had turned red. I had been preoccupied with searching my mind for clues to Laszlo's age. Before I could find any, Rosie declared Hudson the winner and instructed me to serve dessert.

★　★　★

'Could you beat up a kickboxer?' asked Hudson. Despite it being a fine day, he had asked me to drive him to school. I guessed that the question related to Blanche's father, Gary the Homeopath. While a professional fighter of any kind would be a formidable opponent, I had no

254

information as to whether he had maintained his skills and fitness.

'It would depend on his or her proficiency. The world's best kickboxer would almost certainly defeat me, and the world's worst kickboxer would presumably defeat themselves without any action on my part.'

Hudson laughed at my joke. 'You said 'almost certainly'. How would you fight the world's best kickboxer?'

'As quickly as possible. Ideally before they realised that the fight had begun. Probably commencing with a leg sweep. Boxers are generally ineffectual on the ground.'

★   ★   ★

'*Why are you asking?* That's all you had to say.' Rosie was annoyed that I had answered Hudson's question without interrogating him about his motives.

'When I was at school, there were frequently discussions about whose father would be superior in a fight. In some cases, there was evidence to draw on.'

'You could be right, but how many kickboxers do we know? Maybe Hudson *is* afraid of him.'

Rosie raised the topic with Hudson while we ate crumbed barramundi and forty-five-per-cent celeriac mash. 'You should invite Blanche around for dinner sometime. Maybe we could ask her family.'

'Her brother's probably too little. Anyway, not for a while. She's pretty mad at her dad.'

Rosie nodded like a psychiatrist and Hudson remained silent.

'Why?' I said.

'He did the worst thing. He hacked her computer.'

I did not look at Rosie. Doing so might convey some non-verbal indication of guilt. I decided it would be less risky to focus on the facts than on the moral dimension.

'When?' I asked.

'Yesterday.'

'How? I predict he took advantage of human fallibility rather than technology.'

'Wrong. Technology.'

I felt an irrational annoyance that someone who might be better at martial arts than me was also an information-technology expert. 'Continue.'

'He had a video camera in Blanche's room.'

'What?' said Rosie.

'It's part of the security system. It's been there since she was a baby.'

'Is Blanche okay with — '

'Not anymore. She's put tape on it. But it was pointed at her desk. So he could see what her fingers were doing to get her password. Easy because her tablet's so big.'

I was impressed but decided not to share that assessment with Hudson and Rosie. 'A well-known technique,' I said. 'And highly immoral. Did he find anything?'

'She'd been looking up stuff about albinism. Der. And vaccination. That was a while ago, but he found it. Probably autocomplete. I think her mum defended her. That's why . . . ' Hudson stopped suddenly.

Rosie gave me an urgent *zip it* message.

Hudson looked uncomfortable. 'Can I be excused?'

'No,' said Rosie. 'I think there's something you need to tell us.'

Hudson did not speak for several seconds, and I did not need a second signal to remain silent myself.

'You promise not to say anything? Not like with the nickname, when you blabbed?'

'No,' said Rosie. 'We're not going to promise. Some things aren't right to keep quiet about. If you're going to tell us he's violent — to Blanche or her mum — we're going to do something about it. Do you understand why?'

Hudson said nothing.

'You made a promise, right?' said Rosie. 'To Blanche.'

Hudson nodded. I recognised myself as a younger person. I might not have seen beyond the rule that promises were not to be broken. Even now, I would need a strong opposing principle. Rosie had one.

'Which is more important? Keeping a promise or preventing someone from being hurt?'

Hudson nodded. He was 'taking it in'. Unlike most of the time when I delivered advice to him.

'I don't know for sure. She didn't say exactly what happened. But please, please, *please* don't get her into trouble with her dad.'

★ ★ ★

257

Rosie wanted to call the police. After a debate with herself, she decided that she had insufficient evidence to motivate any useful action. But she phoned the school the next day.

'Bronwyn listened. As you'd expect. And said all the right things: thank you, it's important that we know, and so on. She says they haven't seen anything with Blanche, but I got the impression she wasn't totally surprised. From what you said about his behaviour at the swimming, he doesn't exactly hide his anger.'

'Do you think we should still allow Hudson to go to their place?'

'What do you think? You're the one who's been there.'

'Blanche's father doesn't appear to interact with them. Hudson's only there for two hours maximum. And Allannah's always present.'

'I've made Hudson promise to tell me if there's anything that worries him. Oh, and there's a bit of a silver lining for him. They're moving Blanche into Ms Waddington's class for the last term. With him. There'll be some excuse, but they think she'll be better than Rabbit at picking up if anything's amiss.'

33

We were approaching the school holidays, when I would have more time with Hudson. And I had now met his two new age-appropriate friends.

I drove him to visit Dov, the autistic child. Although Dov's home was accessible by public transport, I needed to meet at least one parent or guardian and make an assessment of the home environment, as recommended in a document issued by the school. It was fortunate that I had not seen the guidelines before allowing Hudson to visit Blanche: insisting on an inspection of Gary's office might have been awkward.

On the way to Dov's, we discussed Phil's car. Phil had needed the Toyota, and I was driving the Porsche again. It was noticeably shiny, following panel beating, repainting and polishing. Phil had made me promise that I would not let Rosie drive it unless human life was at stake and there was no other option.

Dov had an impressive knowledge of the model. He noted that the vehicle had a 'turbo' body, which was wider than standard. I now had an explanation for its susceptibility to parking damage.

It was hard to detect anything unusual about Dov beyond a weight in excess of the healthy range (BMI estimated at thirty) and his knowledge of cars. As a child, I had studied particle physics, collected coins and developed a chess-playing computer program with similar intensity.

Dov's mother's name was Becca and she was *delighted* that Dov had a friend visiting. I conducted the house inspection and she accompanied me for the full forty-seven minutes, talking primarily about Dov, who had encountered similar problems to Hudson in dealing with the school environment and forming friendships. Dov had been diagnosed as autistic two years earlier, following unspecified problems with his behaviour.

'The diagnosis was unambiguous?' I asked.

'Oh my God, I wish. Our GP referred him to a psychologist, and she referred him to a psychiatrist, and we've been through every diagnosis under the sun: ADHD, OCD, anxiety disorder, bipolar disorder, early onset schizophrenia, personality disorder. They even asked if he was on drugs. Well, he is now, of course: they've thrown everything at him.'

Undoubtedly, 'everything' was an exaggeration, but I was reminded of my own experience with the psychiatric profession. Things did not appear to have changed much beyond the list of possible diagnoses and treatments being extended.

'But the current diagnosis is autism?'

'That's what his psychiatrist wrote for the school. To get the aide. Who, by the way, is great.'

'So, do you now consider the diagnosis sound and the treatment effective?'

Becca led me back to the kitchen before answering. 'How can we tell? He had a speech impediment, and he got a lot of teasing about it. He saw a speech therapist for a year, and he didn't like doing the exercises, but now he's happy he did.

'But the drugs. He's put on all this weight. He was difficult before and now he's less so, but he's lost something as well. You know, my mother was on this shopping list of medication: it had just grown over the years, and then she got a new doctor and he took her off everything and started from scratch.'

It took me a few moments to realise that Becca was not changing the topic but making an analogy between her mother and Dov.

'If you're intellectually capable, it's advisable to become an expert on your own body and treatments,' I said. 'Medical practitioners observe you far less frequently than you observe yourself. Also, they care less. With children and people with diminished cognitive function, we may need to take that role on their behalf.'

'It's good advice. I keep thinking, really, how bad was he before we started treating him?'

★ ★ ★

Hudson showed minimal interest in seeing Dov again. 'All he wants to talk about is cars.'

'Is it possible that he would make a similar complaint about you? Substituting science fiction for cars?'

'I'm a bit over science fiction. Anyway, I do lots of things.'

'Example?'

'The Library app. The blocks.'

'I thought you'd finished with the blocks.'

'I can't do everything at the same time. Der.'

'So maybe Dov is not locked into cars. Maybe you could find a topic of mutual interest.'

'It would be easier to find another person who was interested in apps dev. Like Tazza.'

*   *   *

I met Hudson's second new friend when I collected him from school to transport him to an appointment with the dentist. He did not walk out with Blanche, as he previously had, but with another girl.

'Where's Blanche?' I said.

He ignored my question. 'Hey, Dad. This is Nadia. Is it okay if I go to her place today?'

'You have a dentist appointment.'

'Today? Are you sure? Can we change it?'

'It's difficult to change. Is it possible to reschedule the appointment with Nadia?'

'Sure,' said Nadia.

'Aaargh,' said Hudson.

Blanche came out alone and I waved to her, but she didn't wave back, presumably due to not seeing me.

*   *   *

In the final week of the term, I received another call from the principal.

'I'm afraid we've got a problem. Quite a serious problem. Hudson's all right, physically, but he's in the sick bay, and I'm going to have to ask you to come and get him.'

'He's had a meltdown?'

'No. It seems he brought a knife to school. And killed a bird. It's not entirely clear. But I'm sure I don't need to tell you that this sort of behaviour is well outside what we can allow.'

It seemed incredible. Unbelievable.

At the school, the principal's assistant made an appointment for Rosie and me to meet with the principal the following day. She gave me the knife, which was in fact a scalpel I had purchased in anticipation of future dissections. Hudson had not asked me if he could borrow it.

The assistant directed me to the sick bay, where Hudson appeared to have been crying. He was now so angry that he was unable to give a coherent account of events. An actual meltdown. There was no point interrogating him until he was able to control his emotions. He had made some progress on that by the time we arrived home.

'What happened?' I asked, when we were seated in the kitchen.

'I broke the rules and now I'm going to be expelled.'

'This is definite?'

'The first part is.'

'We should restrict the discussion to the facts first. Table the evidence, then consider our options. Understand the problem, explore solutions.'

'You're not mad?'

'Mad-angry or mad-crazy?'

Hudson actually laughed, which suggested that he might be the one who was at least temporarily crazy. 'As a dad, you're pretty mad-crazy. Not to be mad-angry.'

'Do I generally get mad-angry with you?'

'I guess not, but I was sort of expecting it. Do you care that I might get expelled?'

'Obviously. But it wouldn't be a disaster. Like being fatally injured by a kickboxer.' It was probably a bad example.

'You remember the pigeon we dissected?'

'Of course. Blanche and I dissected it. You observed.'

Hudson nodded. 'Same thing happened at school. I didn't see it hit the window, but it was definitely dead. I didn't kill it. There's no knife mark. Proof. I bet they've got rid of it, so they can say there was a knife wound.'

'You consider you've been framed?'

'Someone must have dobbed. Only kids knew.'

'Possibly the student who threatened to get you — the one you didn't consider physically dangerous. He may have found a non-physical solution.'

Hudson nodded. 'I was going to dissect it, so it was in my locker.'

'Until you got the scalpel.'

Hudson nodded. 'Sorry I took it.'

'You didn't ask, so you knew it was the wrong thing to do.' I recognised my father's voice as I spoke.

'I *said* I was sorry.' That was *my* voice of forty years earlier. I needed to update the conversation.

'I thought you weren't interested in dissection.'

'I wanted to see if I could do it.'

'To impress classmates and win friends?'

'I just wanted to do it.'

Rosie spoke to Hudson independently and formed a different conclusion. 'I don't think he was trying to prove anything to his classmates. He's been uncomfortable about doing dissections — which I'd think would apply to ninety-nine per cent of primary-school kids. Blanche is a weird kid and you shouldn't take her as representative of anything. I think he wanted to prove to himself that he wasn't afraid of it. Without you looking over his shoulder, judging him.'

It turned out, as it invariably does when analysing human motivation, that there were more possibilities. I had scheduled coffee with Claudia, intending to review progress on the Hudson Project. I related the events and, at her insistence, the entire history of dissection training, even though most of it had involved Blanche rather than Hudson.

'Sometimes, if you want to understand a situation where things seem to have gone wrong, it's helpful to imagine that what has happened is exactly what the person — in this case Hudson — wanted to happen.'

'You're suggesting Hudson wanted to get into trouble and possibly be expelled? It seems totally irrational, and Hudson is not generally irrational. Unless overcome by emotions.'

'I'm not suggesting it's conscious.'

'Of course not. You're a psychologist.'

'Look at what's happened. He's demonstrated he's prepared to do a dissection, without actually having to do it. He's got a reason for leaving the school. And he's got yours and Rosie's attention: whatever else has been on your plates, for the next day or two it's all about Hudson. Proving you love him.'

'You think he might have doubts about that? Incredible. We — '

'Do you ever have doubts that Rosie truly loves you? Irrational doubts?'

'Excellent point. Possibility accepted.'

'It seems to me that you've been giving a lot of encouragement to his friend, but you've been critical of him. Maybe that's because you're more concerned about his development than hers, but all he's going to hear at his age is the criticism. And he'll translate that as you loving him less than her.'

Cycling home, I reflected on Claudia's theory that we have more control over our lives than we acknowledge. Was it possible that I had subconsciously engineered my suspension from the university? That I knew my class demonstration was likely to result in disciplinary action, and that I had then walked away rather than present an excuse which I had been assured would be accepted? That I had *chosen* to work in a bar and spend time with Hudson rather than continue what I had been doing all my adult life?

The more I thought about it, the less ridiculous it seemed.

266

34

Rosie took emergency leave the following day to meet with the principal. She was furious when she hung up the phone after advising Judas.

'So *fucking* predictable. First he gives me chapter and verse about why I need to be there — as if I didn't know.'

'Is there some unusual reason to be at work today?'

'It's our preliminary meeting with the funding body. Judas wanted me there as the lead researcher, obviously, but there's also a difficult person on the committee . . . '

'You didn't tell me that last night. It would have been — '

'Another argument for you to throw at me. I need to be at the school: it's not negotiable. Anyway, then he switched. 'We understand completely. *Of course* you can take whatever time you need.' We. Him and fucking Stefan. He might as well have just come out and said, 'Walk out and leave us in the shit — Stefan and I will deal with it. We get that you're a mum before you're a researcher.''

'I thought that was exactly your reasoning. Putting motherhood ahead of work.'

'You're not being helpful.'

'I'm being incredibly helpful. I offered to go alone. The offer is still in place. But you don't trust me.'

'I trust you, but I don't trust the school not to . . . '

'Fool me?'

'Shit, Don. It's a big deal. It needs both of us.'

I had one argument left, an argument based on empathy. 'If you had been Hudson's primary carer and I had been required at work, I probably wouldn't have considered attending.'

'Thanks. That's what Judas said.'

Hudson had the day off — Rosie assessed that he was informally suspended — and we had dropped him at Jarman's Gym after establishing that, with one term remaining at primary school, he did not want to change schools again: 'I just moved class.' He was significantly less distressed and correspondingly more rational.

We agreed that our goal should be simple: explain that Hudson had not killed the bird, that he was motivated by scientific curiosity and that he had been tutored in dissection. Unconscious motivations were not to be raised.

Rosie had, surprisingly, endorsed Claudia's analysis, even to the extent that I was routinely critical of Hudson. 'No worse than your dad was of you,' she said. I did not regard this comparison as a compliment.

We needed the school to agree that Hudson should not be subject to any undue punishment, which was unlikely to have any beneficial effect. Hudson already knew he had done wrong and was hugely regretful.

'If he'd killed the bird, it'd be different,' said Rosie, 'but he was just repeating something he'd been taught at home. He may be doing it in a few years in the high-school science lab, right next door. And they say he's not ready to move up. They can't have it both ways.'

I recommended that Rosie not project her anger towards Judas onto the principal. I thought it was an excellent insight on my part, but Rosie responded by projecting it onto me. She was calmer by the time we reached the school.

The principal, who in the past had seemed reasonable and open to discussion and argument, was noticeably unfriendly. There was another woman present — estimated age twenty-five, BMI not estimated due to stress — whom the principal introduced as a student counsellor.

'Ms Keen works with the senior school, but she helps us out in cases like this one, where we need some professional expertise. She's a qualified psychologist.'

'You're a clinical psychologist?' said Rosie. 'I'm sorry, I didn't catch your name.'

'It's Kellie. I've got a degree in psychology and — '

'Mr and Ms Tillman. We're not here to discuss Ms Keen's qualifications. She's a school counsellor and we trust her — '

'That's fine,' said Rosie, 'but I'm Hudson's mother and I like to know who's assessing my child.'

'Ms Tillman . . . '

'I'm Dr Jarman or Rosie, Bronwyn. I don't see that what happened yesterday needs a counsellor involved.'

'Well, you'll have to excuse me if I disagree.

Hudson brought a knife to school . . . '

'A scalpel,' said Rosie. 'A scientific instrument.'

'We're not here to — '

I interrupted in my role as good cop. 'The term *knife* is sometimes used as a synonym for *scalpel*. As in 'she went under the knife.' We understand that Hudson broke a rule, but we assume the purpose is relevant in determining the penalty. If he brought a knife to assist with eating his lunch . . . '

'He brought it to kill an animal. Your son cold-bloodedly killed a pigeon. If he were my child, I'd be concerned. I might be pleased to have some professional help.'

'Incorrect. He brought it to dissect the bird. A scientific experiment.'

'Mr Tillman, I'm afraid you're not listening. He killed a bird. Tell them what you think, Kellie.'

'I understand your son might have autism. If so, killing a bird would make sense.'

'You're an expert on autism?' I asked.

'Mr Tillman, *please*,' said the principal. *Bronwyn.* That was helpful in reducing the intimidation factor.

'No,' I said. 'Kellie is correlating autism with cruelty to animals. That will inform her judgement of Hudson. I want to know the basis of that correlation.'

'I'm not a scientist so I can't give you . . . data,' said Kellie. 'But I think we all know that people with autism don't feel empathy. Not like . . . people without autism. So, him not caring about how the bird would feel makes sense.' She smiled and nodded as though she had solved an equation that she had initially considered too difficult. 'Psychopaths would do that too. They don't care about other people's feelings either.'

'Aren't we missing something?' said Rosie. 'He didn't kill the bird.'

'I'm afraid he did,' said Bronwyn.

'You found a knife wound?' I said.

'Mr Tillman . . . '

'It's Professor Tillman,' said Rosie.

'*Professor* Tillman. This is not *CSI* and the bird has been disposed of. But I'm advised that Hudson killed it.'

'By whom?' said Rosie.

'The child who reported it was understandably traumatised. I may well hear from . . . their . . . parents. But they were absolutely clear that they saw him kill the bird. I have no reason to disbelieve them. And everything else was consistent with that: the knife and the bird in the locker. Hudson's story changed when he was challenged.'

Bronwyn's argument was compelling. But Kellie's had a flaw.

'Do you think Hudson lied?' I said to her.

'Well, it does seem that he hasn't been open and honest . . . '

'I thought that autistic people were incapable of deception,' I said.

I could see that Kellie was struggling to find an answer to my statement, which was, of course, a simplistic generalisation, consistent with her understanding of autism. But Bronwyn refused to be distracted.

'Professor Tillman,' she said. 'Let me cut to the chase. Hudson is suspended for the final week of the term. If he wants to come back, we expect him to get an autism diagnosis — which we are prepared to concede may be negative. But you heard Kellie say what the alternative is.'

'You think Hudson's either autistic or a psychopath, is that it?' said Rosie. 'Because a child claims he killed a bird. Do you — both of you, in your professional roles — realise what getting that wrong might mean for an eleven-year-old? *Do you have any —* '

I knew Rosie well. She would shortly insert a profanity, and the conversation would become emotional.

'I think we need a time-out,' I said.

'I'm sorry,' said Bronwyn. 'I chose my words poorly, and I can see that you are both trying to defend your son, as any parents would. But we've been having this conversation all year, not just because of one incident, and now it's come to a head. If we don't have a clear idea, from a professional — someone you're prepared to trust as well — about what we're dealing with, we can't ask our teachers at the senior school to manage him. I think that's fair, don't you?'

'When do you need the assessment?' I asked.

'We need to know by . . . no later than the end of the year. And, I'm sorry, but I have to be quite clear, if another incident like this — even slightly like this — occurs in the meantime, before we have a diagnosis, we'll have to ask you to withdraw Hudson from the school.'

★　★　★

We did not go to the bar that night, despite being scheduled to do so. Hudson had another meltdown, triggered by Rosie conveying the information that we had been unable to overturn the charge of pigeon killing. This was despite her telling him that we had not reached any conclusion ourselves, that we expected he would be able to remain at the school at least until the end of the year and that we would support him whether or not he had initially lied.

His anger did not seem to be directed at Rosie, me, the principal or even the informant: it appeared to be with the sum of the people and events that had resulted in what he perceived as a miscarriage of justice. 'Totally unfair.'

Hudson was insistent that he had not killed the bird. He admitted that he may have claimed that he saw it die: he had assumed it had been killed in the manner of the bird in our yard.

As a child, I had never killed an animal, but if I had, I was reasonably certain I would have lied to my parents, through shame at performing such an act. There had been a parallel situation when I had lost my watch through carelessness. I had to accept that Hudson might be doing the same.

While we were talking to Hudson, I had missed a call from Allannah's number. When I checked my messages, the voice was not Allannah's, but the one I had heard behind me at the swimming carnival and from the top of the stairs in the shop. As in both previous instances, it was belligerent.

273

'Gary Kilburn. We haven't met, but you know who I am. Calling to let you know that our daughter won't be having anything to do with your boy in future. I don't need to explain why. I hope you get some help for him before he does what he did to that bird to a human being.'

⋆   ⋆   ⋆

The following night, Rosie arrived at the bar with Hudson.

'You're not scheduled to work tonight,' I said.

'I know. Hudson wanted to talk to his friends and I need to talk to you. Maybe you too, Minh. I might need to work here full-time.'

'What happened?' said Minh.

'Judas.'

'It's always the boss who gets blamed. Rightly so.' Minh laughed.

'We had our first meeting with the funding body. Yesterday. I couldn't go because . . . it doesn't matter. A colleague went in my place. Afterwards Judas called his inside contact and apparently they loved him — the colleague.'

'So? They'll probably love you more,' said Minh.

'Judas has an issue with a woman on the selection panel. She's the consumer representative — which means she has a mental-health history herself. Judas translates that as unstable. Stefan won her over, so why risk someone else?'

'He can do that?' I asked. 'Put Stefan back in charge?'

'He can do whatever he likes from here on in.

274

I'm resigning tomorrow.'

'Why?' said Minh. 'Besides punishing your boss.'

'It's a good start.'

'I get it. But the work you're doing is so important.'

'Which is what he's blackmailing me with.'

'Wait till you've got another job lined up. One day someone with bipolar disorder who would have killed themselves or maybe just not been who they could have been is going to have made it because of you. And she's not going to care if your boss was a jerk or what your job title was or even who you are. Do the best for yourself and your dreams and the world. Forget about punishing your boss.' Minh laughed and sipped her mojito. 'I would say that. I'm a boss.'

'Does it make you behave like a jerk?'

She laughed. 'Ask my staff. They'd probably tell you I'm drunk on power.'

★ ★ ★

Lying in bed, I assessed the overall state of our lives. Three months earlier, I had been faced with a series of apparently insurmountable problems. I had, I believed, found a strategy for solving all of them, plus the unrecognised problem of not participating sufficiently in my family.

That problem had been solved: I was seeing more of Hudson, and Rosie and I were spending time together. I had seen my father more often before his death and learned something about him and our relationship. The bar — in hindsight, the riskiest part of my solution — was a success. If it continued to grow, and I paid off my share, I could one day be making as much money as I had as a stressed and underqualified researcher. The racism charge had presumably resumed its path towards being forgotten after the setback of the newspaper article. Dave was in Australia, earning money, losing weight and regaining self-esteem.

The problems I hadn't solved were, unfortunately, the most important. Rosie's work situation had reverted to what it was before. Hudson was unhappy, on the brink of being expelled from school, and banned from visiting his closest friend. I expected that our family situation would be dominated by these new problems for the foreseeable future. And though much of the Hudson Project was outsourced, it was obvious that the fault was mine.

35

Minh came into the bar again two nights later and I thanked her for her advice on the Judas situation, which Rosie had decided to take.

'It's easier to see what needs to happen when you're not part of it,' said Minh. 'What's going on with Hudson?'

I outlined the series of events.

'Maybe he killed the bird,' she said. 'Maybe not. A lot of weird shit happens in school. Maybe some other kid did it and he's protecting him. How was he going to catch a bird, anyway? I wouldn't worry about it, except for the trouble it's got him into. He's not the sort of kid who kills animals for kicks. You can trust me on that.'

Hudson was sitting alone reading a book. For the first time, he had not asked for *App Help* to be written on his head.

'You're familiar with children's behaviour?' I asked.

'I'm familiar with Hudson. And I've got two of my own.'

I was astounded, for no logical reason. It had never occurred to me that Minh would have children.

'Who looks after them?'

'How many times have you been asked by a business colleague, 'Who looks after Hudson?''

'Rosie has raised this topic previously with me. I shouldn't have asked. Apologies for the sexism.'

'You can pay me back by calling it out when someone else does it. But about Rosie and Judas: I think he's playing her. Anyway, you wanted to know about my children.'

'Inappropriately. Is there an appropriate way to ask? Since I'm interested and unlikely to use the information to oppress you?'

'The world's best grandmother,' she said, and laughed. 'I see them between getting home from work and coming here. They're in bed by then.'

'Do you have a partner?'

'The kids have a father and he's good, but no, I don't have a partner. You can tell Amghad if he hasn't worked it out yet,' she said, and laughed again.

Twenty minutes later, Minh interrupted me while I was muddling a lime. 'So now you guys have got yourselves a week of holidays where you don't have to compete for accommodation with all the other families with schoolkids.'

'Except Rosie still has her job and I have to work here.'

'You've got the week off if you want it. I just spoke to Amghad. I'll cover for you and he'll be around if I need help. Maybe Rosie can get some leave. If not, it can be a men's trip. Fishing and beer.'

Rosie authorised Hudson and me to be absent from the Monday to the Friday preceding the school holidays. *Encouraged* us.

'We should have put it in the marriage contract,' she said. 'Occasional time out isn't such a bad thing. Have you asked Hudson?'

'Not yet.'

'Take Dave,' she said. 'If it's just you, Hudson's going to feel he's under the microscope. And you hardly see Dave. After they came all this way.'

Rosie was right. Since the birth of Hudson, I had seen my friends less frequently. The move back to Australia had exacerbated the situation, as I had fewer friends here, especially with the deletion of Gene. With the block-making equipment installed at his residence, Dave was no longer visiting regularly.

Also, I recalled, Dave had fishing experience. I had avoided boating with my father due to seasickness.

Rosie had one more suggestion. 'This might be a good chance to bring up the autism thing.'

'It might.'

'Let me rephrase that. You need to bring it up. I think it's best that it's just one of us, so if he's upset he can speak to the other.'

I was becoming familiar with this protocol. 'So I'll be bad cop.'

'Your turn.'

'You get to be bad cop with the principal and I have to be bad cop with Hudson. The situations are not equivalent.'

'You get to have more time with Hudson to make up. So, mandatory task: tell Hudson about the school's desire to have him evaluated. Find out what he thinks. Choose a good time to raise it from his perspective rather than getting it out of the way as soon as you get in the car.'

'Can Dave be present?'

'Your call. I'm not going to tell you what to do.'

★ ★ ★

Hudson agreed to the trip, under certain conditions: route designed to include second-hand bookshops; meat at every meal unless we caught fish; no requirement to dissect fish. He strongly endorsed the inclusion of Dave.

I had assumed Dave would be required at home for child-minding duties, but he and Sonia had engaged the services of a specialist who could increase her hours for the week. Dave's income from block-making would cover the cost.

'You can invite Zina,' I said. 'Assuming she enjoys fishing and talking about baseball. And watching her father drink beer.'

'She's in school, remember?' said Dave. 'She was a bit righteous about Hudson being suspended and then going on a trip. You know how girls are.'

I had no idea how girls were, but the outcome was excellent. We took Phil's Toyota and drove towards Shepparton to collect equipment.

Dave plugged his phone into the car's USB port.

'No requirement for electronic navigation,' I said. But music began playing through the sound system.

'What's that?' I asked.

'Music,' said Dave. 'I figured you wouldn't have any.'

'I have podcasts, but I presumed they would not be of interest to all passengers, so I didn't plan to play them.' *Empathy*. Empathy would also suggest not playing hard-rock music that

280

would not be of interest to all passengers.

'You're okay with this?' said Dave.

'What era is it from?'

'It's Guns N' Roses. Early nineties.'

'Bad influence on Hudson. His musical tastes will be forming, and if he imprints 1990s music, he will lack common ground for communication with peers.'

'The voice of experience.'

'Correct. I didn't have any musical interests of my own and failed to advance from my parents' music.'

'Good point,' said Dave. 'We don't need the Rolling Stones handed down to a third generation. What sort of music do you like, Hudson?'

'I don't really listen to music.'

'You've got a phone? Get on the internet and see what station is playing music that's hot right now.'

At Tillman Hardware, there was some confusion.

'I've sorted out three rods and reels,' said Trevor. 'It's good gear, just a bit old, plus a couple of boxes of lures. It's in the garage at Mum's.'

'We have to go to Mum's?'

Trevor smiled. Something had changed in him since my father's death. I am relatively insensitive to body language, so the difference must have been dramatic. Dave was examining the stock.

'You're gay, aren't you?' said Hudson to Trevor.

'How did you work that out?'

'Dad told me.'

'Good. Because that's what I am. I hope you're okay with that.'

'Sort of. I get called gay at school because my two best friends are girls. Which is a bit weird, right?'

'I suppose they say it like it's a bad thing. It's not, unless you're ashamed of what you are. That's not a good way to live. Do you think you're gay?'

Hudson looked at me.

'I can probably tell you if you're gay or not, but not in front of your father. So, Don, go and help your mate choose the sandpaper. Like old times.'

★   ★   ★

'Are you gay?' I asked Hudson as soon as we were back in the car. Dave, in the front seat beside me, was surprised at the question, being unfamiliar with the earlier discussion.

'Probably not,' said Hudson. 'Uncle Trevor says nothing's certain, but he'd bet on me being straight.'

'What questions did he ask?' I doubted Trevor, despite his personal experience, was qualified to determine sexual orientation in an eleven-year-old.

'Basically, if I was attracted to girls or boys. I told him, and he said, 'Probably not gay.' He said he knew when he was my age.'

'There must have been other questions. You were talking a long time.'

'I wanted to know if he was going to have kids.

282

That's why I asked the question about being gay.'

'You'd like to have cousins?' said Dave.

'Not really. Actually, no. They'd just be little kids. And they'd have inherited the hardware shop.'

'Always the businessman,' said Dave. 'You're the only grandchild?'

'Uh-huh. But it doesn't matter. Uncle Trevor's selling the shop and moving to Sydney.'

I was shocked. My father's death; the sale of the hardware store after Trevor had achieved his lifelong ambition of owning it; Trevor moving away. The only reason for visiting Shepparton would be my mother.

★ ★ ★

'I'm thinking I'll move to Melbourne,' said my mother. She had insisted we stay for lunch, which consisted of processed ham and a salad containing canned beetroot, canned pineapple and canned asparagus. I explained to Dave that Shepparton was famous for its canning industry.

'I've had an offer for the house and I'm going to sell it. Trevor's moving out and it's too big for me.'

'But . . . you want to live in Melbourne?'

'I'll just get a little flat somewhere trendy. Where there's a bit of life. People, shops, things to do. Maybe near you and Rosie, so I can see a bit more of my grandson.'

'You could give us all your money and we could get a huge house with a granny flat,' said

Hudson. 'Nadia — she's a girl at school — her grandma lives out the back. Nadia doesn't like her but that's the price you pay.'

My mother laughed. 'You might all be a bit organised for me. I've had fifty-five years of that and I think I'm due for a break.'

★　★　★

Back in the car, Dave was using the contact time with Hudson to familiarise him with current popular music. I knew from my own experience that this would be an extended project: repeated listening was necessary to make sense of the complexities. The music playing on the radio was unfamiliar and hence impenetrable to me. But it reminded me that I had omitted an item from my list.

'Can you clap your hands in time with the music?' I asked Hudson.

'Why?'

'Because rhythm is crucial to dancing without looking incompetent. Basic social skill.'

Rosie and I had taken dancing lessons, and my principal challenge had been learning how to detect and synchronise with the beat.

'Can I do it some other time?' said Hudson. 'This is supposed to be a holiday.'

'Got my vote,' said Dave.

36

Although it was still light when we arrived at the lake, we decided to defer fishing until the morning. The house we had rented included a backyard, and Dave recommended that Hudson take a fishing rod outside to practise casting.

'I don't know how,' he said.

'That's what old men used to be good for,' said Dave. 'Now you've got the internet.'

Hudson and I began unpacking the vehicle. Dave was of limited use due to one arm being required for his crutch, but he seemed to be relying on it less.

'What's in this box?' I asked Dave.

'Blocks and chisels. I'm going to play with a couple ideas. Stop me snacking.'

'No risk of snacking. Due to absence of snacks.'

'Buddy, I've gotta thank you. You've saved my life. I mean, the weight's coming off; I've got a job. If the orders keep coming in, and I work regular hours, I could make more than I did in refrigeration. And Sonia's happy.'

Dave removed the cap from a 330 ml bottle of craft beer and raised it in my direction. 'You want one?'

'Too early. Alcohol shouldn't — '

'Doesn't apply to the fishing trip. Thanks, buddy. And to Hudson, too. I couldn't have done it without him. Junior partner in size only.'

Partner seemed an inappropriate label for an eleven-year-old who had offered some input to block design and set up a website, but in the interests of supporting Dave's positive outlook, I opened a bottle for myself and clinked it with his.

Hudson returned from the backyard. 'Can't do it.'

'Dave can show you how,' I said.

Dave put his beer down. 'I can't show you how, but maybe we can figure out these internet instructions.'

They were gone for an hour while I conducted pre-dinner preparations.

'Any improvement?' I asked when they returned.

Hudson laughed. 'The video was pretty bad. But we worked it out.'

'Good enough to get the lure in the water,' said Dave. 'After that, it'll be up to the fish. Are we going to barbecue this meat? There's a gas barbecue on the deck. You know how to operate these things, Don?'

'I can operate one, but I don't know how to calculate cooking times.'

'Hit the net again, Hudson. We're not cooking indoors when we can barbecue. What are we cooking, Don?'

'Kangaroo.'

'No way,' said Hudson.

Hudson had previously liked all forms of meat that he had tried but had not been exposed to kangaroo. Dislike of certain foods was a reported characteristic of autism. But if I used Hudson's behaviour as an excuse for raising the topic, I would be commencing the discussion with an item of evidence for a positive diagnosis — evidence that could be interpreted as a fault. This was going to be more difficult than I had anticipated.

'Never eaten it,' said Dave to Hudson, 'but I've got a trick. Works for all meat. Pretty much everything. You like ketchup? Mustard? Chilli?'

'Ketchup,' said Hudson.

Dave went to the pantry. 'We're in luck. Once you've slapped this on it'll taste the same as anything else with ketchup.'

I was horrified. Dave laughed. 'Look at your dad. He's in shock. You've gotta do it now.'

'You have to go first,' said Hudson.

'Sure,' said Dave. 'You want to cook it for us?'

⋆ ⋆ ⋆

The following morning, we went fishing. The ketchup trick with the kangaroo had been necessary only initially, and both Dave and Hudson had evaluated the meal as successful. They seemed in a positive mood, and I was confident we would now not have problems with the rabbit and the calf liver.

I had been surprised by Dave's lack of knowledge of fishing, but he explained that his experience had been from a boat and was not applicable to a lake setting.

'I thought *you'd* be the expert,' said Dave. 'You're expert at everything. Isn't he, Hudson?'

To my amazement, Hudson nodded. Dave's statement was entirely at odds with my own assessment of my capabilities, in particular those

287

requiring physical co-ordination. I shook my head.

'C'mon,' said Dave. 'Computers, karate, setting up a lathe. You're Einstein in overalls.'

'I wasn't naturally talented at anything physical. It took considerable practice.'

'Makes it even more impressive. When I was trying to lose weight, I was embarrassed because you seemed to be able to do anything you put your mind to and I couldn't even stop myself from eating a burger.'

'But you've succeeded.'

'You want to know how hard it's been? I've got a list by my bed. It's the first thing I see every morning when I wake up. Stuff to eat, stuff not to eat. And my weight. Updated every day. I need to see that number to keep me going.'

'Did you bring it with you?' said Hudson. 'The list?'

'Yep. But you don't get to see it. It's too embarrassing. Stuff like *Don't buy pretzels.*' He paused. 'And *Sonia doesn't like fat guys.*'

'She likes you,' I said. 'You've always been overweight.'

'This stuff isn't about logic. It's about motivation. Look at you. You've lost weight too.'

Keeping busy at the bar had reduced my alcohol intake and the weight loss had followed. Phil's advice had been correct, even though I had not consciously followed it. With the resumption of martial arts, I was in the best shape I'd been in since the Oyster Knife Incident.

Dave looked at Hudson. 'If you work at it, you can do anything you want.'

To someone watching, my attempts at casting a lure would probably have been comedic. The scenario was not hypothetical, as Dave and Hudson were watching — and laughing.

Their efforts were more successful: in fact, Hudson appeared to have acquired the skill more quickly than Dave. We stopped to eat the lunch I had packed, and, to my surprise, Hudson was interested in continuing afterwards. I was still having zero success.

'Get Hudson to show you,' said Dave.

Hudson demonstrated the technique, and, after multiple attempts, I managed to hit the water. 'Good work, Dad,' said Hudson. 'Now just keep practising.'

As the sun began to set, Dave got up. 'Need a bit of time out,' he said and walked away, leaving behind the crutch, which had been sitting on the bank.

He returned about ninety minutes later. He had caught two trout. He and Hudson high-fived. 'Had to get away from the tall guy scaring the fish with all his splashing,' he said.

While I prepared the trout, Hudson went to the backyard and practised casting. 'He did all right,' said Dave. 'Early start tomorrow?'

'I recommend finishing at lunchtime,' I said. 'I can use the afternoon to prepare a more interesting meal.'

Dave laughed. 'You having fun?'

'I am now. Rosie will be impressed by Hudson eating fish in non-crumbed form.'

'It's always different when you've been part of it. Like the roo on the 'cue. But you're still stressed. Trying to figure out what to do about Hudson, right?'

'I need to discuss the autism problem with him before the end of the trip. So we can proceed to solving it.'

'There's no solutions to that sort of thing. I mean, people stuff. Anyway, you solve one thing, another comes along. I hope what I said to Hudson about being able to do anything you want was okay. I don't really believe it anymore, but you have to when you're young.'

Dave opened two beers. 'By the way, the rhythm thing. Reason I pulled you up was he'd been keeping time on the back of my seat before you said anything. Slap-slap, tappity-tap, right on the beat.'

'Are you competent to judge?'

'My great-grandma was African-American. It's in my genes. Right?'

'Highly unlikely. But why didn't he demonstrate? He would have passed the test.'

'He likes to keep a few things to himself. Like the swimming. If you'd known he'd been training, you wouldn't have been so impressed.'

Hudson joined us. 'How about you and I let your dad catch up on his reading tomorrow?' said Dave.

'I need to be there,' I said. 'To — '

'Relax,' said Dave. 'We've got this.'

★   ★   ★

290

For the next two days, Dave and Hudson fished and returned for dinner. There were two more trout on the first day, both caught by Dave. On the second, Dave left his crutch behind and there was a total of five fish, two of which had been caught by Hudson. 'Dave helped with the first one, but the second one was totally mine,' he said.

'And he cleaned both of them.'

'Not as gross as a pigeon,' said Hudson.

'That reminds me,' said Dave. 'I've got a challenge. We can each ask the other guys one question, and they've gotta tell the truth. But it's between us. What gets said on the fishing trip stays on the fishing trip.'

'Unless it involves potential harm to somebody.' I remembered Rosie's concern about Gary the Homeopath. And I needed to clarify the process. 'As there are three of us, that means each of us asks the other two participants one question, hence a total of six questions. Correct?'

'You got it. Don, you can ask Hudson the first question.'

'I think I know what it's going to be,' said Hudson to Dave. 'Since you said, 'That reminds me' when I said *pigeon*.'

'You think it's about whether you killed that pigeon at school, right?' said Dave. 'You think that's the most important thing your dad wants to know? And you think we set this up so he could ask that, right?'

'Uh-huh.'

'You're wrong. On three counts. First, we didn't plan it. Second, it's not the thing your dad

291

cares about most. Third, we both know you didn't kill the pigeon, and your dad isn't the sort of guy to waste a question. If we're wrong, you'd better tell us now, and we'll both have to apologise for being idiots.'

'You're not idiots.'

By Dave's criteria, I had been an idiot, because I had been about to waste a question.

'You should go first,' I said to Dave.

'Come to think of it, it's probably not a great idea. We want to share something, we share it, and it stays here. We don't need to play games. I've got one question, though. For you, Don. You got another fish recipe?'

'You didn't like it?'

'It was great. Just good to have variety. I don't want to go out looking for trout tomorrow knowing I'm condemning us to the same meal three nights in a row.'

Hudson selected a trout recipe from the internet and, as we sat down to eat, on the outside deck, Dave made a serious — probably illegal — error of judgement.

'Would you like to try a beer, Hudson? If that's okay with your dad.'

It was definitely *not* okay. I explained, to both of them, about the damage to developing brains and finished by telling them that if I had my life again, I would probably have chosen not to drink alcohol at all.

Dave apologised. 'Sorry, I crossed a line there. Your dad's right.'

'He drinks less than he used to,' said Hudson. 'He was drinking way too much. Mum too. But I don't like alcohol anyway. It tastes disgusting. And burns.'

'Who gave you alcohol?'

'I work in a bar, remember? But Merlin.'

I was amazed that Hudson would dob in his friend, until he added, 'What gets said on the fishing trip stays on the fishing trip.' He laughed, for a long time. Then he added, 'He was trying to teach me *not* to drink. He's a recovering alcoholic — and drugs, when he was a teenager, not now — and he wouldn't go to a bar normally, but he says there's no pressure at The Library. Even when someone's buying a round, you input your own choice of drink and they can only see the price. That was one of the first changes I made to the app.'

'Interesting that we say *recovering alcoholic* rather than *person recovering from alcoholism*. As though it's intrinsic to who he is. Like — '

'He's also gay. Tazza — that's his partner — is gay, obviously, *and* autistic. He says it's easier to pretend you're straight than NT — neurotypical. Because autism gets into everything.'

Hudson had fortuitously introduced the critical subject, but he changed it before I could think of a way of making a connection to his own situation.

'What's happening next term? About the pigeon? Anything?'

'They want you to see a psychologist.'

'To see if I killed it? Could I take a lie-detector test?'

'It's more complicated.'

'They think I'm autistic. And they want me to

have an aide. Right?'

'Correct.' Rosie and I had not prepared a reply for this question but there was no choice unless I lied. 'They think it's possible. But they're not experts,' I said.

'If I see a psychologist, are they going to tell the school what I say?'

'I don't think so. But the intention is to communicate to the school whether or not you're autistic. Or have some other condition that would justify an aide.'

'What if I don't see a psychologist?'

'They say they won't accept you into the senior school. I think the state system is required to take you unless you're a psychopath. Which they might think if they accept the bird story. So, what do you want to do?'

'It's totally unfair.' It was obvious Hudson was angry. 'If the psychologist says I'm autistic and I get an aide, everyone will know.'

'Life isn't fair,' said Dave. 'I got born with the gene for loving food. And no gene for having kids.'

'You've got two kids.'

'Thanks to science. People like your dad. And if you're talking about fairness, he basically got fired for doing his job properly.'

At Hudson's request, I told the full story of the Genetics Lecture Outrage, including my concern that I had added to the daily burden of students who experienced discrimination.

'Mr Warren does that. I don't think he's actually mean, just . . . '

'Insensitive,' I said. 'Lack of empathy for

people different from him. Few people are mean on purpose.'

'But you're not a racist?'

'Who said he was?' said Dave.

'Just some kid at school. It was in the paper, right?'

'Check out his business partners,' said Dave. 'Would you go into business with people you thought were inferior?' He laughed. 'Maybe don't answer that. But we can all work on the empathy-and-kindness thing.'

'You should get a lawyer,' said Hudson to me.

'*You* should get a lawyer for the bird problem,' said Dave to Hudson. 'Maybe that's what you'll end up being. A lawyer. You're a smart guy and a good talker.'

Apparently Dave wasn't satisfied with leading my son into business.

'The ability to argue logically is valuable in numerous disciplines,' I said, 'including science and information technology.'

⋆   ⋆   ⋆

We drove home via second-hand bookshops and, again, Shepparton to return the fishing equipment and eat another salad featuring beetroot, pineapple and asparagus, this time with luncheon sausage.

'You learned to catch fish, clean fish and operate a barbecue,' I said to Hudson as we approached Melbourne. 'And to eat un-crumbed fish and a variety of other unfamiliar foods. Excellent result.'

I had only one issue to finalise before I could report complete success to Rosie.

'Have you considered the possibility of seeing a psychologist? It's optional, but you understand the consequences of not doing so.'

'I don't want to see a psychologist. Not to be assessed for autism.'

'Are you sure?'

'Don't worry,' he said. 'I've got this.'

37

On the first day of the new term, having spent the majority of the official school holidays in his room or visiting Carl, Eugenie and Phil, Hudson appeared for breakfast looking different. He had had a haircut a few days earlier, but there was something else. It took me a few moments to realise that he was wearing long trousers rather than shorts. With socks.

'You have new trousers for a single term?' I said. 'Part of the term will be in summer, when I presume you'll revert to shorts.'

'It's okay,' said Hudson. 'I bought them myself. With my own money. I might wear them even when it gets hot. Like adults do.'

'Some adults,' I said. I wore shorts in hot weather, regardless of season.

'We'll pay for them,' said Rosie. 'I'm amazed the length is exactly right.'

'I got a bigger size and Carl got them taken in. That's what you do when you're tall and thin.'

I remembered Carl's advice and checked Hudson's tie. It was slightly loose at the collar, as recommended.

Then he slung his backpack over one shoulder and headed for the tram stop.

★ ★ ★

That evening I had a phone call from Rabbit, which was surprising, as he was no longer Hudson's teacher.

'I've been meaning to thank you for being so . . . understanding . . . about the nickname,' he said. 'But that's not why I got in touch. There's a girl in Hudson's class who's had a rough holiday break. She's feeling guilty about something she's done, but she's dug herself a hole and she can't see her way out of it. I've pointed her to the student counsellor.'

It seemed odd that Rabbit would seek my advice on a teaching problem. I told him so.

'Mate, I can't say any more. Tell your wife exactly what I said. You want me to say it again?'

I told Rosie. She didn't even need the reference to Hudson's betrayer not being able to see her way out.

★ ★ ★

I persuaded Rosie that we should defer telling Hudson about Blanche's betrayal. Rabbit had spoken to me in confidence, and probably at risk to himself, and it appeared that Blanche was regretting her action. There was no change in the status with the principal, who already knew the identity of the informant. It was hard to see how anyone's life would be improved by sharing the information.

As the term proceeded, it became clear that Hudson had made changes to his routine. He attended the bar only once a week; Merlin and Tazza were always there on that day. They appeared to have a genuinely friendly relation-ship with an eleven-year-old. I guessed that if the conversation was restricted to apps development and science fiction, Hudson could contribute as an approximate equal.

I was required to conduct multiple inspections of homes of other students with whom he had become friendly. Rosie noted that the white shirts that she was washing were not the standard school-uniform-shop variety, but higher-quality branded men's shirts. 'Carl,' she said.

It was hard to judge whether Hudson was happier. At the bar, he seemed to be enjoying himself. When other children came home with him, they spent most of their time doing homework or reading. But neither Rosie nor I was able to observe him during the most critical part of his day — at school.

'He doesn't seem to be doing any worse,' said Rosie. 'Maybe we need to let him chart his own path for a while rather than trying to guide him.'

★   ★   ★

Approaching the middle of the term, Rosie and I had an emotional (on her side) discussion regarding which of us should accompany Hudson to the school sex-education night.

'I'm a doctor,' said Rosie.

'I'm a geneticist, with more experience in reproductive biology than you.'

'In mice.'

'I also participated in the delivery of a calf.' This was during Rosie's pregnancy, when I was acquiring expertise in case of an emergency. That expertise was employed to instruct a medical student in preventing a foetal death, specifically that of Dave and Sonia's daughter, Zina. I pointed that out.

Rosie pointed out that she was the medical student involved in the 'hands-on' role. I pointed out that the sex-education night was likely to be theory-oriented rather than hands-on.

I noted that I had initiated Hudson's sex education with the animal-mating video. Rosie pointed out that it had resulted in us being summoned to the principal's office.

'Don, I'm just a bit freaked out that it might turn out like — what do you call it — the Antenatal Uproar. You lecturing on breastfeeding or whatever the equivalent is. Kids having sex or something.'

'Obviously — '

'Look, the argument's fifty — fifty. So, let me go.'

'The notice said the school recommends a parent of the same gender.'

'Okay, we both go.'

'That gives Hudson no one to complain to in the event of a joint disaster. Which is your recommended tactic for difficult interactions. Also, one of us should go to the bar.'

'Right. You do know I have a day job?'

'Attending the sex-education night is also a job. We should let Hudson choose.'

'Okay, okay. I know what he'll want. But try to avoid saying anything. Nothing, *nothing* that would suggest underage kids having sex. No matter how much it happened in the . . . ancestral environment.'

'You're being controlling. That's not supposed to be desirable behaviour.'

'I'm probably suffering post-traumatic stress from that antenatal thing. We almost split up over it, remember?'

'Obviously. I'll attempt to remain inconspicuous and not mention child sex.'

★   ★   ★

Inconspicuousness should have been easy. There were approximately fifty parent — child pairs, presumably representing most of the students from Year Six. Hudson went to talk to Nadia.

Adults and children were milling around, and I was approached by a woman of about thirty, estimated BMI twenty-four, who introduced herself as Melanie Waddington.

'I saw you come in with Hudson. I was hoping I might catch you. I'm his new teacher.'

'I'm his father.'

'I guessed. I wanted you to know that Hudson's doing really well. When he joined the class, I was told he probably had mild autism — I gather you've had discussions about that — and we have another boy, Dov . . . Anyway, we had a little screen set up to give him some space and Hudson joined him behind that, but, you know, I think he may have been doing it just to be kind and friendly.'

'You don't consider Hudson autistic?'

'I've only seen him for a few weeks, but he's

not what I expected from talking to Neil Warren. He does get a bit excited when he's talking sometimes, but he stops himself. I can see him doing it. I get the sense he's using the change of class to make a fresh start.'

I saw Rabbit Warren as he entered the hall and intercepted him for an update on the Pigeon Betrayal. I was still hoping that some evidence that Hudson had not killed the bird would emerge. Rabbit had no further news but told me I had saved him a phone call on another topic.

'Always better to talk face to face,' he said.

On the contrary, face-to-face communication was likely not to be better if it required long-distance travel for a minor matter or if one or both parties was potentially violent. I could have cited numerous other examples, but I let Rabbit continue.

'I still take Hudson for sport, and I have to say, besides the surprise at the swimming carnival, there's been no great improvement. But Green House has elected him captain for the cross-country race.'

'Athletics?'

'We had that in first term. If I remember rightly, Hudson took the day off sick. This is a one-off event. We try to get all the kids to participate and each house votes for a captain. Hudson put himself forward and the kids chose him.'

'Excellent news. Clearly an indication of improved social standing. Thank you for telling me.'

'Well, to be honest, I'm not so sure. Have you seen him run?'

Hudson's running style was unconventional, with his hands clasped behind his back. Now that Rabbit mentioned it, I realised that it was likely to attract negative attention and should have been on my original list of capabilities.

'You're worried he may not contribute effectively? Surely that's unimportant at primary level.'

'I'm worried they've picked him as a joke. To make fun of him.'

★   ★   ★

Hudson and I sat together a few rows from the front. Allannah arrived and took the seat next to me, with Blanche on the other side.

The sex-education seminar was delivered by two specialist external teachers, one male and one female, with excellent visual aids. There were some simplifications, but they were probably necessary for a primary-school audience. Much of the material addressed physical development and respect for other students regardless of their gender or sexual orientation.

'Now this is an important question. At what age is it possible to become pregnant? Any doctors here?'

Somebody pointed to the person beside them and she said, 'I'm a maxillofacial surgeon. I think that's one for a reproductive-medicine person.'

Allannah whispered to me, 'I bet you know, right?'

'Approximately.'

She pointed to me! The female convenor saw,

as Allannah had obviously intended. My cover was broken.

'You're a . . . ?' said the convenor.

'Geneticist.'

'Aaargh,' said Hudson beside me, quietly.

'Does that mean you're able to tell us how young it's possible to become pregnant?'

'Not as a consequence of being a geneticist, but due to general wide reading.'

There was silence, then a murmur of laughter.

I elaborated. 'So, yes.'

'And the answer is . . . '

'Six weeks. Assuming you're a mouse.'

This time I earned significant laughter.

'Okay,' said Hudson. 'Good one.'

'And if you're a human?'

'Obviously there's a statistical distribution. At the extreme, in cases of precocious puberty, there are documented examples of six-year-old humans giving birth.'

Not unexpectedly, there was a general buzz of conversation.

'But the mean age of fertility in well-nourished human females is approximately twelve to thirteen years. If a girl has sex at that age there is a significant chance of pregnancy.' I had done exactly what Rosie had prohibited. Mentioned child sex. I needed to compensate, and fortunately had the perfect example for engaging the millennial mind: personal anecdote.

'Obviously few people have sex that young. In my case I was forty.'

The room exploded in laughter, and this time I knew they were laughing *at* me.

I was literally back in primary school, uncomfortable about the subject of sex. I had tried being the class clown and now I'd embarrassed myself by revealing personal information that others could use to mock me. And a room full of primary-school children — and, I observed, their parents — was doing that.

This was the scenario I had fantasised about in my twenties: returning to school with an adult's knowledge and responding to a perilous situation with an insightful and apposite statement that would demonstrate my intelligence and maturity.

Ideas were running through my head: statistics about age of commencement of sexual activity, which I did not have; psychological analysis of the personal defects that led to them finding my late start humorous, when it had been a cause of distress over many years; comparison of my own success in forming a long-term partnership with the world's most beautiful woman with their own possibly unhappy relationships.

None of the ideas translated into the required concise and irrefutable statement. Meanwhile, Hudson was saying 'aaargh' over and over. *Autistic people may repeat a phrase mechanically.*

I saw that the two convenors were conferring, and as the laughter finally died down, they began clapping and encouraging the audience to do the same. The male gestured for me to stand.

'I want everyone to understand what just happened,' he said when the clapping had stopped, 'because this is so important. The gentleman shared a bit of personal information that might have been embarrassing to him, and everybody laughed. Because that's what we do when someone talks about the things we're afraid of ourselves. Get them first before they get us.

'So, we got him. We all laughed. But it didn't mean we didn't like him. We're thinking, now if I share what I'm worried or embarrassed about — not with a whole room of people, because we're not all as brave as this gentleman, but with a good friend — it won't be such a big deal. They'll still like me, even if they laugh. And I think everyone here would be a bit happier trusting this gentleman with something personal, because he went first. Give him another round of applause, please.'

I sat down and Allannah squeezed my hand. 'You're amazing,' she said.

After the event, low-quality tea and coffee were served. Allannah and I continued our conversation while Hudson interacted with other children. Blanche was standing alone, eating a biscuit.

Allannah had a bruised eye due to a fall, but was otherwise well. She did not raise the subject of the pigeon but wanted me to know that her husband was now aware of the ophthalmologist visit and my role in organising it. He was not pleased.

'How did he find out?'

'Blanche let it slip. Better than if she'd mentioned the other thing.'

'Immunisation.'

Allannah nodded. 'I'm glad you came tonight.'

'Rosie was worried that I would say something inappropriate,' I said. 'Sex education is a minefield.'

Allannah laughed. 'You're the smartest man I know. No way would Gary have done what you did.'

★ ★ ★

'How did it go?' said Rosie when Hudson and I arrived home. 'Did your dad embarrass you both?'

'Totally,' said Hudson. 'Can I get something to eat?'

Later, I gave Rosie a summary of the evening and she was moderately positive. 'Good save by the facilitators,' she said. We agreed that if Hudson had been chosen as cross-country running captain, he should not be pushed to withdraw.

'Rabbit may be looking out for Hudson,' she said, 'but after the swimming event, he may be more worried that he'll do well and prove him wrong.'

'Possibly. Hudson's aerobic fitness should assist with running. But he'll need to train.'

'Maybe leave that to him and Phil. Did you see Blanche?'

'Briefly. She was with her mother.'

'No more signs of trouble at home?'

'How could I . . . ' Of course. The eye. I should have recognised the situation from my own experiences at school, when victims of bullying did not report it, because the intervention by the authorities would be short-term, but they would continue to encounter the bully daily.

Rosie wanted me to phone Allannah immediately, but I pointed out that she did not have a mobile phone and Gary the Homeopath would probably be monitoring calls on the landline, directly or via the security system.

'Don, this is one sick guy. One dangerous guy.'

'Is it possible Allannah was telling the truth?' I asked. 'About the eye injury?'

'Refer previous statement. Hudson's definitely not going there again.'

38

When I was in primary school, I was frequently sent to the headmaster's office, primarily by the religious-instruction teacher. It became a ritual that I would make some 'unhelpful' or 'peculiar' or 'disgusting' comment about Our Lord or the Holy Bible, be told to sit outside the office, then read a book until the end of the lesson. It would have been easier for everyone if I could have been excused from the class permanently rather than having to prepare an offensive comment every week.

I was again becoming accustomed to visiting the principal: four times already this year. On this latest occasion, I had been told that Hudson was not in any serious trouble, but that Rosie and I might be able to help with a situation that involved him.

'Sounds like one for good cop,' said Rosie. 'But don't give up any ground.'

The principal met me outside her office and took me to the girls' toilets. After determining that they were unoccupied, she invited me in.

'Is it possible you can describe the problem rather than requiring me to enter?' I asked. I had never been inside a female toilet facility in my life, and, despite the principal's assurance that the reason for the rule prohibiting males was temporarily not relevant, my mind rebelled.

'All right. I appreciate your reticence.

Someone has written, on the wall, *Hudson is innocent*. I'm not suggesting it's Hudson: I can't imagine he'd take the risk of going into the girls' toilets. Any more than you would.'

'If it's not Hudson, how can I assist?'

'I'm afraid it's not just this one instance, and it's become a bit of a distraction: it's been brought up in Religious Education. As you know, our classes are more about ethics and the kids think he's been treated unfairly. So now we're getting questions from the RE instructors.'

'*Thou shalt not bear false witness*. Whereas *Thou shalt not kill* is not applicable to birds, so the Bible considers lying a greater sin — '

'Something like that. I suspect Hudson's been encouraging it. And the student who told us about the situation in the first place is now more distressed than Hudson appears to be.'

I wished I'd had such support from my peers for the numerous injustices I had experienced at school. Bronwyn had not answered my question about my role in assisting, so I volunteered some advice.

'I recommend the application of basic legal principles. Hudson has not been proven guilty of killing the bird. You could announce that because of Hudson's denial, it was Blanche's word against his and — '

'How do you . . . What makes you think it's Blanche?' A girl approached the toilet block and Bronwyn led me away. 'Oh, for God's sake, all this secretiveness is doing my head in. The girl's seeing Kellie — you met her, the school counsellor — and she can't breach confidence.

She may just be distressed because she told on her friend, but . . . '

I could see the solution clearly, perhaps because I had analysed the problem for several weeks and discussed it with Rosie. 'The choice is between incorrectly accusing Blanche of lying — '

'Exaggerating.'

'Which is common among schoolchildren — and adults — or incorrectly accusing Hudson not only of lying but of committing an offence which implies a major personality defect, with possible lifelong damage and the immediate impact of him possibly not being accepted into high school.'

'I don't want to revisit the high-school situation. As you know, the problem was there long before the bird. Frankly, I don't know anymore if your son did kill the bird but this isn't a court of law. It's a primary school and we can't give in to this sort of thing.'

It was an unsatisfactory outcome, but I doubted that Rosie would have done any better. As I left, Bronwyn shook my hand and thanked me for being so understanding, given the impact on Hudson.

'I can't imagine it will be as pleasant if I have to call the other child's parents in,' she said.

It was reasonable for her to fear having to deal with Gary the Homeopath. I tried to think of something encouraging to say. 'At least it will help you to build resilience.'

★　★　★

I waited outside the school and intercepted Allannah as she left her vehicle. She moved to hug me, then remembered and pulled back.

'Hey, you were waiting for me,' she said and smiled.

'Did your husband cause the injury to your eye?'

'Don, don't go there. Please.'

'I've discussed it with Rosie. We're here if we can help. We'd like to help.'

'Rosie . . . ' She locked the car and put her keys in her handbag, then bent down beside Blanche's brother and spent an excessive amount of time adjusting his clothes.

'If you need thinking time,' I said, 'you don't need to perform some physical act as an excuse. I can wait while you stand still or walk silently.'

She laughed. 'You're so sweet. And you're very kind, but . . . Gary has an anger problem. It's not the way he wants to be and he's working on it. If he really wanted to hurt me, he would have done more than this. And he does so much good work for people.'

Allannah was using a net-utility argument that she must have known carried almost zero weight in the real world. My good work at the university had not been added to the negative impact of the Genetics Lecture Outrage to determine my overall value. Allannah must have realised her error, because she offered another excuse.

'If you knew what he went through as a kid . . . '

'It's still not a reason for violence.'

'There's a reason for everything. Even killing a

pigeon. Sorry, but he's never hit the children
. . . And . . . please, please don't say anything to
anyone at the school, but when I met Gary, I had
a drug habit. Gary had been there, but he
got into homeopathy and turned his life around.
He got me through it. But not the first time. Or
the second. He stuck with me. Without him, I
wouldn't be here. Whatever you say about
homeopathy . . . Gary and I are living proof.'

'Are you sure we can't do anything to assist?'

'You getting involved would just make it
harder for us to move forward. And Rosie
wouldn't be happy if you did.'

⋆ ⋆ ⋆

Rosie was *furious* with both the Allannah
situation and the principal's position. 'I want you
to call the police. They won't do anything, so
you won't be in trouble with Allannah, if that's
bothering you, but they'll have a note if
something else comes up.'

'Agreed. I'll report the incident tomorrow.'

With respect to the school, she wanted to act
immediately. 'They don't think he did it but
they're more worried about being seen to have
made a mistake than about Hudson's wellbeing.
We're pulling him out. Now. He can go to the
state school; it's only a few weeks and we'll work
it out from there.'

'We should talk to Hudson. Also, there's
probably nobody at the school now.'

Rosie put her phone back in her bag. 'The
voice of reason.'

'And empathy. All decisions about school are ultimately to advance Hudson's wellbeing. As you implied.'

Hudson didn't want to leave the school. 'The kids are okay,' he said. 'I think all schools are the same. Life isn't fair.'

'Tough conclusion to reach at eleven,' said Rosie later.

'He's quoting Dave. But he has surely experienced unfairness before.'

'You're right. I was eight when my mum died. I thought that was pretty unfair.'

I visited our local police station the following morning, and their response was initially as Rosie had predicted. But the policeman, a man of about my age, accompanied me out the door.

'You've done the right thing reporting it,' he said. 'But a word to the wise. Some blokes don't like their wives having good-looking male friends. Especially ones who shop their husbands to the police. Are you with me?'

'No.'

'Just watch out for yourself. If she's more of a friend than you've told us, have a good think about it. And don't tell her you've spoken to us.'

39

Three days after my visit to the girls' toilets, Hudson texted me from Eugenie's: *Can I stay for dinner? It's okay with Eugenie's mum.*

I texted agreement, but when Rosie arrived home, she insisted we phone Eugenie's mum, who was, of course, Claudia.

'Rosie wanted me to check that Hudson was okay. I assume you'd have contacted me if not.'

'Well, yes and no. I'm glad you rang. Hudson had a bit of trauma today, and shared it with Eugenie, and she sent it upstairs to me.'

'Your house has only one storey. Have you moved? Or extended?'

'Metaphorically upstairs. To a more experienced person.'

'He needed the services of a psychologist?'

'He wanted to talk to someone independent. What I wanted to know is whether I can keep what he says in confidence or if you want me to share it with you. I'll have to tell him whatever you decide.'

'What do you recommend?'

'I recommend telling him he can continue to speak to me in confidence, but I'll encourage him to share what he can with you in due course. Does that make sense?'

'Perfect sense. Does it involve a pigeon?'

'I'm afraid so.'

★ ★ ★

I waited until all three of us were sitting at the table the following evening.

'What did you and Claudia talk about yesterday?'

'Don . . . ' said Rosie, but Hudson was already answering.

'She said that you were a bit of a klutz in understanding other people's feelings, especially girls'.'

'That seems to be an incredible breach of confidence for a psychologist.'

'It's all men. It's in our genes. We only look bad because women are so good at it.'

'Claudia said that?' said Rosie. 'She's sounding like Gene.'

'Anyway, I did something klutzy too. With Blanche. She was my only friend, and then I started hanging out with some other kids and I didn't think about how I was *her* only friend. And there's a girl in my class that everyone thinks is the hottest . . . the coolest . . . '

'That would be Nadia, would it?' said Rosie.

'Yeah. That one. Anyway, Blanche didn't think I liked her — Blanche — anymore, and I guess if she had done that to me I would have felt the same. So she told her mum about the eye doctor. Then she dobbed me in about the pigeon. And made up the bit about seeing me kill it.'

'How do you feel about that?' Rosie asked.

'How did you find out?' I asked.

'She wrote me a note. She said she was sorry.'

'That was pretty brave of her,' said Rosie.

'Eugenie's mum agrees with you. So does Eugenie.'

'What do *you* think?' said Rosie.

'We both messed up. We should put it behind us, because being angry gets in the way of everything else. Eugenie's mum basically said that, but I agree.'

'Do you need to take some action?' I asked.

'I talked to Blanche. We're going to try to be friends again, but I can't go to her place and she can't come here, because she hasn't told her parents.'

'Has she told the principal? That she didn't see you kill the pigeon?' said Rosie.

'No. She'd be in huge trouble for lying.'

'Maybe not if she spoke up,' said Rosie. 'Or you could tell the principal about the letter.'

Hudson looked shocked, as I would have been. Rosie might know more about psychology, but she had forgotten the rules of school. In that context, as in the mafia, betrayal was more serious than all other crimes.

★ ★ ★

A disproportionate number of Hudson's classmates seemed to have birthdays in the final term, evidenced by Hudson attending a party almost every weekend, sometimes two. I formed a hypothesis that the children had been conceived as a result of more frequent sex or a careless approach to contraception during the summer holidays.

It turned out that my theory was incorrect.

Birthdays had occurred and parties had been held earlier in the year, but Hudson had in most instances not been invited and in the remaining instances had chosen not to attend.

He had become more popular and socially active since the fishing trip. Via Carl, he had obtained a new costume featuring jeans and shoes which resembled trainers but which were patently not well designed for that purpose.

He had resumed wearing his backpack with both straps, which seemed to be some sort of reversion, but he explained that Carl's advice had been out of date.

'Ever since *21 Jump Street*, it's cooler to double-strap,' he said. 'And that's forever ago.'

Rosie intercepted him as he prepared to depart for a party celebrating the birthday of Blake, the boy he had defeated at the swimming carnival.

'What did you buy him?' asked Rosie. She pointed to a long parcel which Hudson was carrying by a string tied to both ends.

'Just a bat.'

'A cricket bat?'

Hudson nodded.

'Are you sure it's the right size?'

'He told me which one he wanted. It's a good one.'

'For forty dollars?'

'I added some of my own money.'

'How much did it cost?'

'I can't remember.'

I would have abandoned the conversation at that point, but Rosie persisted. 'About.'

'A hundred.'

'It cost a hundred dollars?'

'No, that was what I added. About.'

'Where did the money come from?'

'Dave pays me for helping with the blocks. I have to go or I'll miss the tram.'

On the phone, Dave explained that Hudson had been modest about his contribution — and the compensation. 'He didn't just set up the website. He had the idea, he came up with the brand, he was the one who pushed me to charge about four times what I thought they were worth. He's earned his fifty per cent.'

'Fifty per cent? Of what?'

'Profit. All sales minus cost of materials. We're partners. Fifty-fifty. To be honest, I didn't think we'd make much, but now I'm looking at saving for Zina's college fund and I guess he's saving for his own. I thought you knew that.'

'Seems incredible. You're doing all the work.'

'I'm making more money than if I'd set it up myself. Not complaining. We shared the risk. I've had a business; I know how it works. But he'll be running Microsoft one day.'

I told Rosie.

'He's buying friends,' she said. 'And now he's done it for some of them, the others are going to expect it.'

'We can order him to discontinue the practice.'

'We can. He can tell the other kids that he's not allowed to buy expensive presents anymore. And I guess the invitations will stop.'

'Possibly that will be an important lesson

about human behaviour,' I said.

'I'm sure he knows it already. It'd be a better lesson if he stopped buying expensive presents and the invitations kept coming anyway. It'd be better if the world was like that.' She put Hudson's plate in the dishwasher.

'We were worried that he didn't have friends,' she said. 'Now at least he's mixing. He's found a way to do it, even if it's not the way we'd like. Maybe it'll kick-start some real friendships.'

We agreed that the ban would not come into force until the end of the school year, now only six weeks away. New rules could be set for high school. It seemed a logical decision, but I went to bed feeling uncomfortable. Hudson was in danger of becoming the sort of person I had disapproved of all my life.

40

'Come here,' called Rosie.

'What are you doing in Hudson's bedroom?' Based on what I believed Hudson would want — i.e. exercising *empathy* — I avoided entering his room. The exception was when Rosie had persuaded me to hack his computer, an action I continued to feel guilty about. He was currently absent, configuring my mother's internet access in exchange for homemade caramel slice at her new flat in Fairfield.

'*Cleaning*,' said Rosie. 'Which was one of the tasks my husband volunteered for when he gave up his day job. The room's a pigsty. And you can tell him that he needs to take a shower more often.'

I had arrived at the bedroom door. 'I thought we were letting him be himself rather than trying to mould him.'

'Tell him to shower every day and buy him a can of deodorant. Anyway, the reason I called you is this. Come and see.'

I needed to lie on Hudson's bed to read the sheet of paper that he had attached to his bedside table.

Run every day
Talk to Blanche
Parties
Don't talk about the app

No meltdowns
Nobody likes a show-off
SHUT UP

Beside *Parties* was the number eight, with earlier numbers crossed out. Presumably this was the number of events attended, at a cost to us of $320 for gifts and, extrapolating from the price of the cricket bat, approximately $800 to Hudson. The second half of the sheet was a series of integers in descending order, starting from sixty-four. The numbers above twenty-three had been crossed out.

I knew what it was immediately. I had kept the same count mentally as a child.

'Number of days left of term,' I said. 'I think he got the idea from Dave. On the fishing trip. Dave monitors his weight and — '

'Okay. I hear you.' Rosie spoke louder than was necessary and I sensed frustration. With me. I got up from the bed.

'This is so sad,' said Rosie. 'What are we doing to him?'

'It's about fitting in,' I said. 'We've tried to help him, but he's realised that he needs to do it himself. Psychologists agree that change needs to come from personal commitment . . . '

'Don, I've got a PhD in psychology. I don't need a lecture on motivation. I'm sad that he needs to do this at all. I love him as he is.'

'Agreed. Me also. But the world doesn't. The school world. A lot of the rest of the world.'

'That was your life, wasn't it?'

'When I was young. It wasn't just the world

that didn't like me. *I* didn't like me. I *wanted* to change.'

'You might not have wanted to if you'd been accepted. And you're okay now, aren't you?'

'Of course.' The answer was automatic: I was happy with Rosie, Hudson, the bar. But I needed to add, 'Except for losing my job and my best friend and almost losing you following the Antenatal Uproar and living in fear that I'll be accused of harassment or racism or misogyny or shot by the police due to a social error.'

'Wow,' said Rosie. 'I'm really sorry. Again.'

'Only one of those incidents involved you. But if Hudson is attempting to avoid problems of that kind, despite them being due to the human environment rather than him, we should support him.'

⋆   ⋆   ⋆

'Dov's going to St Benedict's next year,' said Hudson. 'It's a special school, but not just for . . . intellectually disabled. They take smart kids who have trouble reaching their full potential in the traditional school environment.'

It was Hudson's evening at the bar, but his friends had not turned up yet.

'Sounds like you know a bit about it,' said Rosie.

'Dov's mum had a spare brochure. He really wants me to go there.'

'Why you?'

'Because I used to go behind the screen with him. We're sort of friends. Actually, friends.'

323

'Would you like to see it?' said Rosie. 'Have a chat with one of the teachers?'

'Maybe.'

I was shocked. Despite the resistance that Hudson's school had displayed to enrolling him for the following year, I had no doubt he would be accepted in the government-school system, where principals were, according to the press, unable to expel drug dealers, knife wielders and apprentice terrorists.

And there were other private schools. But a 'special' school? It would be final proof that the Hudson Project had failed. And it seemed Rosie was encouraging the idea.

When Hudson had gone, I shared my reaction with her.

'We should let him have a look,' she said. 'I'm not saying he'll want to go there, but wherever he ends up, he's going to have some challenges. We don't want him thinking there's somewhere else that would've been better that he didn't get a chance to see.'

★　★　★

The headmaster of St Benedict's, whose name was Barry O'Connor, made the appointment for 5.30 p.m. so Rosie could attend without taking time off work. Hudson accompanied us.

'I'm sure you realise this is a Catholic school,' said Barry, whom I guessed was in his fifties and slightly overweight (BMI approximately twenty-seven). Rosie laughed, as though the school's religious affiliation had been obvious to her. 'But we get children from all backgrounds. I'm guessing Hudson's friend Dov may have a Jewish heritage.'

Barry gave a short speech emphasising the school's acceptance of human diversity. It was similar to the speech we had been given by Bronwyn the Principal prior to enrolling Hudson, but Barry illustrated it with numerous examples, including some featuring autism.

Whether or not Hudson met the diagnostic criteria for autism, it was encouraging to know that individual traits would be treated with understanding. I had observed that neurotypicals criticised autistic people for lacking empathy — towards *them* — but seldom made any effort to improve their own empathy towards autistic people.

My reflections had distracted me from the conversation. Hudson was speaking.

'What sort of ATAR scores does the school achieve? The top students.'

'Are you thinking of a particular university course?' asked Barry.

'Maybe Law.'

Law! I blamed Dave.

'And what has attracted you to the legal profession?' said Barry.

'Stuff that happens, everywhere — even at school. People get accused of things and don't get a fair trial.'

Rosie had been right. The Pigeon Betrayal had changed the course of Hudson's life.

'I must say that's an encouraging explanation,' said Barry. He looked hard at Hudson. 'You need good academic results — really good results — to get into Law straight from school. Some of our students do, but if that's your focus, you'll probably be better off where you are. If you can manage the social aspects.'

He turned to Rosie and me. 'A lot of our students are late bloomers: they go on to great things, sometimes very mainstream things like Law and Medicine and business careers, but often after a rethink in their late twenties or thirties. We're just as happy to claim them as our own.'

Back to Hudson. Barry was an expert focuser. 'Do you have any questions?'

Hudson nodded. 'What's the proportion of males and females?'

'We haven't always been co-educational, and it's taking a while for girls' enrolments to catch up. When you're talking about kids who have trouble dealing with mainstream schools . . . well, we get a lot of boys.'

'What are the proportions?' asked Hudson, again.

'We're about eighty per cent boys.'

Driving home, Rosie asked Hudson about the gender question.

'I need practice . . . interacting . . . with girls,' he said. 'So I'm not a late bloomer.' He laughed. 'Like Dad.'

'But overall?' I asked.

'I think it'll be good for Dov. Probably I'll go to the state high school. Unless my school changes its mind.'

41

For two weeks before the cross-country event, Hudson was focused on his role as team captain, to the extent of suspending work on the bar app, which was now reasonably stable. The race was over two kilometres, including some uneven terrain, according to the form we were required to sign.

'I'm not going to win,' he said. 'I've been training, but there are a few kids who've been doing athletics since they were about two, so they'll be faster. It's done with points: ten points for the winner, nine for second, eight for — '

'I've deduced the system. Seven points for fourth, correct?'

'Correct. But every finisher scores one point. I need to get everyone in the house to run and make sure they don't drop out, which can happen if you go too fast too early. That's the most common mistake. First step is permission forms. I'm making sure they've all been done.'

Hudson was still running through his plans as Rosie arrived home.

'Steady pace is best, with a sprint at the end. But going slow at the start is better than going fast. You should run the second half faster than the first. It's easier to catch up than to try to keep a lead.'

'Whew,' said Rosie, when Hudson took time out for some other task. 'I guess he's got something to prove. If his team wins, Rabbit will have to back down on his 'no good at team sports' thing.'

'Which was a major factor in the school's informal diagnosis of autism.'

'If you're thinking he'll change his mind . . . and persuade Bronwyn . . . I wouldn't count on it.'

★   ★   ★

Rosie took time off work ('I've stopped caring what Judas thinks') to attend the race. Phil was also there in his role as Hudson's coach. We gathered in a small grandstand at a public sports ground. The competitors would be required to complete a lap of the field after covering the dangerous 'uneven terrain'.

Phil looked around. 'Can't see Blue House Jerk,' he said.

'I suspect his daughter's vision would be inadequate. Fortunately, she's not in Hudson's house.'

We heard the starting gun, and about eight minutes later the first runners arrived — one in front, followed by a bunch of three — and began their lap.

'Should see Hudson soon,' said Phil about two minutes later, checking his phone, which was in stopwatch mode.

More competitors arrived, but not Hudson. Phil was becoming agitated. The winner crossed the line, followed by the three runners — two females and one male — who had accompanied her into the final stage. I assumed these were the athletes that Hudson had mentioned, and they provided a dramatic demonstration of the value of proper training. The next runner still had more than half a lap to complete, and a large number of children were spread out behind him.

Finally, Hudson entered the stadium, and the reason for the delay became apparent. He was holding the hand of a girl I immediately recognised as Blanche, due to the dark glasses, white hair and blue shirt indicating her house affiliation. On Hudson's other side was an overweight child — Dov, wearing a green shirt. He was clearly tired. Hudson patted him on the back and pointed ahead.

There was a huge round of applause and cheering, presumably for Blanche's courage in participating. But there was further drama to come. As soon as they commenced the lap of the field, Hudson released Blanche's hand and increased his pace. Dov took over the hand-holding role, and Hudson began overtaking runners. Phil was cheering loudly, but so was the remainder of the crowd.

'C'mon,' said Phil, not to Hudson but to us, and began pushing his way through the crowd in the stand. We followed as he broke into a run towards the finish line. 'They'll try to hug him,' he said. 'Don't want to spoil it for him.'

Hudson crossed the finish line and put his hands on his knees as he regained his breath. Phil spread his arms to shield Hudson from unwanted contact, then, when he straightened up, shook his hand. I noticed Hudson looking directly at Phil and concentrating on getting the handshake correct.

'Great work,' said Phil. You went past everyone on that last lap.'

'Where did I come?'

'Fifth. Perfect run for you. You were never going to beat the first four.'

'Did you see a girl with a green shirt? A super-tall girl?'

'She won.'

Hudson punched the air, then waited by the finish line until everyone had crossed. Blanche and Dov were not the last. Hudson shook both of their hands expertly, and then Allannah appeared and hugged Blanche and Dov, giving Hudson enough warning to allow him to have his hand out instead. There was a bigger cluster of people around Hudson than around the individual winner, and Rosie, Phil and I were now standing back.

'That's the mother, is it?' said Rosie.

'Correct.'

'She's young but . . . I had some amazing goddess in mind. Given what you've said about her.'

'She appears to be crying. Presumably with happiness that Blanche completed the course.'

Behind me, a male voice that I didn't recognise said, 'I can see why he's captain. Puts us all to shame, yelling our heads off for our kid's team and he looks after a girl from another house. He'll be prime minister one day. At least I hope so.'

'We'd like to think so, too. Unfortunately he

has a few challenges. But it's a lesson for the other kids. They see him doing this, with all that he has to overcome, and, well . . . it's quite inspiring for them.'

The second voice I did recognise. It was Bronwyn, the principal.

Two days after the run, Hudson brought home a notice.

Parents may be aware that a student was suspended for a week last term for bringing a sharp instrument to school. Parents and students should know that it is strictly forbidden to bring knives or any object that might pose a danger to staff or students. However, there has been some misinformation circulated about the incident, and we want to clarify that the student did not threaten or harm any person or animal, nor do we have any reason to believe that this was intended. The student has returned to school after receiving a week's suspension and there will be no further action.

'Blanche fessed up,' said Rosie. 'Has Hudson seen it?'

'Of course.'

'What did he say?'

'He wanted to know if he was now entitled to attend the high school without an autism assessment.'

'And . . . '

'Bronwyn considers the resolution of the Pigeon Betrayal to be irrelevant to the high-school question.'

Rabbit thought otherwise. 'Sorry I didn't get a chance to talk to you at the cross-country,' he said on the phone.

'Alligators,' I said.

He laughed. '*Correct*. But I wanted to encourage you to talk to Bronwyn. The story on the pigeon's no surprise to me, but I think she was having a bet each way. And we've had a lot of positive feedback from parents about what Hudson did for Blanche.'

He paused, then asked, 'Did Hudson know it was Blanche who shopped him?'

'Yes, but he had forgiven her.'

'Pretty good case to go in with. I'd make an appointment to see Bronwyn.'

'Excellent advice.'

'We do care about these kids. If you've got a minute, I've got a story that you'll probably appreciate more than I did at the time.'

'You can have longer than a minute if it allows the inclusion of interesting detail.'

'Right. Well, we were playing cricket — and by the way, Hudson's not the worst catcher in his year anymore. I had both classes of boys, and one of them said about something they didn't like, 'That's so gay.' I have a problem with that expression, so I sat them all down and laid it out, nuts and bolts, what being gay really means.

'We had a family member ... It doesn't matter, but you know, they listen to the sex-education stuff, but they don't really get it. Well, by the end of my little talk they got it.

'So, there's a kid who used to give Hudson a bit of a hard time, when he was in my class, and he'd planted himself behind Hudson and was apparently fiddling with his hair, and Hudson blurts out, 'Hey, that's why Jasper plays with my hair. He's gay.'

'You know what kids of that age are like. They just laughed and laughed and wouldn't stop — absolutely not at Hudson but at Jasper. It was hardly an ideal outcome as far as I was concerned but — ' Rabbit stopped suddenly.

'Is there some problem?'

'Obviously I wasn't happy with the idea that being gay was a negative, but I think the reason there was so much laughter is that the kids see Hudson as a sort of truth-teller. But now I think about it, I wonder . . . whether it could have been deliberate. As though he was . . . using it. Sorry, you've probably no idea what I'm talking about.'

I knew exactly what Rabbit was talking about.

★   ★   ★

We didn't need to visit the school. When I called Bronwyn, she indicated that the autism-assessment requirement had been lifted.

'I've had it pointed out to me, by people who know more than I do, that what he did for Blanche — especially after what *she'd* done to him — doesn't fit with autism. Nor does helping out someone from another house when he had his mind set on getting the points. Kellie was quite embarrassed to have got it wrong.'

'Presumably the school will be arranging some education to prevent her getting it wrong in the future. With possibly devastating consequences for students.' Kellie's assumption that autism was not compatible with altruism and care for others had worked to Hudson's benefit but was patently false. Laszlo was one of the most selfless and generous people I knew.

'I ... Actually, that's a fair point,' said Bronwyn. 'But there is one thing. Kellie did ask me to check with you that he wasn't coached.'

I hesitated, but I could see no reason not to tell the truth. 'I don't understand why it's a problem, but he was coached.'

Bronwyn breathed in, quickly.

'His grandfather is a personal trainer. I understood that other participants had received athletics training for much longer.'

Bronwyn laughed. 'I was thinking about him helping Blanche.'

'I would never have thought of that idea.'

'I believe you.'

Kellie's concern with Hudson being coached seemed unreasonable. None of us is expert in all situations. It is a sign of intelligence to recognise our limitations and of maturity to seek help when required. The school had zero problem with him being coached in the physical aspects of the cross-country run but apparently would have thought him deficient if he had sought help with the psychological component.

★ ★ ★

I waited until dinner to tell Rosie and opened a bottle of sparkling wine.

'What are we celebrating?' said Rosie.

'The completion of the Hudson Project.' I felt I could use the name in front of Hudson, now that we had achieved an unqualified success: not only acceptance into high school, but withdrawal of the autism conjecture by the counsellor, the principal and Hudson's teacher. I had advised Hudson of the principal's decision and he had appeared pleased. Correction: triumphant, as indicated by air-punching.

The school's decision was the ultimate goal, but it had been accomplished through improved social skills, as evidenced by his negotiation of the Pigeon Betrayal and leadership of the cross-country team; improved physical performance, as evidenced by his sporting successes; and improved empathy, as evidenced by his understanding of the Blanche problem.

He had acquired other important competencies, many of which were relevant to social interaction and hence acceptance: fishing, ball catching, bike riding, running, swimming, gift selection, barbecuing, computer programming and requirements analysis, costume selection and use, and business entrepreneurship. Reflecting on the last of these, which would not have been on any list of competencies devised by me, I added 'independent thinking'.

The school appeared, finally, to have acknowledged his progress. 'I'm giving a speech on graduation night,' said Hudson. 'Only a few kids get to do it. I wasn't on the list, but Ms Williams added me.'

'How do you feel about that?' asked Rosie.

'Good. Most of the other speakers are scared.'

'You're not?'

'I like talking.'

'Can Dave and Sonia attend? Possibly with Zina,' I asked.

'Sure. Why?'

'They've known you since you were a baby,' said Rosie. 'They'll want to celebrate with you.'

'Also, we've agreed to go to Zina's play. They will be obliged to reciprocate.'

42

Zina's school play was almost a disaster, given that our sole reason for attending was her involvement. There had been some issue with her costume, and she had refused to participate until it was resolved, which had apparently involved significant effort on Sonia's part.

Hudson took a book and read during all of the proceedings except Zina's play, which Rosie compelled him to watch. It was *terrible*, as was to be expected of a production written and performed by primary-school students. Zina played the role of a teenager visiting from New York, which did not require, as far as I could observe, any special costume.

We left Hudson at Dave and Sonia's place in the care of the child minder and had dinner at a Greek restaurant. It was the first time we had eaten together since Dave and Sonia's arrival in Melbourne and they were scheduled to leave shortly before Christmas.

'That's what you get with a job and kids,' said Sonia. 'But you've been with us in spirit all the time, in what's happened with Dave. You saved us, you know.'

'I think Dave saved himself,' said Rosie.

Since the fishing trip, Dave had been walking without the crutch. 'But I'm not going back to refrigeration,' he said.

'Do the blocks provide sufficient income?' I asked.

'That's the way it's looking. If it drops off, I'll find something else to make.'

'And you don't need to share the profits if you do,' said Rosie. 'This is Hudson's mother speaking in his own interests.'

'Dave's kept me up to date on the problems you've been having with him,' said Sonia to Rosie. 'I guess you must have thought about going back to part-time?'

'I did for a while, but he's doing a lot better. And Don's been great with him.'

'He's grown up a lot,' said Dave.

'Zina's growing up too,' said Sonia. 'Eleven going on seventeen. It's a shame the two of them haven't had more to do with each other.'

'Why?' I said. 'They seem to have completely different interests.'

'You're probably right,' said Sonia. 'Girls mature a lot faster.'

'What did Hudson think of her performance?' said Dave.

Rosie answered. 'Don't ask what an eleven-year-old boy thinks of an eleven-year-old girl's performance at the school concert. You're coming to see Hudson?'

'Yep. But I gotta say, it'll be tough to match what the kids put on tonight.'

★ ★ ★

'I think Hudson's freaking out a bit about his talk,' said Rosie as we showed Minh how to make a Smoked Sazerac. The bar had been running well with less involvement from us, and we were becoming like her — enjoying our ownership without having to work too hard. Having criticised Hudson for making money as an entrepreneur, I was at risk of doing the same.

'He indicated that he was confident,' I said. 'Have you seen evidence to the contrary?'

'I have seen evidence to the contrary. Balled-up paper.'

'He's using paper to write his speech?' Something was wrong.

Hudson was currently in the process of intercepting two women who were walking towards the bar. We still took some orders through personal interaction, but Hudson would draw new customers' attention to the app and offer assistance.

The two women had a conversation with Hudson, brief but long enough for me to notice something.

'I think the woman on the left is the one who asked me the question at the lecture. And recorded the video. It's possible that her companion was sitting next to her.'

'Are you sure?' said Rosie.

'No.'

'Get out of sight. Let me do this.'

'What are you going to say?'

'I don't know yet. Out of sight.'

I moved into the space between the bar and the kitchen, where, due to the low noise level, I was able to listen to the conversation. Minh was working behind Rosie.

'Excuse me,' said a voice that I was reasonably certain was the one that had asked me about the genetic basis of race, 'I was wondering — the woman making the cocktail, can you tell me her name?'

'Why?' asked Rosie.

'This is going to sound strange, but I just interviewed for a job . . . '

'Her *dream* job,' said the other woman. 'And she's going to get it.'

'Don't. But she looks so like the woman who interviewed me . . . '

'For a job here?' said Rosie.

'No, actually in a genetics lab. I've just finished my qualification and I want to work in genome editing. My second interview was with the CEO . . . ' She gestured towards Minh.

'Hard to imagine a senior geneticist working in a bar,' said Rosie. 'She's Vietnamese, and I guess they all look a bit similar, right?' Rosie laughed and kept laughing till the two women joined in.

'Go on,' said Rosie. 'You have to admit it.'

'I guess.'

'Come to think of it,' said Rosie, 'I shouldn't have said that. Sounds racist, doesn't it? But you agreed with me. What do you think, Don?'

I stepped up to the bar.

'Oh shit,' the first woman said.

'Don lost his job in genetics after being accused of racism. You have to be so careful. Now he owns this bar. With Dang Minh, who I understand you've met. They're partners. Let me get her for you.'

'Oh shit,' she said, again.

'Small world, genetics,' said Rosie.

'Please,' she said. 'I was only trying to . . . just

. . . Like, this job, it means so much . . . '

'Don's job meant a lot to him,' said Rosie.

What Rosie said was true, but now there seemed to be an implied threat that I might use my relationship with Minh to exact some kind of revenge.

'Obviously I won't interfere with the process of job selection,' I said.

'You won't? Oh God, do you really mean that?'

'Of course. It would be totally unethical. If you're the most suitable person for the job, I hope Minh is able to employ you. We need the best people working in genetics. Did you want to order a drink?'

'You realise how frustrating you are, don't you?' said Rosie when the two women had left without ordering a drink. Then she laughed. 'I'm sort of glad you let her off the hook. I used to be a lot like her.'

'Used to be? Are you suggesting there's been some change?'

★   ★   ★

'Do you require help with your speech?' I asked Hudson.

'You can't help. It's impossible. What they want.'

'What do they want? If we have a clear specification we can evaluate whether there is likely to be a solution. If not, we can advise the school, and seek a more reasonable specification.'

341

'They want me to talk about why I held Blanche's hand. In the cross-country. Instead of just trying to win. That's *all* they want me to talk about.'

'Is there some problem with providing the reason? The audience would be interested in why you did it. Presumably it was a result of friendship or altruism.'

'Great. You want me to say, 'I helped Blanche do the cross-country because she's my friend.' Or 'I helped Blanche do the cross-country because of alt . . . ''

'Altruism. Performing an act because of its intrinsic merit rather than any benefit to yourself. Such as making a donation to charity. An anonymous one.'

'Dad, I have to speak for *two minutes*.'

'Is the content non-negotiable?'

'*Technically*, I can say whatever I want. But it's what the principal suggested. We all had to go into her office, together, and she 'suggested' what we should talk about.' Hudson used air quotes. 'Guess what Blanche is supposed to talk about?'

'I only know about Blanche's interest in becoming a scientist.'

'That's because . . . you don't think like the principal. It's about overcoming her disability. I'm just trying to fit in. Not do anything that sticks out and looks weird.'

'You've already qualified for high school. You can take a break from fitting in.'

It was possibly not the best advice, but it was automatic. Any break from the pressure to fit in

342

was to be exploited without hesitation.

It was never easy to interpret Hudson's expressions, but I sensed relief. We were on the way to solving the problem. Father and son.

'Can you drive me to Eugenie's?' said Hudson. 'I'll talk to her.'

43

On the day of Hudson's school graduation, Rosie arrived home from work at 2.46 p.m. 'I've had enough for today,' she said. 'Done my duty.'

'Was the presentation a success?'

'It was weird. Stefan presented, and then the committee asked me most of the questions. Stefan figured that they were happy with him and just wanted to check out his number two to make sure of the depth, but . . . '

'Do you think you'll get the funding?'

'I don't know. Like I said, something was weird.'

Fourteen minutes later, my phone rang: Simon Lefebvre's number. Judas. Rosie had gone to the hairdresser.

'Don, can you talk?'

'There's some problem?'

'I need you to speak to Rosie. Urgently.'

'She's not answering her phone? I can probably find the hairdresser's telephone number.'

Simon hesitated. 'I'd rather go via you. I can trust you to be . . . rational.'

'There's a problem?'

'I need her back in front of the committee in an hour. Look, this is good news; I'm going to let her front the project. She's told me that's what she wants, and I've reconsidered. Apparently, she did brilliantly in the presentation today and she's been a real trouper . . . '

'Why did you demote her originally?'

'Does that matter now? Look, I thought with all the problems with . . . your son . . . I was doing her a favour.'

I reflected for a few moments. The reason he had given to Rosie involved a potentially unreliable committee member, not concern for Hudson.

'Don?' said Simon.

'Tell me the truth,' I said, 'or I'll terminate the conversation. It's impossible to reach an optimum solution based on false information.'

'Don, that doesn't sound like you. Not taking someone's word. We've known each other — '

'Correct. It's atypical for me. My default position is to assume honesty, but obviously that has to be modified by evidence. You're a habitual liar and hence not trustworthy.' My experience with Gene had provided a valuable, if painful, lesson.

'I think that's a bit . . . ' He abandoned the argument, for obvious reasons. 'All right, Don, you're a rational man, you'll relate to this. I was trying to be gentle with Rosie. It actually is about the problems you've been having with . . . '

'Hudson.'

'Hudson. Rosie's had to take leave, go part-time, come back full-time, rush off to school meetings. Stefan's there every day, on schedule, nine to five. His mind's on the job. Given the choice, who would you have taken?'

'Ridiculous question. It assumes there are no other variables. You considered all parameters and hired Rosie.'

'Stefan's a psychologist. I needed an MD for medical cred. You asked for the truth. And all things being equal, she's the better researcher. But all things aren't equal.'

'Why do you want to reinstate her?' Judas had already given me a reason, but it made sense to ask again, now that I had demanded truthfulness.

'She's . . . The funding body have apparently got another organisation to partner — which means to put in money — and when they advised them of the change to the chief investigator, they threatened to pull out.'

'Why would they care who leads the project?'

'Between you and me, I'd say it's a feminist thing. Affirmative action. The other party's a medical-research company run by some Vietnamese woman.'

* * *

Hudson accompanied me to the hairdresser, where an employee was combing paste into Rosie's hair.

'You need to abandon the hair processing. For a second interview. Simon has re-promoted you.'

'I'm not — '

I explained the situation.

'Too late,' she said. 'And I'm totally pissed off that he phoned you. If he'd phoned me, I'd have hung up on him.'

'Obviously he realised that. Very astute. You could have used the 'washing your hair' excuse. Without deception.'

346

'Anyway, it's Hudson's speech night. This is a chance for me to show what's more important.'

'Aaargh,' said Hudson.

It was easy to translate. 'After Hudson has had to accept a change in parenting because of the importance of your research, it would be extremely annoying — '

'I hear you. But this is a big night. I really need to be there.'

'You have to go to the interview,' said Hudson. 'I don't want people to commit suicide because you came to my speech night.'

'Get this in your head,' said Rosie. 'You are not responsible for the consequences of other people's decisions.'

'Dad said — '

'Enough. I'll go. We'll talk about this later, though. What time are you on?'

'It's the last item,' said Hudson. 'I'm going to be the first speaker because I'm the most confident. Anyway, Dad will be there. Grandpa will video it if you don't make it. Even if you do make it.'

⋆   ⋆   ⋆

'Where's your speech?' I said as we departed for the school.

Hudson tapped his head.

'What if you lose your place?'

'I have a good memory. And it has a structure. The way you remember a speech is to divide it into blocks, which you think of like boxcars on a train — '

347

'Carriages.'

'Carriages, linked together, numbered . . . '

Hudson explained the speech-memorisation technique as we collected my mother and proceeded to the school.

The hall was almost full when we arrived. Phil, Dave and Sonia were waiting for us, without Zina, who was not feeling well.

As we walked to our seats, we were intercepted by a man of about forty wearing a suit without a tie, who introduced himself as Ewan Harle.

'I'm the senior-school principal. The incoming principal. Bronwyn pointed you out. I was hoping to catch you and Rosie.'

'Rosie has a work emergency.'

'Sorry to hear it. She's a doctor, isn't she?'

'Correct.'

'Well, I hope the patient is okay.'

'She's a researcher. Hence potentially thousands of patients will be impacted.'

Ewan Harle nodded. 'Good point. It's funny how we relate better to the idea of someone delivering a single baby than doing something that might have a global impact.'

It seemed odd to bring obstetrics into the discussion, but I let him continue.

'I've been filled in on what happened with your son and wanted to apologise on behalf of the school. Not only about the bird and the knife.'

'Scalpel.'

'Ah, I didn't know that. I gather there was some . . . encouragement to have your son assessed by a psychologist. All I can say is that if you and Rosie and Hudson make that choice, and it gives the school an opportunity to provide some targeted assistance, we'll work together. It's a fine line between encouraging and shaping, but it's our job to find it.'

'I like him,' said my mother, who considers herself able to make judgements of people on the basis of almost zero information. 'He knew Hudson's name.'

Ewan Harle joined the junior-school principal on the stage but seemed only to be there for ceremonial purposes, an incredible waste of a senior professional's time. A hologram or even a cardboard cut-out would have achieved the same purpose.

The preliminary performances were similar in style and content to those we had witnessed at Zina's school but shorter and of a higher standard, due to only Year Six students participating. They included a percussion combo, featuring Hudson playing bongos. Competently, it appeared. Another item on the list successfully completed, without intervention from me.

Dave leaned over. 'Told you he had rhythm.' He laughed. 'That's what he's been doing with George.'

Not stimming, drumming. Even Rosie and I had made the mistake of seeing Hudson's behaviour through the lens of autism.

'Your wife still tied up?' Ewan Harle had come down from the stage, apparently to speak to me.

I checked my phone. 'She's on her way.'

The final item was described as 'Six of the Best from Year Six'. The printed program had not been amended to reflect the recent addition of Hudson. The number could have been returned to six by deleting Blanche, who had received a week's suspension as punishment for her role in the Pigeon Betrayal, but I agreed with the school's decision not to exclude her.

Blanche had acted unethically, but she was only eleven. I had made mistakes at eleven, too. Being judged and punished by adults had not made me any less likely to make them again, any more than it had in later life. And she had undone the harm she had caused, at some cost to herself.

My phone vibrated. *Stuck in traffic.*

Hudson had told us he would be the first speaker. Phil was focusing the video camera, and my mother nudged me with an unnecessary reminder.

But instead of Hudson, the principal introduced Blake, the swimming champion and cricket-bat owner. Blake gave his speech, the audience applauded, then Bronwyn introduced the second student. Then the third and the fourth. Something was obviously wrong. Meltdown? Nerves? Illness, possibly as a result of pressure?

I looked at the program again, with no mention of Hudson's name, and had a terrible flash of insight. Hudson had never been on it. He had wanted to impress us and had tried too hard. Perhaps he had planned to tell us before Rosie's work crisis intervened. But now there was no escaping the deception. What would he do? Where was he? I tried to stifle my rising

350

panic as the fifth speaker was introduced.

My mother jumped to her feet. I looked around for Hudson, but it was Rosie at the side door. She saw us and squeezed past to the seat we had reserved on my other side. I was about to explain the situation, but Rosie pointed to the stage.

There was another expert problem-solver in the room, one who was innovative enough to be able to re-sequence a schedule at short notice. Ewan Harle was looking directly at us, giving the two-thumbs-up signal.

44

The principal introduced Hudson by describing his assistance to Blanche in the cross-country run. Hudson had been right. His speech as specified would have been pointless, since there was little to add to what Bronwyn had already said. In fact, many in the audience would have seen the race.

Hudson stepped up. It was apparent that he was nervous, but less so than the preceding students. They had read from the lectern, but Hudson took the microphone from the stand, removed his glasses, then stepped to the centre.

'God, he's going to give a TED Talk,' said Rosie.

A voice said quietly, but loud enough to be heard by the audience, 'Psycho.' It was *the* voice. Gary the Homeopath.

'He won't hurt you.' My mother's voice was louder and there was a ripple of laughter.

Hudson didn't appear to have heard. He was already speaking, faster and more articulately that the previous students. It was how he normally spoke, but the contrast was startling. I estimated that he would be able to pack seventy per cent more content into his speech.

'Three months ago, I was suspended for killing a bird. Slitting its throat with a scalpel. Some people thought I did it because I was autistic and one day I might kill a person.'

Phil whispered, 'He's got their attention.' I was thinking that *slitting its throat* was the sort of detail Gene would have included to make a lecture more dramatic. Perhaps a lawyer would do the same.

Rosie was holding my hand, firmly. My mother grabbed my other hand. If I was required to applaud, I would be unable to.

'I didn't kill the bird. If I had, I don't think Ms Williams would have asked me to give a speech.' Hudson smiled and paused for the first time. There was laughter. He was nodding his head, and I guessed that it was a rehearsed action: *Stop here and count to some specified number.* Eugenie had done an excellent job in preparing him, but Rabbit had also described him as a competent public speaker.

'This year I learned that I *was* autistic, and I learned that a lot of people think autistic people are weird or uncaring or not good enough to go to a normal high school.'

My left hand — the one being held by Rosie — was suddenly under increased pressure. There was no change to my mother's grip on my right hand.

I concentrated on Hudson. The hand that was not holding the microphone had begun as a fist but now had two fingers extended. Two boxcar topics: the bird; discrimination against autism. Given human anatomy, it was likely that he had a maximum of three more points to make.

Finger number three. 'My parents and teachers tried really hard to help me fit in because they didn't want people to think I was autistic and then assume those things about me. This semester I decided to show that I can do all the things that 'normal' people do' — Hudson illustrated his point with a one-handed air-quotes sign — 'and I think I managed to, because I've been accepted to the senior school.'

There was sustained applause. I didn't clap, and nor did Rosie or my mother, and not only because our hands were being used for connection purposes. Having spent six months helping Hudson to fit in, I was now feeling uncomfortable with the outcome. I was also aware that he had not finished his speech but was waiting for the clapping to finish. His fourth finger had uncurled.

'But it took a lot of work that I could have spent on other things, like getting good marks and going to the bar.' More laughter. 'It's our family business and my dad designed it to be a comfortable place for autistic people.'

Finger number five: 'What I learned from the bar is that autistic people shouldn't have to do all the changing, and my goal is to make the world a better place for people who are different.'

The audience clapped for a long time. They obviously hadn't observed that he had closed his fist again and uncurled another finger. I guessed his time was almost up.

'Next year I'm planning to go to a special school, so I can practise being myself without pressure to act like someone I'm not, and when I'm ready I want to come back here to get the best chance of being a lawyer while still being myself, so I can advocate for people who aren't good at speaking for themselves. If that's okay with Mr Harle.'

He turned to the senior-school principal, and the audience erupted in laughter and clapping. Hudson didn't move until Ewan Harle smiled and nodded his head, and then he walked off the stage as the audience applauded again. There were a few moments of audience discussion while Bronwyn went backstage to retrieve the microphone, which Hudson had taken with him.

'Nice work,' said Phil. 'Put the headmaster on the spot. He'll be a lawyer all right.'

Bronwyn returned with the microphone and reinserted it in its holder. 'It looks like the teachers in the senior school have an exciting time ahead, and maybe Hudson will reconsider coming here next year,' said the principal. 'We say we embrace diversity, and we have had parents and students in the past who have held us to that challenge, and that only makes the school stronger. I'm sure Hudson's parents are proud of the maturity that he's shown in finding his way.'

The phrases were similar to those my academic managers had used regularly, and which I had ignored regularly. But, doubtless because it was our son who was the subject of them, I found that my eyes had become wet. Rosie was now holding my arm. My mother was nodding.

The final speaker was, of course, Blanche, who was guided up the poorly lit stairs by Dov, carrying her oversized tablet computer. The principal introduced her with a reference to her impaired vision, which was obvious to the audience.

Blanche was more nervous than Hudson had been and took a few seconds to get started.

'First of all, I don't want anyone to think Hudson's my boyfriend.' It was the sort of statement that could be expected to provoke laughter in primary-school students, which it did, and also in their parents, who had apparently been infantilised by the environment.

Blanche was smiling. 'She did that on purpose,' said Rosie. 'She's a smart kid.'

'But,' she said, 'we worked on our speeches together, so I knew what he was going to say. Everything he said was right. Also, he's a really good person, except for being obsessed with space travel and computers and not with personal hygiene.'

There was laughter before she continued. 'This year I learned four important things.' I looked to her fingers, but she was reading, so no counting was necessary.

'One was that I want to be a scientist and that it's possible to be vision-impaired, even completely blind, and be a scientist.

'Two was that your parents and teachers know heaps more than you do, but they don't know everything. That's a problem when you're a kid and you're not sure about something important. You have to do research and then decide. My dad is not in favour of conventional medicine, but I decided to go to a doctor about my eyes.' She looked at her tablet for a moment and then looked straight out at the audience. 'And get immunised.'

From several rows behind me, I could hear Gary's breath being blown out from between pursed lips, as it had been when Phil challenged him at the swimming carnival.

'Three: I hung out a lot with Hudson, and I'm probably autistic too. It's not so easy to see in girls, and nobody would notice it in me anyway because my albinism is the big deal. But I did the test and guess what?

'Four is that I learned that people can be super-kind and most of what I just talked about was because of Hudson and his dad, who — Hudson said I could say this — is as good a person as Hudson and maybe even a bit weirder.'

She looked up. 'This wasn't in my speech, but I hope Hudson comes to the senior school next year so he and Dov and me . . . I . . . can help each other. Thank you.'

Again, there was a great deal of applause. Hudson was right about me not caring about being called 'weird'. But, despite the term having been used by others in the past year to describe Hudson, I had never thought of him as actually weird — possibly because we might both be weird along the same dimensions.

'Wow,' said Rosie. 'Did you have any idea he was going to say that? Or Blanche?'

I shook my head.

'Shh,' said my mother, as the principal was delivering platitudes again. Then there was the actual graduation ceremony. It was over before I had finished processing Hudson's revelation that he had self-diagnosed as autistic and chosen to announce it in public. And Blanche also.

357

As we stood to leave the hall, Dave and Phil were congratulating me for Hudson's speech, and Sonia was hugging Rosie in the way people had hugged at my father's funeral. I noticed that Rosie's hair was looking strange: two different shades of red.

Rosie spoke to me over Sonia's shoulder. 'Blanche's father may have mixed feelings about what she said.'

Rosie was wrong. Gary the Homeopath's feelings seemed to be wholly negative. I identified his voice as we walked towards our designated meeting point outside the hall: 'You piece of shit.'

Then I saw who he was speaking to: *Hudson*. He was using aggressive and potentially threatening language to a *child*. *My* child. I was instantly angrier than I could ever remember being: at risk not of a meltdown, but of committing a physical assault.

Finally, I saw Gary the Homeopath in person. He looked almost exactly as I had imagined him, though bigger — not as tall as me but more powerfully built.

If Hudson had studied martial arts, he would have known what to do, which was to run away. Instead he was standing beside Blanche, only a few metres away from Gary. As I approached, Allannah interposed herself between Gary and the children, and Gary half-pushed and half-struck her out of the way.

Phil walked straight up to Gary and grabbed him by both shoulders. Gary expertly broke free, created distance, then kicked Phil in the knee, precisely and extremely hard. Phil went down, and Rosie said, loudly, 'I'm calling the police.'

'They can arrest him,' said Gary, pointing to Phil, who appeared to be in pain. 'I'm entitled to defend myself.' Then he turned to Hudson again. 'I'm not finished with you.'

'Yes, you are,' said Allannah. 'We're going home. Now.'

'You're staying right where you are until I've dealt with this little shit.'

Allannah walked back to Gary and grabbed him by the arm, and this time he held on to her, but didn't move. He turned back to Hudson.

It seemed inconceivable that he would strike a child, but I did not want to take the risk. He had already assaulted Phil and Allannah.

'Go inside,' I said to Hudson.

'Do what your father said,' said Rosie.

Hudson walked but stopped just behind Rosie.

Gary was now looking at me. Angrily. Aggressively.

'You. You're the piece of shit who poisoned my daughter. You had her assaulted.'

'Incorrect.'

'By doctors. And you've been hanging around my wife like a fucking bad smell. You've got a kid on the way, haven't you?'

It took me a moment to remember Allannah's excuse for hugging me in the shop.

Gary pointed towards Hudson. 'Might want to think about skipping the vaccination this time.'

People leaving the graduation had gathered around us, and I had a flashback to my schooldays when students shouting 'rumble' would summon a crowd to observe a fight, until a teacher arrived to separate the antagonists either physically or with threats of punishment.

In this case the teacher was Rabbit. 'That's enough,' he said, and put his hand on Gary's shoulder. Gary twisted and flung Rabbit away, delivering a blow to the side of his head that he could probably claim was accidental.

'Anyone else want to have a crack?' said Gary, looking at me.

'Are you talking to me?' I said. It was a genuine question of clarification, but it came out sounding like a challenge.

'Don, don't,' said Allannah.

I had never used my martial-arts skills in a genuine fight. I had once prevented two bouncers from assaulting me, but that had been the result of a misunderstanding. Nobody was hurt, and we shook hands after they realised that I had not taken advantage of the situation to inflict injury. There had been a low-impact encounter with police in a New York playground, also as a result of a misunderstanding, and no charges were laid. On the occasion that I had broken Phil's nose, we were using boxing gloves, so it was a formal contest — technically, sport.

The first rule of martial arts is to avoid physical conflict whenever possible. I did not know how competent a fighter Gary was. If he had once been a professional kickboxer, he was likely to be superior to me. His disabling of Phil had been swift and expert. Rosie was kneeling beside her father, making a phone call.

'That's enough,' said Rabbit. 'I'm going to

have to ask you all to go home.' Ewan Harle was standing beside him.

There was no visible reaction from anyone. We were not planning to go home but had pizza scheduled, which Rabbit would not have been aware of.

Gary looked at me. 'You want to have a go, do you? That your mate on the ground?' He dropped his arms loosely to his sides, a transparent attempt to appear helpless and entice me to engage in combat. He smiled. 'Didn't think so. You're going to run away like Rain Man. He's watching you, you gutless piece of shit.'

I was familiar with the Rain Man reference and pointed out the problem with using it as an insult. 'Your daughter also considers herself autistic.'

'Piece of *shit*.' He took a step towards me and I stepped back.

'Don,' said Allannah, 'walk away. Please. He's a kickboxer.'

'Shut the fuck up,' said Gary to her, and took another step towards me. I stepped back again.

'If you touch him, I'm leaving you,' said Allannah, presumably to Gary, as Allannah and I were not in a relationship.

If I did not follow Allannah's recommendation to walk away, I would be implicitly agreeing to a fight. Any injuries I sustained would be my own fault.

In my role of martial-arts teacher, if a fight was unavoidable, I would have counselled myself to use a leg sweep, at which I was highly

361

proficient, to defuse the situation. It would be unlikely to cause serious injury and had the advantage that it would be illegal in most forms of kickboxing — hence my opponent might not be expecting it and would not have a practised defence.

Kickboxing skills are of minimal use on the ground, and the humiliation of being dumped would probably resolve the situation. I would win the fight, and the next day I would have the satisfaction of knowing that I had not taken advantage of a person who was agitated and would likely regret his actions.

Unfortunately, the optimum leg for the sweep manoeuvre, given the geometry of our positions, had been injured in the Oyster Knife Incident, and would be at some risk of re-injury. It was always better to walk away.

Gary was positioning himself for the knee kick, carelessly telegraphing his move. Then a male voice behind me said, 'Smack the bastard.' It was probably the use of the word 'bastard', but I was reminded of George and the bully at school who had put him in hospital and not suffered any consequences. I had always trusted the advice of my friends in difficult social situations and, though the real George was in New York, my response was instinctive.

I stepped forward to confine the kick, which Gary would not have expected, as I had previously retreated. I took advantage of his momentary surprise to hit him in the left eye as hard as I could. He was strong and experienced enough not to go down but did not react in time to block my other fist, which I used to deliver an equivalent blow to his right eye. While he was disoriented, I executed the sweep with my uncompromised leg to put him on the ground.

At that point, Rabbit and Ewan Harle intervened, and I indicated that I had no intention of causing further injury. I was shaking, and my hands were hurting, but I did not think I had broken any bones — at least, none of mine.

'You okay, buddy?' said Dave. He put his arm around me, and, oddly, it didn't feel too uncomfortable. Standing beside him was George. The real George, smiling.

'Flew in this morning,' he said. 'Fell asleep in the hotel and almost missed it.'

Dave was laughing. 'I gotta say, I was wrong. You guys had the bigger graduation night.'

45

'You agreed we would get pizza.'

An ambulance had taken Phil to hospital. He was pleased that I had not walked away from the fight and pointed out that his knee was due for a reconstruction in any case. He had given me the keys to the Porsche.

'Please don't let Rosie drive it,' he said.

Gary had accepted mainstream medical attention from the woman who had identified herself as a surgeon at the sex-education night.

'He'll have to tell people he fell over twice,' said Rosie. Her mood had improved since I explained that nobody — including Allannah — was pregnant with my child.

My right hand was wrapped in a handkerchief to prevent blood leaking onto my clothes, but Rosie had confirmed that neither hand was broken.

Rabbit had assured me that if the police or school authorities investigated, he would state, correctly, that Gary had been abusive and had approached me with the intention of committing an assault. Apparently there were multiple video recordings.

But now the uninjured members of our party were standing outside the school fence, and Sonia had suggested that we should go home. Immediately. Without pizza. After all that had happened, she wanted to add further disruption!

'Pizza is unaffected,' I replied to Hudson.

★　★　★

I had made a reservation at our preferred pizzeria and elected to drive there alone in Phil's car to allow time for reflection. I was still shaking from the violence, which I knew had been excessive. It was a terrible example for Hudson and any other children watching, except in terms of the symbolic triumph of science over pseudo-science. Fortunately, I could blame George. It was not surprising, given the stress, that I forgot to take into account the unusual dimensions of the Porsche.

The remaining members of our party were seated in the restaurant with drinks on the table by the time I had given Phil's contact details to the driver of the other vehicle.

'Was the speech okay?' said Hudson.

'I've already told him it was great,' said Rosie. 'So have Dave and Sonia and George and your mother, and I've told him that Phil thought it was worth going to hospital for. Your son got virtually a standing ovation, but he'd like to hear from his father as well.'

I had time to prepare my answer, as the waiter arrived to take orders.

'Disaster,' I said, when the waiter had completed her task. 'You failed to mention altruism.'

Hudson looked surprised, then smiled. 'Ha ha.'

'You recognised I was joking?'

'Der, Dad.'

'So how can you be autistic? Autistic people don't get jokes.'

365

'That's a stereotype. People think that because someone's autistic, they have to have every — '

'Hold on, Don,' said Rosie. 'You haven't answered the question. Properly.'

'World's best primary-school graduation speech,' I said. 'Vast amounts of information considering the two-minute limit, logical, transparent structure . . . and succeeded in engaging the millennial mind. Mine also.'

Hudson looked incredibly pleased, which was strange, as he had apparently already had six positive responses.

'I got a lot of help.'

'From Eugenie?'

'Uh-huh . . . her whole family. Not just with the speech. With all the stuff I did this term. Would it be okay to invite them to have pizza? I told Eugenie I'd ask, so they haven't eaten. She's waiting for a text.'

'Go on,' said Rosie to Hudson.

Hudson looked at Rosie and Rosie looked at Hudson. Then Hudson looked at me. 'Eugenie and Carl's dad helped me. A lot. I checked with Mum and she said it was okay.'

It took me several seconds to process the information. 'Eugenie and Carl's dad' was *Gene*. My son was in contact with him. With Rosie's permission.

Rosie must have seen my confusion. 'Eugenie thought that Hudson had a big challenge and that her father knew more than anyone about . . . playing the system.'

She refilled my wine glass. 'He coached *you*, didn't he? I wouldn't be getting lace-up runners for our wedding anniversary if it wasn't for him, would I? I wouldn't be married to you. There would be no Hudson.'

'Correct. But — '

'But you still can't forgive him after eleven years, because 'nothing has changed'. Well, now it has.'

'You've held onto a grudge for eleven years?' said my mother. 'Donald.'

'Can I text them?' said Hudson.

I nodded.

When Hudson had finished texting, I asked him, 'What did Gene teach you?'

He shrugged. 'Lots of stuff.'

Rosie looked at him for a while. 'When you held Blanche's hand in the cross-country, was that Gene's idea?'

Hudson nodded.

'That's why you didn't want to explain it in your speech.'

Another nod.

'So, was it to look good?' said Rosie. 'To impress everyone that you cared about her?'

'Hey,' said Dave, 'what does it matter? Sounds like Hudson did a good thing . . . '

'But,' said Sonia, 'I think Rosie's concerned that he didn't do it for the right reasons.'

I was becoming annoyed, not at Gene, but at Hudson's motivation being questioned. For some people, it mattered not only that an initiative was effective, but that the *feelings* behind it met with their approval. These were the people who considered Mother Teresa's contri-bution to addressing poverty more important than that of the Bill and Melinda Gates Foundation.

'I got into senior school,' said Hudson. 'If I hadn't held Blanche's hand, it wouldn't have happened. I had to show I cared about other people.'

Rosie nodded, slowly, and Hudson continued.

'Blanche wanted to run, but she was scared of falling over. She was in Blue House, and I was the captain of Green, but she was my friend, so I wanted to help her. I was going to just get Dov to hold her hand, which he wanted to do because he likes her, and that was why he agreed to run. He was Green, so that made up for the extra Blue, but Gene said I should do the hand thing myself, even if it slowed me down, and then everyone would know that it was my idea. Because we couldn't lose sight of the big goal, which was getting into senior school. So, I said, maybe I could run faster at the end, because Grandpa — '

I interrupted. 'Incredibly complex problem. Involving assumptions about how multiple people would respond. Obviously, Hudson needed input. And the solution was highly successful.'

'We made a list of factors,' said Hudson.

I could see that Sonia was going to speak again and did the *cut* sign to indicate that the subject was closed. I had many criticisms of Gene, but zero doubt about his expertise at self-aggrandisement, which he had successfully transferred to Hudson in a situation where it was needed to counterbalance prejudice. In any case, there was a more important question.

'Are you sure you're autistic?' I asked Hudson.

He did not get a chance to answer, as food arrived, and then Gene, Claudia, Eugenie and Carl — the entire Barrow family, reconstituted — walked in. Dave and George, who knew Gene from our New York men's group, immediately embraced him, which was incredible after so long. Carl and Hudson high-fived.

Rosie took advantage of the confusion to whisper to me: 'You were right. About Blanche and the run.'

Claudia approached me. 'What are you doing with Gene?' I asked. 'Has there been some reconciliation?'

Claudia laughed, which did not answer the question. 'I gather the talk went well.'

'How did you gather? You haven't spoken to anyone who was there except me and we've exchanged zero information.'

'Hudson texted Eugenie as soon as he finished. So, how are *you* feeling? I gather there was an . . . altercation.'

This was becoming ridiculous. Vast numbers of questions were unanswered, vast amounts of information needed to be exchanged and now Claudia was introducing further topics. It was fortunate that I was among friends and family, or I would have had some sort of brain-overload-related breakdown. We needed to prioritise the issues and deal with them one by one.

I began with the most urgent. 'What variety of pizza do you want?'

Rosie instructed the waiter to extend the table to create places for a total of fourteen customers.

There were only twelve of us, but two further people appeared at the door: Merlin and Tazza, Hudson's friends from the bar. There was a risk that they had brought further subjects for discussion. And everyone was beginning at different levels of knowledge.

Rosie had a solution. 'Don, I'm going to bring everyone up to speed while you and Gene sort yourselves out. Over there.' She pointed to a table in the corner.

'What about our pizza?'

'I'll send it over.'

'Who's going to bring Gene up to speed?'

'Give him a summary. Second thoughts: Claudia can tell him later.'

'But Claudia and Gene . . . '

'Don: table. Gene. Go.'

★   ★   ★

'You're looking well,' said Gene.

'My appearance is a poor indicator of how I'm feeling. I've been in a fight that I should have avoided.'

Gene laughed. 'Don, thank you for letting me be here and share in Hudson's big moment. He's a terrific kid and I've missed watching him grow up. I did get him to check with Rosie, but . . . I wanted to do something to make up.'

'Make up for what?' I said. 'I was the one at fault.'

'Hardly. You spoke the truth. As you've always done.'

'I destroyed your relationship.'

'I sowed the seeds myself. If Lydia couldn't accept my past ... And before that, I manipulated you into lying for me. All I can say about that is that it gave me some breathing space to be accepted by Carl while he needed a father.'

My mind was drifting back to Hudson's self-diagnosis as Gene continued.

'You know, I encouraged Hudson to make peace with his friend Blanche, even though it didn't particularly advance his cause with the school, which was notionally my brief. A bit of projection, Claudia would say.'

'Have you two made up yet?' It was my mother. She didn't wait for an answer. 'You're always over-thinking things. Just shake hands and come back to the table.'

Gene smiled. I had no choice but to do what my mother told me.

Pizza consumption was in progress. Rosie explained that (1) all guests were now familiar with the events of the evening, (2) everybody was very happy for Hudson, and (3) nobody was discussing definitions of autism. It seemed that they had waited for me.

'How can you be sure you're autistic?' I asked Hudson.

'I did the test, online. I'm definitely on the spectrum.'

'The Autism Spectrum Quotient is only one of numerous instruments. And not intended for self-administration by an eleven-year-old ... '

I stopped, because Hudson had adopted an expression that I had not seen since the evening I told him Rosie would be returning to work and I would be his primary carer. And prior to that, when we had announced we would be leaving New York. Even before he spoke, I had worked out the problem. There were multiple tests for autism. But I knew which one he'd used.

'You hacked my computer. *Dad.*' He put his head in his hands.

I had no answer. I could blame Rosie, but that would only alienate Hudson from both of us.

Rosie began to speak. 'Hudson . . . '

'I don't want you to speak to me.'

'Wait.' It was Gene. 'It wasn't your dad, Hudson. It was me. The night you had dinner with us. You left your computer on when you went to the bathroom and . . . '

'What? Why?' said Hudson.

'Are you surprised? You should know me well enough by now. You think I wouldn't check your computer if I thought you were holding out on me? And you think I wouldn't tell your mother what I found to win me a few points?'

'Pleased to see you haven't changed,' said George.

As Gene continued his lie, Rosie and I looked at each other. Ethically, I had no choice but to stop him. My brain was *wired* for honesty. But . . . tonight was a night of celebration. If I corrected Gene, Hudson's trust in me would be destroyed.

I stood up and walked out to the street. A few seconds later, Rosie joined me.

'I'm so sorry,' she said. 'I really screwed up . . . '

'I agreed to do it. But then we failed to act on the information.'

'What do you mean?'

'That he was considering the possibility of autism.'

'The school had brought it up already, remember? Don, you're not really happy about what he said tonight, are you?'

'Eugenie, Carl, Phil and I, and George and Dave — and Claudia and Gene — worked to assist him in developing the skills to . . . '

'Fit in?'

'Correct. We thought we'd achieved success. He had multiple friends, succeeded in conventional school activities, overcame rejection from the senior school . . . '

'I was part of that too.'

'Of course,' I said.

'Well, I'm not upset with what he said tonight. I'm still taking it in, but everyone's so proud of him. We should be too. Did we want him to be like Trevor, pretending for half his life?'

What Rosie said made sense, not only logically but in explaining my emotional reaction to Hudson's declaration that he had succeeded in passing for 'normal'. I mentally reviewed the last six months, when I had walked away from my job in the hope of assisting Hudson to *fit in* — by conforming to neurotypical norms of behaviour.

'We were working against what Hudson really wanted,' I said. 'All our efforts made it harder for him.'

'You are *so* wrong,' said Rosie. 'Whatever

mistakes we made, he's come out of it with the confidence to make his own call. He's resourceful; he's got integrity; he's okay with who he is. And it wasn't what you taught him from any list; it was being who you are. What you did with the bar. Being willing to talk about your own stuff. What you did tonight. You're his hero.'

'You don't think that the autism classification is going to have negative consequences?'

'It's bound to. But so would trying to be something he isn't. And attitudes are changing. Look at Blanche. I don't know if she's technically autistic or not, but she wants to be part of your tribe.'

'I'm opposed to tribalism. It's . . . ' I stopped, realising what Rosie had implied. 'My — '

'Whatever. You are who you are. I know who you are, so no label is going to make any difference to me. The same with Hudson. The important thing is that you don't think Hudson's some sort of failure just because you don't want a label yourself.'

'Of course not.'

'Not 'of course not'. We'd better go inside. But you need to think about it.'

On the way back to the table, I thought about it. And made two decisions.

The first was to give Gene a hug. It was not comfortable, especially as he was seated with pizza and wine in front of him, but I needed to thank him for lying to protect my relationship with my son. And remind myself that I had learned to do many things that were not natural to me. As had Hudson. And that I was pleased to have those capabilities.

Merlin tapped his glass. 'Can everyone be quiet for a moment. Tazza would like to say something.'

Tazza cleared his throat. Several times. 'I want to congratulate Hudson on coming out. It's a brave and good thing to do. But there's something else that's great: whether we're out or not' — he waved his hand to indicate all thirteen of us, or possibly just George, Gene, Dave and me, seated together — 'we manage to find each other.'

The rest of the group just wanted to talk about the fight.

'What did Mr Warren say?' said Hudson. 'He's the sports master — he played cricket for Victoria — and Blanche's dad brushed him off like a *fly*. And then — ' Hudson mimed two punches and fell backwards in his chair, presumably from attempting to demonstrate the leg sweep without creating enough space.

'He was extremely surprised,' I said when Hudson was reseated. 'He had classified me as a geek and subscribed to the stereotype that geeks lack physical skills. And Allannah — Blanche's mother — had announced that my opponent was a kickboxer. Rabbit expected that I would lose.'

'Rabbit. You called him Rabbit. Ha. He was so wrong.'

'Correct.'

I needed to say something more, to implement my second decision. I had the attention of the whole table: my partner, my son, my mother, my closest friends. And allies: Tazza and Merlin. If I didn't do it now, I suspected I never would. I took a deep breath, but couldn't find the words, or possibly the courage.

People were restarting their conversations. The moment had passed. But then George, deploying skills I would never have, sensed what was happening and began a drum solo with his cutlery, on the wooden table, plates and glasses. And, as everyone in the pizzeria focused on the former rock star, the words formed in my mind. George finished with a drumroll on the table and pointed a hand towards me.

'Always a mistake to underestimate an aspie,' I said.

Epilogue

I took the job with Minh. It offered the possibility of exciting work, and I realised that for years I had been afraid to move from an environment in which I felt socially safe.

Following an interview with Ewan Harle, Hudson decided to continue to the non-special high school. My mother volunteered to assist with after-school activities.

Almost zero had changed externally since I'd decided to identify as an aspie — as *autistic*. I had little doubt that I shared a set of attributes with many other humans, including Hudson, Laszlo, Liz the Activist, Dov, Tazza the Geek, and possibly Blanche and Gene, and that the best available label was *autism*. The questionnaires and checklists that showed me to be neurotypical were addressing, at best, a subset of these attributes, focusing on problematic behaviours — behaviours which, in my case, had been modified by a lifetime of trying to fit in.

Since my self-diagnosis, I was, as Rosie had observed of Hudson, 'more comfortable in myself'. I had also made a mental shift. In the past, I had wished the world was different, but assumed that it was my responsibility to fit in. Without Hudson, perhaps I would have continued on that path, but Hudson might have eighty or more years of life ahead of him. In that time the world could change, and, ethically, I was obliged to contribute to that change. I had my answer to Liz the Activist's question: *Which side are you on?*

★ ★ ★

On the first day of my new job, Minh assembled the company's thirty-eight employees in the meeting room.

'Everyone except Don has heard this talk before. So . . . ' she spun around with her eyes closed and one arm extended. When she stopped, she was pointing to the woman whose question six months earlier had incited the Genetics Lecture Outrage. It appeared that her job application had been successful. I hadn't noticed her presence, due to engagement in a technical conversation with another new colleague.

'You're it, Laura,' said Minh.

Laura looked at me, then Minh. 'Sorry, I haven't had a chance to learn it yet. I . . . '

Minh didn't wait for her to finish but spun again, this time selecting a tall male of approximately thirty. 'Faraj.'

Faraj recited what I presumed was a standard introduction, which could just as easily have been printed and given to me. Except it would not have been possible to print the enthusiasm.

'This is likely to be the most important work you — we — will ever do. One day, out of this lab, is going to come something that changes the world for the better, in a big way. Maybe it will end malaria or amoebic dysentery, or wipe out

AIDS or schizophrenia. Maybe some problem that hardly anybody thought that genome editing could solve. Like climate change. And all of us are going to be part of it. Even if it doesn't come out of this lab, we'll be part of the global effort, part of the community that pulls it off. And when our work makes money, we'll invest in other research initiatives to make the world a better place.

'We're not going to let anything smaller than that stand in our way. If we have problems — with technology, with resources, *with each other* — we solve them, we get past them, and we're never afraid to ask for help to do that, because what we're creating matters so much more.'

In another profession, Faraj's speech would have sounded overblown, but this was genome editing. I felt *uplifted*.

I had been taking notes, and when I finished, the room was empty. Except for Laura. She walked over to me and I detected unhappiness. Possibly anger.

'I can't believe you're here. Nobody told me. I mean, I withdrew my complaint after that . . . woman . . . set me up in the bar. You got what you wanted. I thought you'd go back to your old job.'

'Is there some problem with me being here?'

'I wanted to move on. I thought you would too. You knew I'd applied for this job. I don't want to come to work every day and deal with your anger about what happened.'

'I'm not angry.'

'You can't not be. I thought you might just have quoted some racist paper or study result. That's all I wanted, something for a blog. And then you did that exercise and handed me something that I could use to make a difference. It wasn't about you personally. But you lost your job. Of course you're angry.'

Something had fallen into place. 'You asked the question with the intention of entrapping me?'

'I wanted you to say what you believed. And I planned to share that.'

'My wife and my support person suggested that you had some motivation other than academic curiosity. It seemed implausible to me because I assume sincerity by default. It's possibly related to being autistic.'

'Shit. Oh shit . . . I didn't . . . ' Laura crossed her arms. 'I was doing it for a bigger cause.'

'With minimal effect.'

'Thanks for reminding me of that. As you can see, everything's turned to shit. I get hated on by half the university, nothing changes, and now this. And what you just said: I'm sorry if I took advantage of something I didn't know about you . . . '

'Approaching systemic problems via individual cases is inefficient and involves people — hence uncontrollable effects at the level of intervention. High-level action is vastly more effective. Like modifying the mosquito genome rather than treating individual cases of malaria.'

'Not all of us have the power . . . '

Intellectually, I was trying to move towards

reconciliation, but Laura was right about my emotional state: I was angry. She had lured me into causing distress to my students so she could complain about it. She had damaged my reputation and cost me my job. And now she didn't want to work with me, and I didn't want to work with her.

We had a problem.

★ ★ ★

Seven months earlier, I had identified five problems and set out to address them using the skills and experience that had led me, in a moment of arrogance, to label myself World's Best Problem-Solver. As I prepared to begin a new phase of my life working with Minh, I had conducted a post-project review with the two 'key stakeholders'. We had opened sparkling wine to toast the approval of Rosie's funding application and it seemed sensible to use the remaining wine to celebrate the resolution of the original problems.

'What problems?' said Hudson.

'Number One. The job-incompetence problem. Solved by resigning and nominating Laszlo to replace me.'

'Just like that,' said Rosie.

'Correct. Problem Number Two: The Genetics Lecture Outrage, solved, as predicted, by the Gordian-knot-cutting sword.' I explained to Hudson. 'Multiple problems solved by a single action.'

'Walking away,' said Rosie. 'Which relied on

the bar being a success. For which you can thank Minh and Amghad, with a bit of help from Hudson and me.'

Amghad had received an attractive offer for the business, but The Library had become an important part of our lives and those of numerous patrons, and he needed a reason to stay in touch with Minh.

'Agreed. Hudson's intellectual input to the app was critical, and you provided free labour.'

'Right. *And* called out your ex-student . . . without which you'd still have a complaint hanging over your head.'

'Probably. Problem Number Three was Dave. Completely solved.'

'By me,' said Hudson. 'Plus your tools.'

'The sword of Dad didn't work there,' said Rosie. 'Dave was supposed to work in the bar . . . '

'But the problem was solved. Problem Four: The Rosie Crucifixion.'

'What?' said Hudson.

'Your mother's requirement to work full-time.'

'Solved by you and me,' said Hudson. 'You quitting work; me dealing with it.'

'Right,' said Rosie. 'All I had to do was run a world-class pilot project, develop a bid and sell the package to a funding body that accepts one in ten proposals. Hardly anything.'

'You should still take some credit,' I said. 'You definitely made a contribution. Number Five — '

Rosie made a double stop sign. 'Sarcasm alert. Reprocess.'

Right at the beginning of a statement was a

clue which Hudson and I should have noticed. Rosie clarified that she had made a greater contribution than might be appreciated from a literal interpretation of her words, but did not dispute the fact that the problems had been solved.

'Excellent,' I said. 'Number Five was the most important problem. The Hudson Adjustment Problem.' I explained to Hudson. 'Not liking school, not fitting in.'

'You thought that was the most important thing? You quit your *job* because of that?'

'Correct. I wanted you to be happy.'

'And that's a problem you can never say 'solved' to,' said Rosie. 'If you can even call it a problem.' She addressed Hudson. 'Your dad just wanted to help you, like all parents do. You're the one who's done the hard work.'

Hudson ate a piece of un-crumbed fish and a forkful of one-hundred-per-cent celeriac mash. 'Things are better,' he said. 'Everyone helped. Just for a while I thought you wanted a different kid, like Zina or Blake or . . . Blanche.'

'You really thought that?' said Rosie.

'Not now. Zina would be pretty annoying.'

'How's Blanche doing?'

'I'm not supposed to see her, remember? So how would I . . . She phones me sometimes. She's definitely going to the high school next year. So is Dov. We have the numbers.' He laughed. 'Blanche's parents aren't splitting up. Her mum says her dad's like he is because of genes and . . . something else.'

'Environment,' I said. 'Including upbringing.' I

was not happy to have my arguments used in this context.

'Uh-huh. Anyway, she says he had all his buttons pushed at the same time and that won't happen again.'

'I should talk to Allannah.'

'Blanche's dad wouldn't like it. Obviously.'

'I think,' said Rosie, 'you may be right. Your dad's done more than enough.'

She finished her glass. 'But I think the lesson with your dad's problem-solving is that there are seldom easy solutions to people problems. Sometimes we just need to . . . '

'Muddle through,' I said.

Rosie laughed. 'I'm not disagreeing; it's just not a term I ever thought you'd use.'

'On the contrary, muddling through is a recognised problem-solving technique. Lindblom, 1959.'

'Well, that's what we've done. And we've done it as a family.'

That had been the problem I almost missed — the biggest problem of all. Family cohesion. I judged us as currently cohesive, but continued monitoring, problem-solving and muddling through was likely to be necessary.

★ ★ ★

I had activated the espresso machine and offered to make a coffee for Laura. Her need for caffeine apparently overrode her urge to escape me. Or perhaps she was hoping I would find a solution. Which was what I was trying to do.

I *viscerally* did not want to work with her.

When Gene exploited me, with far less impact, I had terminated our relationship. It was an emotional reaction, and I was aware that I was not good at making decisions while swamped by emotions.

I was a scientist. I was autistic. *These* were my key strengths. I needed to distance myself. What would I want myself to do? Better, since I had spent six months thinking about it every day, what would I want Hudson to do?

I had a flash of insight. Hudson had already faced a similar situation: the Pigeon Betrayal. His failure to understand the complexities of human dynamics and his consequent insensitive behaviour had provoked a disproportionate response that put his future in jeopardy.

With help he had found a solution, and, uncomfortable as it would be for me to apply it here, I had to acknowledge that it had worked.

I gave Laura her coffee. 'We both messed up,' I said. 'We should put it behind us, because being angry gets in the way of everything else.'

'Easy to say — '

'I would be unable to function professionally if I was angry. Hence, I am highly motivated to eliminate that emotion. If I failed, I would resign. In embarrassment.'

'So that's your solution? Just forget about it and move on?'

'If there are outstanding disagreements, we can discuss them later. As scientists, rationally. While we continue to work on changing the world.'

Laura shook her head, but I diagnosed

bewilderment rather than rejection and resisted the urge to add further arguments.

She finished her coffee and put the cup down. 'All right. If you can do it, so can I.'

'The problem is resolved?'

She laughed. 'The problem is resolved.'

★ ★ ★

It would have been a disaster if Laszlo's Asperger's had prevented him from contributing to a cancer cure; if Rosie's status as a mother had resulted in her removal from the bipolar-disorder project; and if Hudson's autistic traits had blocked his journey to high school, human-rights advocate and possibly — as suggested by the anonymous voice at the cross-country race — prime minister, where he would have the power to change the system. And if Laura and I had been prevented from changing the world by our failure to resolve a personal issue.

I would never have the intuitive sense of others' emotions that supposedly is needed to deal with interpersonal problems, but I had done my best using rationality, experience and hard-won learning about human behaviour, and those skills had been sufficient.

I was reasonably certain that my son would be proud of me.

Acknowledgments

Once again, I have a long list of people to thank.

First, as always, is my wife and writing partner, Anne Buist. Screenwriting taught me that two heads are better than one in story development, and hers was the second head. Her reward has been Don Tillman's disparaging comments about her profession, but even she would acknowledge that psychiatrists have not always done well in identifying and responding to autism.

The last few years have seen a significant escalation of the discussion around autism and in the participation of autistic people in that discussion. Thanks to conferences, seminars and social media, I've been able to hear and communicate with many in the community, and get a sense of the issues and the state of play both clinically and socially. I hesitate to name anyone, lest a 'thank you' be interpreted as endorsement of a particular view (it should not), but I do want to acknowledge Tony Attwood, Stephanie Evans, Kerry Magro, Katherine May, Jeanette Purkis, Louise Sheehy, Thorkil Sonne, and T. Rob Wyatt.

My early readers provided me with their customary diverse and helpful feedback. Thanks to Tania Chandler, Robert Eames, Irina Goundortseva, Cathie Lange, Rod Miller, Rebecca Peniston-Bird, Jan Phillips, Dominique Simsion, and Tony Stewart.

The team at Text Publishing have now shepherded me through five novels and I thank publisher Michael Heyward for his continued faith. My editor, David Winter, is a consummate professional — and I've come to anticipate his feedback with enthusiasm rather than trepidation. Kirsty Wilson, Shalini Kunahlan and Jane Watkins have kept my books visible in the Australian marketplace, and Anne Beilby, Emily Booth and Khadija Caffoor have ensured that they will be read around the world — forty languages and counting. W. H. Chong again designed the Australian cover.

Thanks also to my international publishers, particularly Cordelia Borchardt (Fischer, Germany), Maxine Hitchcock and Jillian Taylor (Penguin Random House UK), and Jennifer Lambert (HarperCollins Canada), for their insightful feedback.

And thanks, for diverse reasons, to Krysia Birman, Kerrie Hancox, and Lee Kofman.

Finally, this series of novels was inspired and informed far more by life experiences — my own and others' — than research. Thanks to everyone — all of you — who contributed to those.